W9-BLY-792

THE SPLENDOR

BREEANA SHIELDS

PAGE STREET
PUBLISHING CO.

PAGE STREET
PUBLISHING CO.

Copyright © 2021 Breeana Shields

First published in 2021 by
Page Street Publishing Co.
27 Congress Street, Suite 105
Salem, MA 01970
www.pagestreetpublishing.com

All rights reserved. No part of this book may be reproduced or used, in any form or by any means, electronic or mechanical, without prior permission in writing from the publisher.

Distributed by Macmillan, sales in Canada by The Canadian Manda Group.

25   24   23   22   21   1   2   3   4   5

ISBN-13: 978-1-64567-322-4
ISBN-10: 1-64567-322-7

Library of Congress Control Number: 2020952659

Cover and book design by Laura Benton for Page Street Publishing Co. Cover images: Background texture © Shutterstock / Magenta10; frame © Shutterstock / MicroOne; mask © Shutterstock / Extezy; butterfly © Shutterstock / Skiline Design Co; girls © Shutterstock / paw. Author photo © Justin Shields

Printed and bound in the United States

Page Street Publishing protects our planet by donating to nonprofits like The Trustees, which focuses on local land conservation.

DEDICATION

TO JACOB: WHO I CAN ALWAYS
COUNT ON FOR GREAT CONVERSATION

CHAPTER ONE

J ULIETTE WISHED SHE'D NEVER HEARD OF THE HOTEL
Splendor.

If she'd known then what she knew now, she would
have ripped her sister's reservation into bits and tossed the
pieces in the fire.

But she didn't, and so on the morning Clare turned twenty,
Juliette tied a bright yellow ribbon around the envelope and
waited by the door of the tiny flat they'd rented just a year
earlier when Clare was taken on as a governess.

The two of them had dreamed about a night at the
legendary hotel for years. It was a bright glimmer of hope
in an otherwise dismal existence, whispered about during
sleepless nights in the damp and drafty bedroom they shared
at the children's home. Juliette and Clare would lie, fingers
entwined, under the questionable warmth of a threadbare
quilt, imagining the wonders they would encounter when they
finally entered the grand double doors.

"If we ever make it to The Splendor, what will you

wish for?" Juliette asked once.

Clare sighed softly in the dark, a contented sound that warmed Juliette from the inside out. Clare was a dreamer and a brighter future was her favorite dream.

"So many things," Clare said. "It might be fun to be a princess. Or to ride an elephant through the streets of some faraway city." The girls had been young then, and their dreams were young too.

Juliette wriggled her ice-cold toes beneath Clare's calf. Her sister shivered but didn't move away.

"You could do both."

Clare laughed. "You're right. I could."

Their parents were long gone, and they had no friends besides each other, but at least they had this wild, glittering dream: a visit to an enchanted hotel that promised to turn their fantasies into realities—at least for the duration of their stay.

They'd heard the legends—everyone had. But was it true that The Splendor could make you feel like you were falling in love? Like you were singing on a stage in front of thousands of adoring fans? Like you were flying? Everyone said The Splendor could give you things you didn't even know you wanted.

She hoped they were right.

When Clare finally made it home, her shoulders slumped with exhaustion, Juliette didn't even wait for her to shrug off her coat before thrusting the envelope toward her.

"Happy birthday!"

Clare's lips curved in a gentle smile. "You remembered." The way she said it—both touched and surprised—made Juliette wonder if *Clare* had forgotten the date. Typical. She was always so focused on making sure Juliette was taken care of that she rarely thought of herself.

Clare worked a finger under the seam and tore open the envelope. She was likely expecting something homemade—a card scrawled in Juliette's messy script or a coupon that could be redeemed to skip her turn doing the dishes. It was the only kind of gift the girls had ever been able to afford. But when Clare unfolded the creamy paper, she froze. Her green eyes widened, and her chin dropped, shaping her lips into a soft pink circle. Then her entire expression melted into something between awe and ecstasy. Juliette's throat got thick. She didn't need The Splendor to feel like she was flying.

But then Clare's gaze went to the broom closet and a flicker of panic sparked in her eyes. "Jules, how did you do this?"

"Don't worry. I didn't touch our rainy-day stash." Juliette knew it would be the ultimate betrayal to dip into the fund the girls had carefully set aside for years. *Someday money* Clare called it each time she tucked another coin into the false bottom of a box filled with cleaning rags. *Someday we'll have a better life, Jules.*

"Then how did you do this?" Clare asked.

Juliette gave her a small enigmatic smile. "I won't give away my secrets."

She didn't want to tell Clare about the dozens of odd jobs she'd taken over the last year when she was supposed to be studying—taking in laundry for wealthy women who lived on the east side of town; making early-morning bread deliveries, the scent of yeast so tempting, it was all she could do to keep from tearing the loaves apart and devouring them herself; hours spent sanding newly carved rocking chairs at the carpentry shop, her lungs raw from breathing in sawdust.

She didn't want anything to temper Clare's joy.

"Do you like it?"

Clare's eyes glimmered. "But . . . we were supposed to go together."

Juliette's heart seized. Had she miscalculated? Was Clare disappointed? But then Clare pulled Juliette into a fierce embrace, her tears mingling with Juliette's own.

"I love it."

It was one of the last times Clare touched Juliette. The last time she looked at her like they were a team.

The memory made Juliette's chest ache, and she forcibly shoved Clare from her mind. A crust of anger had formed over her heart like a frozen lake in winter. But one wrong step—a too-tender memory of Clare, a moment too long thinking about how things used to be between them—and the ice would crack. Juliette would slip beneath the surface to the frigid shock of loss and betrayal lurking below. She could survive the anger, but she couldn't survive the emotions it concealed. They would crush the air from her lungs.

And so, as she hurried through the streets of Belle Fontaine, heels clicking on the cobbles as she passed chocolate shops and cafés with striped awnings and delicate wrought iron tables, she fed her anger a different set of memories.

Clare was only at The Splendor for a few weeks, but to Juliette, it felt like a lifetime. Their lives were a pair of clasped hands—connected, intertwined—and Juliette's days were empty without her sister.

Each night, Juliette lay awake and thought of everything she wanted to tell Clare when they were reunited. She'd been carefully collecting bits of gossip like they were the small treasures she used to gather on her childhood walks—shiny rocks, abandoned coins, colorful leaves—stuffed in her pockets to share with her sister later. She saved stories the same way. A handsome stranger had visited Mrs. Cardon three days in a row at precisely noon, leaving an hour later with his hair and clothes noticeably disheveled. The corner bakery changed their recipe for scones—they were now studded with morsels of cranberries—and Juliette hadn't decided how she felt about it yet. A robin had taken residence in the tree outside the girls' bedroom window and insisted on waking Juliette with birdsong at an offensively early hour.

When the end of Clare's vacation finally approached, Juliette waited at the bottom of Splendor Hill, breathless with anticipation.

She spotted Clare climbing out of the carriage, her expression wistful, as if she were waking from a particularly lovely dream.

Juliette called her name. Clare turned, scanning the crowd, but her gaze slid past Juliette. She craned her neck to look for the source of the noise.

"Clare!" Juliette shouted again, louder, more insistent.

Finally, Clare's gaze settled on Juliette. Her brow furrowed, as if she were trying to place someone vaguely familiar. But then her eyes cleared, and she waved.

Juliette ran forward and flung herself into Clare's arms.

Clare stiffened and pulled away.

Juliette's ribs collapsed around her heart. She assumed Clare would be as desperate to see her as she was to see Clare.

Juliette blinked back tears. "What's wrong?"

"Nothing," Clare said. "Everything is fine." And then, after a beat: "Why are you here?"

Juliette twisted her fingers together. A nervous habit. "I thought . . . I wanted to see you." A storm of confusion raged in her chest. Was Clare angry with her? Did she have a terrible time at The Splendor? Why was she acting so strangely?

Clare gave a polite laugh. "Well now you've seen me. But I better get home. I have work tomorrow."

She turned and walked away, leaving Juliette scrambling to catch up.

Juliette tried to rationalize away Clare's behavior. Maybe

she was tired. Maybe after living inside a fantasy, the return to real life was disorienting. Things would get better.

But they didn't. They got worse.

Clare treated Juliette like she were nothing more than an acquaintance, edging around her in their flat as if they were strangers who happened to share the same space. When Clare acknowledged Juliette at all, it was with a distant, infuriating politeness. It would be easier if Clare were openly hostile; at least a strong emotion—even a negative one—would reveal some depth of feeling. But Clare wasn't angry at Juliette; she was simply indifferent.

And that was so much more painful.

Juliette spent several weeks trying everything she could think of to repair their bond. She wrote loving notes and tucked them in Clare's shoes. She took over all the chores Clare used to do, scrubbing the floors and making her sister's bed with the corners of the sheets folded into tight envelopes just the way Clare liked them. She prepared a dinner of all of Clare's favorite foods.

But Clare greeted these niceties with a formal kind of civility, expressing gratitude in the same tone she might use to thank a waiter arriving at the table with her food—kind, but impersonal.

Finally, Juliette resorted to trying to antagonize Clare.

She borrowed a dress without asking, criticized her sister's hair, left dirty dishes in the sink. In the past, Clare never let Juliette behave like a pest without correction.

But not anymore.

Now each time Juliette annoyed her sister, she watched Clare's eyes narrow, saw her jaw tighten and her lips press together. But then Clare would take a deep breath and visibly shove away her irritation, as if someone had bumped into her on the street and she was determined to avoid an overreaction.

The Splendor had created a gulf between them, and Juliette didn't know how to build a bridge to cross it.

And then Juliette's world came crumbling down around her. She'd been trying to make small talk with Clare all morning. *How did you sleep? How is work? Are the children in your charge still difficult?* But all she got in return were one-word answers and distracted noises of assent.

Finally, Juliette lost her patience. "Clare!"

Her sister froze, a piece of toast halfway between her plate and her mouth. She raised her eyebrows and waited.

"Please talk to me," Juliette said, her voice full of desperation. "Ever since you got back from The Splendor, things have been different. *You're* different."

Clare set the bread down on her plate. Brushed the crumbs from her fingers. Her gaze was steady as she met Juliette's.

"I've been trying to find a way to tell you—" Relief sagged out of Juliette. Clare was finally going to trust her with the truth. She leaned forward. And then Clare finished the thought. "I think it's time you got a place of your own."

Juliette reared back as if slapped. "You want me to move out?"

Clare pushed her plate away. She stood and grabbed her coat. "You've been entirely too needy lately. This is for the best. You'll see."

After Clare left, Juliette sat motionless for a long time, tears streaming down her cheeks and dripping from her chin. She cried until there was nothing left. Until her eyes and cheeks were bone dry. Until her whole body felt parched.

But dry things catch fire quickly, and when Juliette's gaze went to the broom closet, something inside her sparked, and suddenly she was ablaze. She stood and retrieved the box from the shelf. Opened the false bottom. If Clare could spend a few weeks basking in luxury, Juliette could too.

She stole every penny.

Now her steps slowed as she approached the edge of the cobbled circular drive where horse-drawn carriages—bright white and trimmed in gold—waited to whisk their guests to luxury.

Juliette tried not to look up, tried to keep her gaze pinned to the candy-colored flowers that bloomed along the path, to the other guests milling about the circle chatting with one another in excited tones, but in the end, she couldn't help herself. She lifted her eyes toward the sky where The Splendor perched above the city like a giant bird with gilded wings— magical and imposing.

Her pulse sped—the familiar awe the hotel always inspired was now tinged with dread. And more than a little panic.

Juliette's courage faltered.

Maybe she should turn around and go back to the flat. She could get a refund on her ticket and put the *someday money* back before Clare got home. Her fingernails curled into her palms. But then what? Without Clare, she had no one. Her throat grew thick. She needed to find her own path forward. Maybe a week of luxury would give her clarity about what she wanted.

"Do you have a reservation, miss?" The driver closest to Juliette watched her with a curious expression, perhaps unaccustomed to witnessing worry instead of anticipation. His gaze dropped to the creamy page she held, and he extended a white-gloved hand, palm up. His dark eyes were kind, but his mannerisms were all business. He wore a short, well-trimmed beard. His suit was expertly pressed, and his shoes so shiny Juliette imagined she could use them to style her hair in a pinch. He was the very image of perfection.

Just like The Splendor itself.

"Miss?"

Juliette's fingers trembled as she gave him the reservation. He examined it closely and then smiled. "Welcome."

Juliette took the driver's outstretched hand, and the frantic spinning in her stomach settled. She climbed into the carriage and closed her eyes as she sank against the plush purple velvet. Moments later the driver clicked his tongue and the horses started forward. The rumble of the wheels over the cobbles soothed her nerves.

She could do this.

Several minutes passed until a collective gasp arose from the surrounding carriages, and Juliette's eyes flew open.

Her breath caught.

She didn't know where to look first. The view from the ground, majestic as it was, hadn't done the hotel justice.

Not even close.

The Splendor was not one building, but three. The main structure stood straight ahead at the highest point on the mountain. It was constructed of pale, sand-colored limestone that reflected the light of hundreds of fountains—water in hues of violet, blue, and green—spouting directly from the floor of a marble courtyard near the base of the steep steps that led to the grand entrance. The facade boasted hundreds of rows of evenly spaced arched balconies so each guest could enjoy the breathtaking view of the city below. The effect was sophisticated and magical.

Flanking the main building were two identical wings facing each other. In the center stood an enormous pool. An elegant bridge arched over the impossibly blue water.

It looked exactly like the kind of place where dreams came true.

A memory floated to the surface of Juliette's mind. It was years ago. Juliette had been searching for Clare for over an hour—the girls were on kitchen duty that week at the children's home, and even though Juliette was more skilled with a knife than her sister, she wasn't about to peel ten pounds of potatoes by herself.

She found Clare resting under the shade of a maple tree, an open book perched on her knees.

Juliette waited. She knew better than to interrupt when Clare was like this—jaw tight, the tip of her tongue poking between her front teeth as her hungry eyes roamed over the page.

It took a few moments, but finally Clare's expression relaxed. Whatever danger lurked inside the story must have passed for now.

Juliette gently lifted the book from her sister's hands. "Time to come back to reality."

Clare's eyes took a moment to clear, but when they did, the joy melted from her face like a dish of butter left too close to the cookstove. Guilt wormed through Juliette to have ruined something so lovely.

"What if I don't want to come back?" Clare said, snatching the book and clutching it to her chest. "Fantasy is so much better than reality."

The memory pierced Juliette. Grief pushed up her throat, making it hard to breathe. Clare finally got to live in her fantasy, and it must have been so wonderful that it made living with Juliette even bleaker by comparison.

What if Clare's greatest wish was that she'd never *had* a sister? Perhaps within the walls of The Splendor, Clare always got the last bite of bread because no one else was hungry. Maybe she slept more soundly without Juliette's cold feet brushing against her own. Maybe removing the burden of a younger sister—if only for a few weeks—made it unbearable to return.

Juliette should have known Clare would leave her eventually. Everyone always did. But it didn't stop the ache her absence left.

Another awed murmur from the surrounding carriages pulled Juliette's attention back to the present. She cocked her head to one side and listened.

Music floated on the air—at first so faintly Juliette could have been convinced she was imagining it. But as the carriages approached the main entrance, the music grew and swelled until it seemed to be coming from nowhere and everywhere at once. And there was something captivating about the tune, as if it held a promise in the melody.

Juliette took a deep breath. Maybe being drenched in luxury would be just the common experience the two sisters needed to reconnect. Maybe she could find an answer to the question that had been thrumming through her mind for weeks: *Why?*

But if all else failed, she hoped The Splendor could give her the next best thing: Maybe it could make her stop loving Clare the way Clare had stopped loving her.

CHAPTER TWO

S UNLIGHT STREAMED IN THROUGH THE SMALL ATTIC
window on the top floor of The Splendor, illuminating
a single slice of buttery air filled with lazily rotating bits
of dust. Henri sat on the edge of the bed—the patchwork
quilt rumpled from his too-brief nap—and pinched the bridge
of his nose with his thumb and forefinger. A headache was
brewing behind his eyes.

He longed to curl up and go back to sleep, but he'd
already been gone too long.

He picked up the steaming cup of matcha tea from
the bedside table and took a sip. Stella had it sent up from the
kitchen, claiming it would boost his energy, but as far as he
could tell it wasn't working. Or maybe he was just exhausted
beyond help. What he really needed was more sleep—just one
solid, uninterrupted night—but there wasn't time.

The new guests were due to arrive any moment, and
everything had to be perfect.

Henri stood and rolled his shoulders. A pitcher—a sheen

of droplets glittering on its cool metal surface—rested on the bureau. Henri swiped at his forehead with his sleeve—he was sweating too. He scooped up the pitcher and took it to the worn stone washbasin in his suite—not nearly as lavish as the gold leaf ones in the guest rooms—and splashed a bit of cold water on his face. Then he grabbed a tall glass, filled it to the brim, and drained it in a single swallow.

Better.

He examined his reflection in the mirror above the basin, frowning at the dark circles under his eyes. He combed his fingers through his thick mop of black hair. Tugged on the hem of his jacket. Plucked a piece of lint from his lapel.

Not that it mattered. The guests would see what he wanted them to see. But it was important to Henri. He preferred reality over illusion, even though the latter was his specialty.

Henri left his suite and took the stairs two at a time.

The moment the staff quarters gave way to the guest areas, Henri felt the pressure in the air change. It crackled with magic. His fingertips itched with anticipation and his exhaustion fell away like a discarded coat in an overly warm room. He felt lighter. Freer.

Henri passed a console table topped with roses in a crystal vase. He dragged a single finger along the blooms, and they stood up taller, their hue changing from a dull, dark red to a vibrant scarlet. The vase glittered under his touch. Not good enough. He ran a palm along the surface of the table, and a delicate inlay of emerald unfurled along the border.

Henri continued through the corridors' brightening colors, polishing surfaces, making sure every square inch of The Splendor was drenched in luxury.

He knew he should leave these details to one of the other

illusionists. He could ill afford to spend his limited energy on minutiae when he would need to draw on deeper reserves of magic in the coming days, but he couldn't resist. Theo and Stella were counting on him, and he couldn't bear to disappoint them.

Henri descended the grand staircase into the main ballroom, and the gold leaf banister gleamed under his touch. The marble brightened beneath his feet as if freshly mopped.

The room was buzzing with activity. Illusionists polishing silver, turning ordinary rugs into intricately woven masterpieces, adding another layer of flickering candles to the giant chandelier above.

Stella stood in the corner, overseeing the work, arms folded across her chest, lips pressed together in a disapproving line. For just a moment, Henri saw her as the others did. Stern. Intimidating. There was nothing soft about Stella. She was all angles—sharp nose, pointed chin, close-set eyes that always seemed to be narrowing into a scowl. But when she spotted him, her face relaxed, and the harsh image of her vanished. He saw her as she really was—the woman who had saved him, had given his life purpose.

She strode toward him and planted a brief kiss on his cheek. Her lips were cold. "Feeling better?"

"Much." Though he knew it was only the magic in the air, not the nap. Not the tea. Which meant he'd fall into bed exhausted in the morning. But no matter. As long as the evening was perfect, it would be worth it.

"Good. I want you in top form when the guests arrive."

"Do you have the final registry?" Henri asked.

Stella turned her attention to a slight girl who was vanishing small scratches in the heavy walnut concierge desk. "Carmen!"

The girl spun around, wide-eyed, as if she were a child

caught misbehaving. She pushed her hair out of her eyes. "Yes, Miss Stella?"

"Henri needs an updated guest list."

"Oh." Her gaze swept over the jumble of clutter behind the desk, searching. "Yes, of course."

Stella snapped her fingers impatiently. "Now, please. We don't have all day."

Carmen startled. She snatched a stack of paper and scurried in their direction.

Henri gave Stella a reproachful look. "This is why everyone steers clear of you on arrival day."

"They *should* steer clear," Stella said under her breath. But her expression mellowed as the girl drew near. Carmen's hands trembled as she handed over the document.

"Thank you, that will be all," Stella said. She didn't sound particularly sincere, but Henri supposed it was better than nothing.

He flipped through the pages, scanning the list of names, which were all familiar by now. He'd spent weeks researching each guest. It was imperative to know them well in order to make their experience at The Splendor unique and unforgettable.

But when he reached the final page, he let out a groan.

"A late booking?" Stella guessed.

Henri nodded. A new name glared at him from the bottom of the page. Juliette Berton.

Stella clucked her tongue. "Well, that's not ideal. You better manage her yourself. I have no doubt you'll rise to the occasion."

Henri started to answer, but Stella wasn't looking at him. She'd spotted something across the room that made her eyes flash. "Bernard, what are you doing?" Her voice echoed in the cavernous space. A young illusionist on the opposite side of the ballroom froze, a bundle of fabric clutched to his chest. He opened his mouth and then closed it again, fishlike.

"I have to handle this," Stella said. And then she waggled her fingers at the guest list. "See that you handle that."

She hurried away, heels clicking on the marble floors. Henri wasn't sure what Bernard had done to earn Stella's ire, but he didn't envy the boy. Arrival day was tense for everyone, but especially Stella and Theo. The Splendor was a lifelong labor of love for the couple. They demanded perfection for every guest—a stay filled with pampering, luxury, and enchantment. So, while Stella might be prickly now, once the carriages arrived, she'd be as charming and accommodating as the rest of the staff combined.

But Henri was under the most pressure of all. If he failed, they all failed. He tugged at the back of his neck. Late bookings were always challenging, but he couldn't remember the last time a guest had booked *this* late. What prompted such a spontaneous vacation? A lost job? A cheating spouse?

He sighed. He'd hoped to sneak away tonight for a catnap, but now he'd have to spend it trying to ascertain the hopes and dreams of a random stranger. He had to turn Juliette's fantasies into realities even if he didn't know what they were yet.

Despite being surrounded by magic, Henri's head started to pound again. He took a deep breath and forced his spinning thoughts to still. He needed to deal with one thing at a time.

And next on his list was food.

He moved through small clusters of illusionists, each creating a different wonder. He slowed near a pair of fountains in the foyer. Gold and silver fish leaped from one stream of water to the other, arching elegantly in the air.

"Nicely done," he said without stopping.

He made his way to the kitchen at the back of the hotel. Here the magic hung so thick in the air he could nearly taste it. Dozens of cooks were bustling about, pulling dishes from the ovens, whisking bowls of fluffy cream, dusting confections with magic and finely milled sugar. Hundreds of small plates, each with a different dessert, covered every surface.

Amella—the head chef—leaned over a bowl, stirring a bright yellow batch of pie filling. Her black curls were pinned back from her face, her brown skin smooth and unlined, despite the chaos surrounding her.

"Which guest?" Henri asked, dipping his finger into the bowl.

Amella swatted his hand away. "Simon George."

Henri licked the pie filling from his finger and was instantly filled with overpowering nostalgia. Simon's happiest memories were summers spent with his grandmother—lying in a hollow log watching ants scurry above his head, building forts in the meadow behind her house, sitting with her on the porch swing, a giant slice of her signature lemon meringue pie perched on his knees.

Henri closed his eyes and savored the feeling. "It's perfect."

He sampled several other desserts—a crème brûlée designed to imitate the feeling of falling in love, decadent chocolate mousse that felt like celebration, a red velvet cake that perfectly captured the blissful sensation of waking up to check the time and finding you still have hours left to sleep.

A pang of longing hit Henri square in the chest. Sometimes he wished he could sink into the fantasy world of The Splendor. But even more, he longed for a reality—a past—that was full of the kind of love and nostalgia so many of the guests were trying to recapture at the hotel. The wild dreams of fame and fortune never tempted him, but this— the nostalgia, the memories of love—always filled him with a kind of bittersweet grief.

"Is everything all right?" Amella touched his wrist. Her hands were soft, gentle.

Henri blinked. Shook his head, as if to clear the cobwebs from his thoughts. "I'm fine. But we had a last-minute booking."

Amella's forehead finally wrinkled in concern. She set the bowl on the countertop and sighed heavily. "What would you like me to prepare?"

"The only information I have right now is a name. Juliette Berton. Once she arrives, I'll get close to her and find out more."

Amella drummed her fingers on a wooden cutting board. "So, something generic for tonight?"

Henri bit his lip. If Juliette were coming to The Splendor for adventure, a universal emotion—like kindness or acceptance—might be a misstep. She might want a dessert with an edge. One that produced an adrenaline rush. Then again, if she were risk adverse, that kind of experience would ruin her evening.

Amella was watching him expectantly.

"Something chocolate and laced with love," Henri said. A generic dessert was the safer option. Once he knew Juliette better, he could tailor her stay.

Amella scooped up the bowl and resumed stirring. "I'll get started right after I finish this."

Henri nodded a quick thanks before leaving. He needed to talk to the clothiers, the ambiancers, the weavers. The entire staff needed to be warned about the last-minute adjustment. But the most difficult task rested on Henri himself. Each guest received a signature experience during their stay. A fantasy-fulfillment only he could provide.

If he failed, the reputation of The Splendor was at stake.

Henri knew nothing about Juliette, but it was his job to make her dreams come true.

CHAPTER THREE

JULIETTE

JULIETTE'S EYES WERE BRIGHT AS THE CARRIAGE CAME TO a stop.

Impossibly, dusk had melted into full darkness in a span of moments instead of hours and now the hotel and the grounds were bathed in moonlight.

The driver climbed down from his perch and offered his hand. "Welcome to The Splendor."

Juliette barely glanced at him as she slid her fingers into his, her gaze held captive by the majesty around her. She could scarcely drink it all in.

The cobblestones beneath her were paved in shimmering gold. A ribbon of crimson carpet unfurled from the grand double doors at the top of the steps and stopped just shy of Juliette's feet, as if it had been placed for her alone. It beckoned her forward like an invitation.

The air was warm and faintly scented—a fragrance so divine it made her wish she could tell where it was coming from so she could lean in, breathe deeply, and capture it more fully. But just like the music floating on the breeze, it was simply there, surrounding her with no clear source. Burbling fountains illuminated by soft golden light flanked the staircase.

Several other guests—dressed in fine silks and fancy shoes—glided up the steps. The sight froze Juliette in place. She tugged on the sleeve of her dress, suddenly self-conscious of its thinning fabric and patched elbows.

Maybe she should ask the driver to take her back down the hill. She glanced over her shoulder and their gazes met. The man's eyes filled with sympathy, as if sensing the source of her hesitation. He rested a hand between Juliette's shoulder blades.

"Nothing to worry about. They'll take good care of you. Head on up, now." He gave her a gentle nudge forward.

The first step was the hardest, but once she took a deep breath and started climbing, the knots in her muscles began to unwind. She did her best to ignore the other guests who moved with more certainty, unintimidated by so much opulence.

As Juliette reached the top of the stairs, a young woman— probably only a handful of years older than Clare—waited. She was dressed in all black: tailored pants, a silky top, and low-heeled leather boots. Her skin was the color of fresh cream, and her eyes were nearly colorless, like chips of ice. Her pale hair was gathered at the base of her neck and tied with a satin ribbon.

The woman stepped forward. "You must be Juliette. I'm Caleigh. I'll be your personal concierge for the duration of your stay."

Anxiety bloomed in Juliette's chest. Was she supposed to know what that meant? She swallowed, unsure how to respond.

Caleigh tilted her head to one side, birdlike. Curiosity flitted across her expression, but she recovered quickly, replacing the look with a warm smile. "I'm here to help you with anything you need. My job is to make sure your stay is unforgettable."

"Thank you," Juliette said softly, grateful both to have a concierge and that Caleigh hadn't forced her to reveal her ignorance.

"My pleasure. Shall we get started?"

Juliette took Caleigh's offered elbow and allowed the woman to lead her toward the entrance. A seed of hope took root in her heart. She hadn't expected to have such close contact with someone who worked at The Splendor. Maybe Caleigh remembered Clare. Maybe she could help Juliette understand why staying here had altered her sister's affections.

As the guests approached, the huge doors swung open and all the worries flew out of Juliette's thoughts like startled pigeons.

It was as if she'd walked into a fairy tale. A vast marble floor, polished to a mirror sheen, stretched to the far end of the space where twin staircases curved in opposite directions toward a balconied upper level. A huge candelabra—flickering with hundreds of individual flames—hung from the ceiling. Vases of flowers were sprinkled liberally throughout the room, and as Juliette passed them, she marveled at the unlikely scents wafting from their blossoms. Yellow roses that smelled like freshly squeezed lemons, pink peonies scented like ripe strawberries, white dahlias redolent with vanilla. Servers—dressed just like Caleigh in all black—circulated with trays of goblets filled with bubbly pink liquid. Guests lounged on cut-velvet sofas in rich colors of sapphire and plum. Light conversation and laughter floated on the air like music.

"What do you think?" Caleigh's voice made Juliette startle. She'd forgotten for a moment that she wasn't alone. She felt like a little girl with her nose pressed to the glass, observing without belonging. She couldn't believe she was really here.

"It's breathtaking."

Caleigh's gaze swept over Juliette's threadbare dress. "Would you like to change before you explore?"

"Oh." Heat crept into Juliette's cheeks. She crossed her arms over her stomach. "I didn't bring anything nicer."

Caleigh laid a reassuring hand on Juliette's arm. "You misunderstand. Our dressmaker will prepare something perfect especially for you."

"Does it cost extra?"

The woman frowned slightly, as if offended by the question. "Of course not. Come, let me show you to our clothier."

Juliette followed Caleigh as she threaded her way through the crowd, past an indoor waterfall that tumbled down a wall of stone, an ice sculpture of the entire city of Belle Fontaine rendered in exquisite detail, and a glass enclosure filled with thousands of colorful butterflies.

Everywhere she looked was a feast for her eyes.

And then her gaze landed on a man across the room. He was young—a few years older than Juliette at most. His all-black attire suggested he worked at The Splendor, but unlike the other staff, who were bustling about attending to guests, he leaned casually against the far wall, watching her intently. It startled her so much, she stumbled and nearly fell.

Caleigh spun around. "Are you all right?"

Juliette went hot from her scalp to her toes. "I'm fine. Just clumsy."

She snuck a look from the corner of her eye. The stranger was still watching her. There was something compelling about him, though she couldn't quite put her finger on what. He wasn't classically handsome. He was a bit too lean, his features a bit too sharp. And yet . . .

He noticed her watching and smiled. Like magic, it transformed his face. Juliette was staring. Quickly, she looked away. She'd fallen behind Caleigh and she rushed to catch up.

But she couldn't resist darting a glance over her shoulder. The stranger's face had changed yet again. He looked perplexed. Worried.

"Right through here." The voice pulled Juliette's attention back to Caleigh, who held open a heavy walnut door. Juliette stepped over the threshold and sucked in a sharp breath. At first glance, the room looked a bit like a library, with its high ceilings and dark, rich woodwork. But instead of shelves, the cabinets were outfitted with layer upon layer of rods, which were loaded with more clothes than Juliette had seen in her entire life, all of them in sumptuous fabrics: satin ball gowns, soft cashmere sweaters, shimmering silk tops. And the colors—Juliette was certain she'd never seen so many vibrant hues. Vivid jewel tones, soft pastels, sparkly metallics.

An older man with a heavily lined face and a shock of white hair appeared at her side. He was wearing a smock with at least a half dozen pockets, each stuffed to overflowing with various supplies: scissors, thread, scraps of fabric, seam rippers, pencils.

"You must be Juliette," he said, taking her elbow. And then, without waiting for a reply: "I'm Armond. Favorite color?"

Juliette blinked. "I . . ."

Armond waved his hand in front of his face as if swatting away the question. "Never mind." He took her chin in his hand and studied her face. "You'd look fetching in green." He raised a bushy eyebrow. "Unless you don't approve?"

"No. I mean, yes." Juliette shook her head, flustered. "Green is fine."

Armond made a noise halfway between a grunt and a

sigh. "Wait here." He disappeared through a doorway at the far end of the room.

Juliette shot a nervous glance at Caleigh, who shrugged. "You booked late," she said as if this explained everything.

"I'm sorry?"

"Usually your dress would have been ready weeks ago. But you made the reservation so last minute that there wasn't time to prepare."

A flash of irritation went through Juliette. "So sorry to inconvenience everyone."

If Caleigh noticed her clipped tone, she didn't let on. "It's no trouble. We could use a little excitement around here from time to time." A server came through carrying a silver tray laden with delicate cups shaped like blooming flowers. Caleigh snatched one as he passed.

Juliette thought of the children's home and bit back a sharp reply. Wouldn't it be nice to spend every day working in a fantasy world where the biggest worry was a rushed dress fitting? She took a deep breath and pushed away her annoyance. She was letting her bitterness over her fight with Clare steal her enjoyment. Maybe she should just come right out and ask if Caleigh remembered her sister.

Caleigh handed her the flower cup. "Try this. I think you'll like it."

"Do you enjoy your job?" Juliette asked, trying to keep her tone light. She sipped the drink. It tasted like chocolate laced with cinnamon and her whole body warmed pleasantly as it slid down her throat.

Caleigh pulled her ponytail over one shoulder and twisted the gathered hair around her palm. "Most days. It's nice meeting new people."

Something itched at the back of Juliette's mind. A half-formed question appeared, then floated away before she could grab it. She'd been about to ask Caleigh something related to meeting people. Juliette pressed her lips together. Why couldn't she remember? But then Armond returned, a satin gown slung over his forearm, and she lost her train of thought.

"You can change back there," he said, dipping his head toward a low wooden screen that didn't offer nearly enough privacy. Juliette took the dress and stepped behind the partition, which only came up to her neck. She crouched a little as she stripped off her old dress and pulled the new one over her head. The fabric slid against her skin like water. She skimmed her palms along the skirt. It felt decadent.

"Are you waiting for an engraved invitation?" Armond asked. "Come out and let's have a look at you."

Juliette stepped around the screen and Armond's face split into a grin. He didn't say anything as he fussed with the hemline and tugged at the waist. She thought he would ask her to remove the dress for alterations, but he didn't. Instead, a gust of magic blew over her like a warm breeze, and she felt the dress cinch tight at the middle and shorten at the bottom.

Then Armond took her shoulders and spun her toward a mirror. "What do you think?"

Tears prickled at the backs of her eyes.

The dress was a deep emerald, sleeveless with a sweetheart neckline, and it fit Juliette perfectly—skimming over flaws and accentuating assets.

Like magic.

But of course, it *was* magic. A laugh bubbled up her throat.

"Would you like me to change anything?" Armond's voice was tinged with just a bit of vulnerability that made him instantly more likable.

Juliette let the fabric glide through her fingers, marveling at the transformation. And then she noticed her hair—it had been loose when she arrived, hanging down her back in a long curtain, and now it was swept into an elegant updo. But how? And her skin . . . normally she was so pale, she looked almost sickly, but now there was color in her cheeks. She appeared lit from within.

Armond studied her, still waiting for an answer.

"Please don't change a thing," she said, touching the emerald necklace resting against her collarbone.

"Very well." Armond shooed her toward the door. "Off with you then. A magical evening awaits."

Juliette followed Caleigh through a series of wide, lavish, seemingly never-ending corridors. The Splendor was even more enormous than she first thought.

"Where are we going?" she asked.

"To the ballroom," Caleigh answered without turning around. "It's a lovely evening for dancing."

Juliette had never been to a country dance in a barn, let alone a formal ball. A knot of anxiety wedged beneath her breastbone.

She stopped walking. "I don't want to."

Caleigh faltered. Turned. "Why not?"

"Should it matter? I thought this place was supposed to fulfill my wishes."

A spark of panic flashed in Caleigh's eyes. "Your rooms aren't ready yet. If we'd had a bit more notice . . ."

Juliette shifted her weight from one foot to the other. "I don't dance." She left the rest—that she didn't know *how* to dance—unsaid.

Caleigh's expression relaxed. "It won't be a problem." Juliette frowned, and Caleigh rested a hand on her arm. "You don't have to dance. You can mingle. Meet other guests."

Juliette bit her bottom lip. She wasn't sure what she was

expecting when Armond dressed her like this. She felt naive that a ball hadn't crossed her mind. But maybe Caleigh was right. Maybe she should give it a chance.

"If you aren't having fun, you can leave," Caleigh said, seeming to sense Juliette's softening resolve.

Juliette sighed. She gave a small nod of consent.

"Good," Caleigh said, taking her elbow. "Because we're here." They stepped through an archway.

But it wasn't a ballroom. It was an outdoor paradise.

Bright stars glittered against a velvet sky. The trees were swathed in hundreds of miniature twinkling lights. Guests refilled fluted crystal glasses from the huge fountain in the center of the courtyard that bubbled with pale liquid the color of sunshine. Some people were dancing, others stood in small groups chatting, and still others were sitting at cozy tables eating a variety of desserts, all of them fancier than anything Juliette had ever seen.

"Enjoy yourself," Caleigh said, squeezing her arm. "I'll check on you later."

Juliette tried to protest—she hadn't wanted to come at all, let alone by herself—but it was too late. Caleigh had already been swallowed up by the crowd. Helplessly, Juliette looked around for someone to talk to. And her gaze landed on him. The same young man she'd seen earlier.

He was moving toward her with a dessert plate in his hand.

"You must be Juliette," he said when he reached her, echoing Armond's words exactly. "I'm Henri."

Henri. The name suited him.

Juliette tipped her head to one side. "Why does everyone seem to know me?"

Henri laughed. "On the contrary. We hardly know you at all." He held up the plate. "Are you hungry?"

Actually, she was. She took the dessert from him. A thick slice of chocolate cake drizzled with caramel sauce sat in the center of a golden plate. It smelled divine. Henri handed her a delicate silver fork.

Juliette took a bite and the flavors burst in her mouth. Rich. Warm. Decadent.

And then a swirl of emotions overtook her. The cake tasted . . . a pit opened in her stomach . . . it tasted like an afternoon with Clare. Like her sister's laugh—high and bright as a bell. Like cool grass sliding between her toes. Like chasing each other through the trees on a bright summer day.

It felt like belonging in one bite and then loss in another.

The cake tasted like love.

The chocolate turned to ashes in her mouth.

Why couldn't she just forget about her sister and experience the hotel the way Clare did—a fantasy so powerful that her mundane reality would never be able to compare?

A bright spark of fear went through her. What if she was incapable of happiness?

What if she was so broken that not even The Splendor could make her whole again?

CHAPTER FOUR

T HE DESSERT WAS A MISTAKE.
Henri's pulse thundered in his ears, and he silently cursed himself. He should have asked Amella to infuse the cake with passion or happiness. He'd forgotten how easily love—once lost—feels like heartache.

Henri gently took the plate from Juliette and set it on a nearby table. "It doesn't seem like you're enjoying this. I'll find you something else."

But she stared mournfully at the cake, as if he'd stolen something precious from her. As if she wanted it back. This was turning into a disaster.

Sweat slicked his palms and he pressed them against the front of his jacket, hoping they'd dry quickly. Maybe it was safer to skip food entirely for the moment. He touched Juliette's elbow lightly to get her attention. "Would you like to dance?"

Her eyes lifted to his. "No."

The response shocked a laugh from him. "No?"

Her jaw tightened with resolve. "No."

It shouldn't be this hard. Guests at The Splendor *wanted* to be here. They longed to be swept away by a fantasy. Why was she so reluctant?

"May I ask why not?" Henri said.

Juliette's gaze darted across the crowd as if she might find an answer among the couples swaying beneath the stars. Her fingers curled into her palms. Was she scared?

Henri raised a single eyebrow, waiting.

Finally, she bit her lip. Her shoulders sagged. "I don't know how."

Her expression was a question mark. Unsure. Vulnerable. A tendril of sympathy unwound in Henri's gut.

"Not a problem. I can make you feel like you were born to dance."

She opened her mouth like she might refuse, but then she snapped it closed. Raised her chin, defiant. "I don't believe you."

"Try me."

She held his gaze for several long moments, but then she slid her fingers into his outstretched hand. Her skin was warm and smooth.

Henri led her to the center of the dance floor. Magic flowed down his arms and into the tips of his fingers. He pressed a palm against the small of Juliette's back. She sucked in a sharp breath as the illusion took over. He wondered what she heard—the lively tune of a dozen fiddles? The wild beat of drums? The high, bright notes of a flute? He could summon the fantasy, but Juliette's imagination filled in the details. Her eyes were wide and startled, and for a moment Henri worried she might bolt. But then her lids fluttered closed and her lips curved into a gentle smile.

Henri took the opportunity to study her. She was

drenched in illusions, but he saw through them all. Juliette's hair was the color of a bright copper penny, and though it was enchanted to appear swept into a fancy updo, in reality, it cascaded down her back in a silky curtain. Her skin was pale and a smattering of cinnamon freckles dusted the bridge of her nose and the tops of her cheekbones, but the illusionist had whisked them away, rendering her complexion flawless.

Henri preferred the original.

Juliette opened her eyes—from a distance he'd thought they were the color of coffee, but he was wrong. They were somewhere between brown and green without quite settling on either color. As if they refused to conform.

There was something familiar about her. He was almost sure he'd seen her somewhere before.

"I never knew dancing could be so effortless." Juliette's voice was filled with a relaxed wonder that shot a spasm of guilt through Henri's chest.

She *wasn't* dancing. She was simply standing in the circle of his arms, swaying gently from side to side, while feeling like she was cutting up the floor with clever footwork. Usually Henri didn't see the result of his illusions so up close and personal.

He didn't like how it made him feel like a liar.

He swallowed. He needed to focus. He couldn't give Juliette what she wanted until he discovered what it was. But he felt off balance. Maybe a direct approach was best.

"So why are you here?"

Juliette shrugged. "Caleigh insisted."

Henri shook his head. "Not at the ball. At The Splendor."

She arched an eyebrow but didn't reply.

"Everyone comes looking for something," Henri said. "Adventure. Fame. Love. So what are you looking for?"

Juliette's expression shuttered. The awe flickered from her

eyes like a candle in a sudden gust of wind. Unease threaded through Henri and he thought she might not respond. But then she sighed.

"Answers," she said simply.

Answers? Henri wanted to press her, but Juliette turned her face away, avoiding eye contact. A clear message additional questions were unwelcome. But he couldn't give up.

"Answers about . . . ?"

Juliette's eyes narrowed. "What exactly is your role at the hotel?"

Suddenly, Henri understood, and his shoulders dropped with relief. Sometimes guests came with a burning curiosity about how the magic of The Splendor functioned. What they really wanted was a peek behind the scenes. A taste of what it would be like to live and work here. The secret was to give them just enough to satisfy their curiosity without destroying the dreamworld he'd worked so hard to create. *Everyone wants to taste the bacon, but no one wants to watch you butcher the pig*, Stella often reminded him. *When a guest asks to know more, give them a tour of the kitchen, not the slaughterhouse.*

Henri had long ago learned how to handle inquisitive guests.

He smiled. "Let me guess: You've always wanted to be an illusionist?"

Juliette gaped at him as if a set of horns had just erupted on his head. "Not in the slightest."

Her reply was a sharp needle that punctured his swelling certainty. Every time he thought he'd finally found his footing, she said or did something that made him feel as if he'd stepped into a patch of quicksand—like he was slowly sinking with no idea how to extricate himself.

How was he going to explain to Stella that he was no

closer to designing a Signature Experience for Juliette than he
had been this morning?

A bead of sweat slipped from the nape of Henri's neck and
inched down his spine. The courtyard had been enchanted
for the comfort of the guests, but Henri was immune to the
soothing sensation of a circulating breeze. He resisted the
urge to let go of Juliette so he could strip off his jacket.

"Did *you* always want to be an illusionist?" she asked.

The question caught him so off guard that he answered it
honestly.

"I don't know."

Juliette laughed, a rich, resonant sound that floated on the
air like music. "How could you not know?"

Panic bloomed in Henri's chest. He summoned another
wave of magic and sent it through Juliette. The music swelled.
A subtle fragrance with notes of orange and vanilla wafted
through the air. Contentment wrapped around them like a
warm blanket.

Juliette closed her eyes and breathed deeply, the question
forgotten.

A headache thrummed at Henri's temples.

This whole evening had been a disaster. Nothing was
going according to plan.

His gaze swept over the courtyard and the myriad of
guests soaking in the atmosphere—lounging in the chairs at
the edges of the dance floor; eating desserts, their eyes closed
in rapture; gazing up at the stars dotting the night sky.

And then there was Juliette. It was as if she needed to be
convinced to stay.

She was clearly heartbroken—her single bite of cake
had told him that much. But usually those were the easiest
guests to manage. They arrived eager to forget, and The
Splendor allowed them to dive headfirst into a fantasy world

of extravagance and distraction. So, why was Juliette so resistant to being swept away? She seemed more intent on asking questions than basking in luxury.

What if that's why she came? For a different kind of adventure?

Maybe he could direct her curiosity in a more productive direction. Give her a mystery to solve. The idea spun around his mind, bumping against all the Signature Experiences he'd created in the past. He'd never allowed a guest to be a detective for the week. To gather evidence and solve a case. A memory surfaced—a card game where players raced to be the first to solve a series of clues. He tried to grab the thought as it floated past—where had he played it? when?—but the details refused to crystalize, slipping away like a half-remembered dream in early morning.

Henri's eyes burned. He needed sleep.

"You never answered my question." Juliette's voice snapped his attention back to the present. She was watching him with a curious expression. "What exactly is your role here?"

"I thought we'd already established I'm an illusionist."

Juliette tilted her head to one side. "You seem like you're something more."

Henri's chest went tight. It wasn't unusual for the occasional guest to ask questions about the hotel, but no one ever showed any interest in Henri himself. He knew he shouldn't read too much into it. Juliette was probably just especially inquisitive. Or maybe she wasn't quite sure what she wanted yet, and her questions were an attempt to discover what was possible. But he couldn't help how it touched something inside him to feel seen.

He tried to keep his voice even. "What makes you think I'm something more?"

She lifted one shoulder in a shrug. "The rest of the staff look at you with deference."

"Do they?" Henri scanned the room—to the waiters carrying trays of magic-laced canapés to the sculptors creating living topiaries to the chefs spinning edible globes of mist for guests to inhale flavors of cheesecake, peppermint, and apple pie. He'd always craved more friendship than they were willing to offer, but *deference* hadn't crossed his mind as the reason why.

Juliette laughed. "So, who are you?"

"My guardians own The Splendor," he said. "They took me in as a boy and I've lived here most of my life."

Juliette's face softened. "I'm an orphan too."

A wave of cold shock went through him. He'd never met someone who had a similar background as him, and he had the instant desire to pull her off the dance floor and ask her a million questions. Did she ever find a permanent guardian? Did she ever dream about her parents? Did she ever feel alone in the world?

His first impression of her shifted, breaking apart and reforming into something new. He was aching to know more, but he was supposed to be focused on her desires, not her past. He couldn't just—

"Did you know your parents?" The question slipped out before he could help it.

Juliette bit her lip and her eyes filled with pain. A sudden vision of Stella's irritated face swam in his imagination. He could practically hear her voice in his head. *Never do anything to break the spell for a guest. The Splendor weaves a tapestry of luxury—don't tug at the threads!*

Henri had just committed the twin sins of losing focus on his steady stream of decadence-creating magic *and* broaching an unpleasant topic. Sad talk was expressly forbidden.

This conversation was exactly the opposite of what he was supposed to be doing. But he hadn't had time to gather information on Juliette before her arrival. If he had any hope of making her visit extraordinary, he had no choice but to do it here and now. Even Stella would have to concede that, wouldn't she?

And he couldn't deny Juliette piqued his curiosity. Even if he put the priorities of The Splendor aside, he wanted to know more about her.

But he couldn't afford mistakes. If Juliette left unhappy, Stella would never forgive him.

He reached for his magic. "Never mind. You don't have to answer." He let the magic flow down his arms, but before it reached Juliette, she started to talk.

"I didn't know them." She sighed. "Not really. I never met my father and I only have vague memories of my mother." Her expression was distant and sad. He should back off. Change the subject to something more pleasant. Let his illusions flow into her and erase the lines between her eyes.

But he didn't.

"So who raised you?" he asked.

"My sister and I lived in the children's home in Belle Fontaine. But she's several years older than I am, so . . ." Juliette stiffened. Swallowed. "If I'm honest, it was"—she hesitated, as if searching for the right word—"it was Clare who raised me."

Clare. The name turned over in his mind like a key in a lock. Suddenly he knew why Juliette had seemed familiar.

A stone dropped into his stomach.

He knew exactly who had broken Juliette's heart.

And it was all his fault.

CHAPTER FIVE

JULIETTE

J ULIETTE WAS FLOATING THROUGH A DREAM.
She followed Caleigh up the curving marble staircase, her thoughts coming and going like gossamer clouds— one moment solid and distinctly shaped but vanishing if she tried to hold them, as if blown away by a strong wind.

It wasn't an entirely unpleasant sensation.

Caleigh glanced over her shoulder. "Did you have a nice time?"

Juliette murmured an assent, though "nice" was an understatement. Juliette had *danced*. She moved across the floor like the performers she'd seen at a festival one summer when she was small—women dressed in jewel-toned silks and delicate slippers, spinning so fast they looked like their feet never quite touched the ground. Tonight she'd been just as elegant. Every bit as skilled.

It had made her feel alive in a way she never dreamed possible.

At the top of the stairs, Caleigh took Juliette's elbow and

led her down a wide corridor lined with vases of flowers and baskets of fruit.

Caleigh stopped at a set of ivory double doors carved with a delicate design of vines and leaves and opened them with a flourish. "Welcome to your suite."

After everything she'd seen today, Juliette thought she was beyond surprise.

She was wrong.

Plush white carpet stretched in front of her like a field of freshly fallen snow, and the moment she stepped over the threshold, she longed to tug off her shoes and let the fabric push up between her toes and caress the soles of her feet.

She spun in a slow circle as she tried to take it all in. The walls were covered in light green fabric dotted with tiny pink rosebuds.

On the far side of the room was a round marble dais encircled by fluted columns in salmon-colored stone. An enormous four-poster bed stood in the center, draped with delicate, filmy curtains.

Juliette moved farther into the room. Directly in front of her, two oversized chairs covered in pale blue velvet flanked a hearth that glowed with a cheerful fire. A low table held a tray of flaky pastries and a small plate of chocolate molded in the shape of a swan. Around the corner was an enormous round bathtub, already filled to the brim; steam curled invitingly from the surface.

"The water will stay warm all evening, so there's no rush." Caleigh's gaze flicked from the bath to the pastries. "Are you hungry?"

Juliette smiled. "Actually, I'm starving." She curled into one of the chairs by the fire. Warmth enveloped her and the cushion seemed to conform to her body, making her feel weightless. Her thoughts went calm and diffuse.

Juliette reached for a knife and delicately sliced a wing from the chocolate swan. She plucked a flaky roll from the tray, smeared it with the chocolate, and took a bite. She let out an involuntary sigh as the combination melted in her mouth. She'd never tasted anything so decadent.

"I saw you dancing with Henri," Caleigh said, sinking into the chair opposite Juliette. "You're lucky. He doesn't often interact with the guests."

A thread of pleasure went through her at the thought of being singled out. "He taught me to dance."

Caleigh smiled conspiratorially. "Yes, I saw."

Juliette felt heat flood her cheeks. The words had slipped from her lips unbidden.

But if Caleigh noticed her discomfort, she didn't let on. Juliette's embarrassment faded as quickly as it had come, and her thoughts circled lazily around the idea of someone like Henri caring about someone like her. It was just a fantasy, wasn't it?

They ate in silence until Juliette didn't think she could manage another bite. She let out a contented sigh.

Caleigh smiled, as if the sound pleased her. "How would you like to end your evening?" she asked. "A bath? A massage?"

"A massage?" The idea felt both foreign and thrilling— something she'd heard about but had always seemed impossibly out of reach. "Is that—" She bit her lip, feeling suddenly shy. "Is it really an option?"

Caleigh grinned. "Of course, it is."

Juliette hesitated. Did she dare? Then again, why was she here if not to be pampered? "A massage sounds nice if you really don't mind?"

"Why would I mind? I'm here to make sure you have everything you could possibly want." Caleigh stood up and poked her head into the corridor. Juliette heard the muffled murmur of conversation, and before she knew what was happening, a young man dressed in a red bellhop uniform entered the room. He wore a rounded pillbox hat and carried a folded table beneath one arm and a basket full of supplies in the other. He must have been waiting nearby just in case. It felt strange to have so many people at her beck and call.

Strange and glorious.

The bellhop unfolded the padded table and placed it in the center of the room. Then he began pulling supplies from the basket—dozens of candles, which he lit and scattered around the room, a variety of oils in small jars, a fluffy robe.

His movements were quick and efficient. When he was finished, he gave Caleigh a quick nod and left the room.

Caleigh reached in her pocket and took out a small silver bell. "I'll give you some privacy to get changed, but don't hesitate to ring if you need anything at all." She gave the bell a gentle shake and a lovely set of chimes echoed through the room. Either she must sleep very lightly and very nearby or the bell was enchanted.

"Thank you," Juliette said, "I will."

Caleigh dropped the bell into Juliette's palm. "Sweet dreams." And then she slipped out the door and closed it behind her.

Juliette set the bell down on the small table beside the bed. She changed into the robe the bellhop had left neatly folded on top of the dresser—it was made from the softest fabric she'd ever felt. She climbed onto the padded table, and the moment she nestled her face into the head cradle, gentle strains of relaxing music began to waft through the room.

Magic.

The door opened softly. She lifted her head to see a short older woman dressed in flowing robes of soft pink. Her silver hair was gathered in a bun at the back of her head.

"Hello, Juliette." Her voice was calm and soothing. "I'm Harriet."

Juliette started to reply, but Harriet lifted a hand. "No need. Just relax and I'll do the rest."

Juliette expected to feel at least some measure of awkwardness—she wasn't used to being touched by strangers, let alone in such an intimate way. But something about the woman's calming presence—or maybe something about The Splendor itself—made her feel completely at ease. Harriet slid the robe from Juliette's shoulders and began to knead her neck and upper back. The masseuse's hands were soft but skilled. Magic flowed through Juliette's muscles, unwinding tension she hadn't been aware she was holding. She lost track of time. She felt weightless.

The longer Harriet worked, the more deeply Juliette sunk into an utterly blissful state of peace. She forgot where she was. Forgot *who* she was. She was serenity itself, and she couldn't imagine worrying about anything ever again.

The last thought she had before drifting off to sleep was this: The Splendor was her favorite place in all the world.

CHAPTER SIX

HENRI

STELLA WAS DISPLEASED.

She stood in front of the floor-to-ceiling windows of the penthouse apartment and stared out over the twinkling lights of the city below.

Henri studied her with a pit in his stomach. The stiff set of her shoulders. The way the cords in her neck pulled taut. He'd just spent the last hour recounting the events of the evening—from the failed dessert to his inability to determine an appropriate Signature Experience for Juliette.

Theo had asked a few questions, but Stella had scarcely said a word. And her silence spoke volumes.

Henri hated disappointing her.

He raked his fingers through his hair. "I'll keep trying. I'm sorry I couldn't—"

"Son." Theo's voice was gentle, but firm. He patted the leather seat beside him. "Sit down and stop apologizing." Theo's feet were propped on the table in front of him. His hands threaded together behind his head as if he didn't have a care in the world.

Henri remained standing.

Theo's eyes flicked to Stella and then back to Henri. "Both of you need to relax."

Stella shot him a withering glare. "Or maybe *you* should show a little more concern."

Theo frowned and gave a heavy, exaggerated sigh. "You're right, dear. Let's throw Henri out on the streets because he hasn't ascertained the hopes and dreams of a stranger in one evening." His eyebrow quirked up playfully. "What a failure."

Stella's expression thawed. She dropped into the seat next to Theo and nestled in the crook of his arm. "I'm sorry. You're right."

This was Theo's magic—more impressive than any illusion. His calm was the counterpoint to Stella's chaos. He softened her hard edges and brought her back from the brink.

Theo's fingers rested lightly on the crown of Stella's head. "I'm not the one who deserves the apology."

Stella stiffened. A weighty hush filled the room, and then finally, she gave a defeated sigh. Her eyes lifted to Henri. "I've been too hard on you. Forgive me."

Henri's shoulders fell, and he let out a relieved breath. He sat. The leather cushion beneath him was supple and buttery soft. Every detail in the penthouse—from the fabrics and furniture to the lighting and floors—was both sumptuous and genuine. Stella didn't care for illusion in her own spaces.

"Of course, I forgive you," Henri said. "I know how much you care about The Splendor."

"It's the most important thing in my life," Stella said.

Theo gave a gruff laugh and sunk his fingers into her hair. "No offense taken."

Stella elbowed him in the ribs. "You know what I mean."

But then her playful expression turned more serious. She straightened and leaned forward, arms resting on her thighs. "We need a plan. Guests who arrive wanting nothing are bad news."

An image of Juliette surfaced in Henri's mind, and a sudden protective instinct rose in his chest like a mother bear alerting to an unexpected threat. "I'm sure she wants *something*. I just don't know what it is yet."

Stella regarded him with cool detachment. "Or maybe she's intent on causing trouble."

Henri shook his head. "I don't think so. She recently suffered a heartbreak."

"Why didn't you say so?" Stella's voice sounded shot through with a sudden burst of sunshine. "If someone broke her heart, then you must *un*-break it. Maybe all she needs is a love story."

A trickle of unease slid down Henri's spine. He didn't say anything about romance. Stella jumped to that conclusion all on her own.

He shifted in his seat. He hadn't mentioned Clare yet. He told himself it was because he didn't want to cause Stella and Theo undue alarm. Maybe one heartbreak was just like another. Maybe it didn't matter that Clare had only been here a few weeks ago. That Juliette really *did* have reason to resent The Splendor.

But in truth, it was more than that. Something about Juliette's face when she took a bite of Amella's chocolate cake had reached inside him and plucked a deep chord of sympathy that resonated in a way Henri couldn't explain. He'd never had his heart broken. Not that he remembered anyway. And yet . . .

"I appreciate your honesty." Stella's voice snapped Henri's attention back to the present and hit him like a pitcher of ice water thrown in his face. He tried to compose his expression but felt—as he always did when Stella looked at him—like he were made of glass and she could see his thoughts on display.

Henri swallowed. "My honesty?"

"You could have told us the evening went perfectly, and we wouldn't have known the difference." She leaned forward and patted his hand. "You're a good boy, Henri. Fortunately, I think this problem is easily fixed. Give the girl a romance she won't soon forget."

"It's getting late," Theo said, stretching and swinging his legs to the floor. "I'm going to bed."

Stella glanced at the clock on the wall, and a crease appeared between her brows. "You better get going, Henri. You have a full night of work ahead."

A full night of work ahead. His head ached at the thought. He kneaded his eyes with his thumb and forefinger. The exhaustion was unrelenting—wave after wave of it, and he felt as if he barely had a chance to catch his breath before it pulled him under again. He commanded his body to stand. If he kept moving, maybe he could outrun his fatigue.

"I'll give you an update in the morning," he said as he headed toward the door.

"Not too early," she said. "You need your rest."

He was grateful she'd noticed.

"And, Henri?"

"Yes?" He looked back, his hand on the door frame.

"Make sure Juliette Berton has sweet dreams tonight."

Henri started his evening in the crypt. He slowly descended the hundreds of roughly hewn stone steps that plunged into the vast underground cavern beneath the hotel. The air grew thick, enveloping him in a warm, soothing blanket of steam. The pounding in his head slowed, and then stopped altogether.

The Splendor's magic came from water.

The hotel was built on a network of geothermal lakes, rivers, and springs—hundreds of them, all bubbling from the earth below and brimming with magical properties. Some were so hot they could disintegrate a person on contact. Others were cold enough to halt a beating heart. But the best was a mix of the two—serene pools where scalding springs and icy ones melded together underground to create the perfect temperature for a full-body soak. Water that bestowed heavy doses of relaxation and power.

And Henri needed both if he was going to work all night.

He reached the final step and took a deep breath. The crypt seemed bled of color. The only light came from the dozens of flickering torches mounted on the stone walls. It was the exact opposite of the world upstairs—dim instead of bright, peaceful instead of bustling, monochromatic instead of bursting with a thousand hues. It was muted in every respect and Henri loved it.

He headed for his favorite spot in the entire underground. Theo once jokingly called the hot spring Lobster Lake because Henri had a habit of soaking for hours at a time, often emerging with bright-red skin that persisted for half a day afterward.

The name stuck.

Henri stripped down to his underwear and lowered himself into the hot water. Instantly, his muscles relaxed, and as the tension melted away, his jumbled thoughts untangled and stretched out, slow and lazy.

Stella's anxious face—which had been at the forefront of his mind since he left the penthouse—faded and his attention wandered to the events of the evening. His thoughts circled around Juliette. She presented a unique set of challenges. Henri had dealt with last-minute guests before. And he'd been forced to create Signature Experiences based on limited information too. But this was the first time two guests had dovetailed quite like this—the first time one guest arrived as a direct consequence of another.

If I'm honest, it was Clare who raised me. The memory of Juliette's words pierced Henri; guilt spread through his heart like a stain. How could he possibly restore her happiness when he'd had a hand in destroying it in the first place? The task seemed impossible.

His throat grew thick. Stella would be furious when she found out he'd withheld information from her. Maybe he could fix it before he had to tell her.

Henri sighed. He couldn't afford to worry about this right now. Not when he had so many other guests who needed his attention tonight. He pushed thoughts of Juliette and Clare from his mind and slowly sunk deeper into the water until his entire face was submerged. His vision fractured and his worries spiraled away. He stayed underwater until his lungs begged for air. Until his mind was empty and clear.

When he resurfaced, he felt better. More well rested than he had all day. He wondered if his renewed energy was real or if it was only an illusion.

He wondered if it even mattered.

Henri climbed out of Lobster Lake and hurriedly dressed. He didn't bother drying off, even though his clothes stuck to his damp skin. The longer he remained in contact with the water, the better. He climbed the long steps, but at the top, he passed over the door he'd come through before. He turned left and entered a different door that deposited him in a secret passageway that ran behind the suites—a mirror image of the main hallways of The Splendor. Much like the crypt, the hidden corridor wasn't decked out in the lavish finishes characteristic of the public areas of the hotel. The walls and floors were stone. The lighting was sparse. Along the length of the corridor—at eye level—were a series of small, evenly spaced plaques with numbers engraved on their surfaces. Above each was a small rectangular opening. Henri stopped in front of the number 124. Gemma Caron's suite.

Henri placed a palm against the stone wall. He closed his eyes and focused until his mind touched Gemma's. She was deeply asleep. Her concierge must have left her hours ago. But then, Gemma had been here so many times before, she probably looked forward to sleep. As luxurious as The Splendor was during the day, the most impressive magic—Henri's magic—happened beneath a blanket of stars.

As tired as he was, Henri felt a bit of relief at the simplicity of the task ahead. Unlike Juliette, Gemma's desires were not a mystery. She was a wealthy woman in her seventies and a longtime patron of The Splendor. Gemma knew exactly what she wanted and presented Stella with detailed instructions before every stay.

Tonight, she wanted to join the circus.

Henri reached in his pocket and removed a small vial made of bright fuchsia glass; a cloudy substance swirled inside. He unstopped the container and the vapor glided out and twisted around his fingers. Henri gathered the substance in his palm and gently blew it into the small opening—a discrete pathway between the hidden corridor and Gemma's room. The mist scattered like dandelion seeds and disappeared through the wall. Henri guided it to Gemma's temples. He couldn't see her, but he'd worked with her often enough that her mind was as familiar as her face.

Henri let the substance sink into Gemma's memory. And then he began to work.

The experience had been carefully crafted over a week ago, but Henri still needed to tweak details as he wove it into Gemma's existing experiences. He needed to make it unique to her, so it would feel as real as if she'd actually been there.

Henri gently guided images into Gemma's mind: a giant circus tent with fat red and white stripes. Butterflies dancing in Gemma's stomach. The silky feel of her lavender leotard against her skin. He reached into her memory for how she felt as a young girl—the parts that were brave and fearless, the parts that were self-conscious and unsure—and he wove them seamlessly into this moment. Gemma stood on the platform high above the crowd, both exhilarated and afraid. Her aerial partner waited on the opposite side of the tent, so far away his face was featureless. He was dressed in bright silver. He climbed on the swing, and a spasm of panic went through Gemma. Could she trust him? Her sleeping mind supplied the question, and Henri scrambled to answer it. He searched her memory for someone she *did* trust—a childhood friend—and borrowed some of his features. The partner folded his legs around the swing, flipped upside down, and launched himself toward Gemma with outstretched hands.

She saw his face and an instinctive feeling of trust settled her nerves. The butterflies in her stomach landed softly. Her partner would never let her fall. She reached for him; he caught her and held her with a steady grip.

And then Gemma was flying.

The crowd blurred beneath her. A few tendrils of hair escaped from her bun and tickled her cheeks.

Gemma pointed her toes. Folded her body in half. Flipped upside down.

With some guests, Henri might focus on the applause. On the adulation of the people below. On making the client feel like a star.

But not Gemma.

What she most desired was adrenaline—the breathless exhilaration of being high above the ground, the thrill of speed, the sensation that her body was without limits—and so he lingered in this moment, stretching it far beyond its natural limits like pastel taffy on a pull, sticky and sweet.

Finally, Gemma's partner deposited her back on the platform. The crowd roared. A warm feeling of satisfaction glowed in Gemma's chest.

Henri brought every detail into focus—the tantalizing smell of popcorn, the delighted yells of children bouncing on their toes and begging for more, the bright spotlight that bathed Gemma in fire.

In her sleep, her heart pounded.

She wasn't ready to climb down from the platform yet, but she didn't need Henri's help to stay. Her imagination had been sufficiently primed to allow her dreams to take over from here, spinning the experience in a thousand different directions, adding details to thrill and delight her until the soft light of morning nudged her awake.

Henri slipped the glass vial back into his pocket. He'd visit again tomorrow—and every night for the rest of Gemma's stay—each time giving her a new costume, a new crowd, a new trapeze routine. By the time she checked out of The Splendor, she'd feel as if she'd lived a rich and full life as a trapeze artist. It wouldn't feel like a dream. It would be as real as the birth of her child. As tangible as the death of her husband.

Henri was very skilled at his craft.

He continued down the corridor, stopping at each room to offer some bit of magic. Not every client would get a Signature Experience tonight. Most only took one evening to complete, and Henri needed to conserve his energy. But every guest got at least a morsel of illusion to enhance their stay. Henri stopped at room 189—Gabriel Martin—who wanted to play the violin on the streets of Paris. His Signature Experience was scheduled for his final night at the hotel, but Henri sent a tiny whiff of magic through the opening above the door. Just enough to give Gabriel dreams of tuning his instrument. Of taking lessons and learning how to shift smoothly between positions. Of hours spent perfecting his vibrato so it resonated with a lush, full sound. These small illusions would make the Signature Experience—when it finally happened—richer and more satisfying.

Henri's energy flagged as he climbed the stairs to the next level and then the next. Floor by floor and room by room, he sent tendrils of magic into every single guest suite until he could barely stand. A headache throbbed at his temples. His thoughts grew muddy and a muted, faraway panic gnawed in his gut. There was a price to his magic, and he was afraid of what would happen when the bill came due.

Henri stopped in front of the door he'd saved for last. The number engraved on the plaque was 718: Juliette Berton's room. He leaned his head against the cool stone and took a deep breath.

And then he released his magic and let it perch on Juliette's mind.

Henri was instantly awake.

Juliette was already dreaming, and her dreams were full of longing—for Clare, for the parents she barely knew, for a group of people she could call family. Her desires were so familiar they robbed Henri of breath. It was like glimpsing into his own depths and witnessing something so raw he struggled not to flinch away. He and Juliette were the same. She thought she wanted a fantasy, but she didn't—not really. She wanted a more satisfying reality.

It was the one thing he didn't have the power to give her. Stella's words echoed in his memory. *Maybe all she needs is a love story.* Stella could be right. Falling in love was a powerful drug and it could treat a variety of ailments. But Henri didn't think it was the right choice.

Not for Juliette.

He let his magic sink into her mind, but he didn't give her riches or adventure or fame. He simply let her feel safe. He filled her imagination with wonderful but ordinary things. Watching a new puppy run through the grass, his too-big paws making him awkward and clumsy. Catching snowflakes on her tongue in the first storm of winter. Coming in from the cold to warm her hands in front of a crackling fire.

Henri gave Juliette the feeling of sitting on a mother's lap to hear a story she'd heard a hundred times before. A father who checked beneath the bed for monsters. The sensation of biting into a perfectly ripe strawberry. He let her dream of birthday cakes, and splashing barefoot through shallow streams, and the feeling of sand squishing between her toes.

He gave her everything he'd always wanted. He fed simple bits of magic through the opening above room 718 until he felt like a wrung-out cloth, all the energy completely squeezed out of him.

Until he had nothing left to give.

Henri was barely aware of staggering back into the main hallways of The Splendor. He climbed up to his attic bedroom and didn't even bother to undress before he fell into bed. He was drifting toward sleep when a horrible thought occurred to him. What if he'd made everything worse instead of better? He'd given Juliette all the joy he could manage, but it wasn't a Signature Experience, so it would simply seem like a very vivid dream to her.

He gave her a happy life that would be snatched away the moment she woke. A feeling of dread settled over him.

He'd made a terrible mistake. Instead of weaving a beautiful fantasy to help her escape, he'd shown her in painstaking detail how lacking her life had been to this point.

And how hopeless it would seem the moment she left The Splendor.

CHAPTER SEVEN

JULIETTE

J ULIETTE WOKE FACEDOWN ON THE MASSAGE TABLE. HER
eyes were coaxed open by the sound of a cleared throat,
followed by a giggle. She pushed herself into a sitting
position.

Caleigh stood at the threshold of the room, holding a
covered tray. Her eyes twinkled with amusement. "Wow, that
must have been some massage if it knocked you out for the
entire night."

"Is it morning already?" But as Juliette blinked against
the sunlight streaming through the windows, she realized the
question hardly needed an answer.

And Caleigh didn't give one. Her eyes flicked to the still-
made bed and then back to Juliette. She gave an exaggerated
frown. "You didn't even get to experience sleeping in your
amazing bed. Well, I guess it gives you something to look
forward to tonight." She winked. "You're in for a treat."

Juliette rolled her neck and shoulders, searching for some
sign of the discomfort that might typically arise from sleeping

in the same position all night, but her body felt as loose and relaxed as it ever had. Her dreams had been full of simple joys and small pleasures. An unfamiliar sensation coursed through her and she tried—drowsily—to identify it. It took her a moment, but finally she found the word. *Contentment.* She was content.

Caleigh uncovered the tray in her arms, revealing a stack of fluffy waffles covered in strawberries and whipped cream. "I'm sorry it's not much, but we're in a bit of a time crunch."

Juliette stared at her, confused. The breakfast looked as delicious as anything she'd ever eaten, and her mouth watered as Caleigh handed her the plate. "Why are you apologizing?"

"It's just that usually we have more variety. I'll bring a better selection tomorrow." She handed Juliette a fork. "You eat and I'll find you something to wear." Caleigh disappeared around the corner and Juliette dug into the waffles. They tasted every bit as divine as they looked. Rich strawberry sauce soaked into the buttery crevices. Each bite melted in her mouth.

"Why are we in a time crunch?" Juliette called out between forkfuls. "What are we doing?"

Caleigh reappeared with a stack of clothes. "Yesterday was all about luxury and relaxation. Today is about fun. We're going to the arena."

The arena was an oval-shaped, open-air theater built into the side of a hill. A light breeze ruffled Juliette's hair as she followed Caleigh down the gentle slope. The weather was perfect—neither too hot, nor too cold. The sky was soft blue and cloudless. As they got closer, the low roar of a crowd drifted toward them. When they reached the base of the hill, the arena finally came into full view.

Juliette's breath caught. It was so much larger than she'd originally thought, and the benches were packed with spectators.

Thousands of them.

Now she understood Caleigh's comment about being crunched for time. "I'm sorry. Did I take too long eating breakfast? It looks like we'll never find a seat."

"Oh, you're not *watching*," Caleigh said. "You're competing."

Juliette's step faltered. "Competing in what?"

Caleigh laughed at her horrified expression. "Magical chariot racing."

Juliette's stomach went tight and she cast a doubtful glance toward the waiting crowd. There were so many people watching. Chariot racing? She wasn't even confident in her ability to race on foot. She couldn't possibly—Caleigh put a hand on her arm, and Juliette felt instantly calmer. "Don't worry. You're going to love it."

Juliette thought back to the ball last night. She'd been convinced she'd hate dancing, but she was wrong—it had turned out to be utterly magical. Maybe she was wrong about this too.

Caleigh guided her to a large single-story stone building nestled behind the arena. They ducked inside and it took Juliette's eyes a moment to adjust to the dimmer light.

A dozen identical chariots marched along one side of the room in two orderly rows. In the center of the room, a large group mingled. Half were dressed in the all-black uniform worn by staff, and the other half donned a variety of clothing from fancy dresses to loungewear.

"So, here's how it works," Caleigh explained. "There will

be twelve teams of two—each made up of one guest and one illusionist. So, the first thing we need to do is get you paired up. I'm happy to offer recommendations, or you can go meet them yourself and choose."

Juliette stared at her, openmouthed. "How would I choose? I'm not even sure what's happening."

"I already told you. Chariot races." As if this answered all possible questions.

Juliette groaned. "Not helpful."

Caleigh took her elbow and guided her forward. "Go talk to them and find someone you click with. All of them are insanely talented, but the team who wins is usually the one who communicates best. I recommend starting with Maura. She's wickedly fast." Caleigh nodded to a girl with waist-length black hair and then turned back to Juliette. "Are you competitive?"

Apparently she wasn't, because Maura seemed to be holding court among several guests vying for her attention, and Juliette had no desire to push in.

She scanned the group for another illusionist, and her heart quickened as she spotted Henri in the throng. His head was bent toward an older guest, who was gesticulating wildly as he talked, obviously in the middle of relating some exciting story. But Henri's eyes kept flicking up toward the entrance, and for just a moment, Juliette had the odd sensation that he was looking for her. She shoved the thought away—it was ridiculous. He probably didn't even remember her.

Caleigh followed Juliette's gaze, and made a low noise at the back of her throat. "Well that's interesting."

"What?"

"Henri's never competed before."

Something fluttery moved through Juliette's chest. "So why is he here now?"

Caleigh gave her a conspiratorial grin and nudged her in the ribs. "Maybe you should go find out."

Juliette's cheeks heated. But she had to go talk to *someone*, so it might as well be an illusionist she'd already met.

She plunged into the crowd, drying her sweaty palms on the front of her pants as she walked. She wondered if the other guests felt this apprehensive. Henri was facing away from her, his thick black hair curling just a bit at the nape of his neck. When she got close enough, she touched him lightly on the shoulder and he spun around. His expression was blank at first, but then it melted into a smile.

"Juliette." So, he *did* remember her. "Nice to see you again."

"I've been told I'm supposed to find a partner for"—she gestured toward the chariots—"whatever this is."

He laughed, low and rich. "This," he said, "is one of the finest games The Splendor has to offer. What do you say we team up and win it?"

"You're not already spoken for?"

His gaze was steady, his dark eyes holding hers. "I'm not. But if you'd rather try for Maura—"

"No." Juliette shook her head. "She seems to have her hands full."

"Because she's the reigning champion," Henri said, "but maybe we can dethrone her."

A series of three bells chimed and the crowd parted as if by magic. Henri rested his palm between Juliette's shoulder blades and leaned down to whisper in her ear. "We now have until the second bell to prepare our chariot," he explained.

"Prepare it how?" The chariots looked perfectly functional to her, and even if they weren't, she didn't have the skill set to get them ready for use and she doubted Henri did either.

He put a hand to his chest and gave her a feigned grave

look. "We can't possibly race in something so plain."

Suddenly Juliette understood. This was less about competition than it was about luxury and magic. A thrill of anticipation went through her as Henri led her to their chariot.

"What are we going to do with it?" she asked, running her fingertips over the smooth brown wood.

"Whatever you want. We're a team. You provide the creativity and I provide the magic."

She glanced around the room. Guests furiously whispered to illusionists as chariots transformed all around her. One appeared to be made of white marble, but the gold veining running through it was animated—moving vines that sprouted leaves; flowers that slowly bloomed, disappeared, and then blossomed anew. Another chariot mimicked the night sky, full of twinkling stars and constellations. Juliette was transfixed. In a matter of moments, the rows of identical unadorned chariots had become a vibrant collection of art. She didn't know if her imagination could compete.

And then she had an idea.

She spun toward Henri. "Could we make our chariot an animal?"

He raised a single eyebrow. "What did you have in mind?"

"A dragon."

Henri didn't respond for the space of several breaths. Juliette shifted her weight from one foot to the other. Maybe it was a terrible idea. But then a slow smile spread across his face like the spill of sunlight over a mountainside.

"That's genius."

He ran a palm over the wood and it instantly rippled into leathery green scales. Juliette gasped. It was entirely realistic. She touched the chariot and it shivered under her hand as if it really were an animal come to life. She leaped back as the dragon sprouted a giant tail that swished in her direction. She circled around to find a horned head had grown on the front of the chariot, as well as a small pair of wings on either side.

Juliette held out her hand and the dragon sniffed at her fingers. Delight bubbled up her throat and she laughed.

"Henri, this is remarkable."

She wasn't the only one who thought so. The room filled with a chorus of murmured awes as the other guests gazed at Henri's creation. Several of the guests openly scowled at their illusionist partners. Juliette was surprised by how much it pleased her to have such jealousy aimed in her direction. Maybe she was competitive after all.

Another set of bells chimed. It was time to race.

C AMARADERIE.

  The thought had startled Henri from a deep sleep. He'd drifted off the night before with questions about Juliette swirling through his mind—why she was here, what she wanted, how he could make sure her visit was a success. He'd sifted through everything he knew about her, from her lost parents to the way she'd questioned him about his role at The Splendor, to the sense of longing he'd seen in her dreams. She wanted so many of the same things he did. Friends. Family. To belong.

  But he couldn't come up with anything to deliver those things in such a short visit. And then the thought that made him bolt upright: Juliette needed to feel a sense of camaraderie.

  And the chariot races were the perfect way to achieve that.

  It had taken some time to arrange. They needed illusionists to manifest not just the arena but thousands of spectators to fill it. And they also needed eleven other guests for whom the chariot races would be an added benefit to their visit.

Henri had been up for hours by the time he and Juliette finally stood together on the back of the chariot. They were waiting at the starting line for the bells that would signal the beginning of the race. He should be exhausted, but he could feel Juliette's anticipation like a pressure in the air. Her cheeks were flushed. She bounced lightly on the balls of her feet. It both relieved and energized him: He may have finally solved the mystery of what she wanted.

A set of chimes rippled through the air and a cacophony of magic erupted all around them. The other illusionists had conjured horses to pull their chariots, but who needed horses when you had a dragon on your side?

"Go, Henri!" Juliette shouted. "Go!"

Henri used his magic to create the sensation of their dragon lurching forward. Juliette sucked in a sharp, startled breath and lost her balance for just a moment. She grabbed Henri's arm to steady herself and then she laughed—it was a wild, joyous sound that demanded company.

Henri laughed too.

He summoned a feeling of speed, of the wind blowing through Juliette's hair. She tipped her head toward the sky just in time to see an explosion of colors shoot through the air—fireworks in a dozen shapes and colors.

The race wasn't just about speed. It was also about distraction. The illusionists were only allowed to summon magic as directed by their teammate—it allowed the guest to feel in control of the illusions. Making the other competitors lose focus so they forgot to give instructions was half the battle.

"Juliette," Henri said, pulling her attention back to him. "What next?"

From the corner of his gaze, he saw Maura's guest lean over and whisper something in her ear. Maura nodded and stood up straight. Her lips pursed in concentration. He'd heard Maura won so often not because she was the most gifted illusionist—though she was excellent—but that she had a knack for choosing the guest with the fiercest imagination.

The game was on.

A moment later, Juliette gasped.

A yawning chasm had opened on the path in front of them. But Juliette didn't miss a beat. She grabbed Henri's arm. "Fly over it." *Yes.* Unlike the other teams, their chariot had wings.

Henri directed his magic, lifting their dragon in the air and sailing effortlessly over the chasm. A chorus of groans sounded behind them. The other competitors were unhappy, but the crowd was going wild—they were on their feet, clapping and shouting.

Henri risked a glance over his shoulder. Most of the other chariots were perched on the edge of the crater. One of the other illusionists conjured a bridge to span the gulf and the chariots raced across it. But Henri and Juliette were far ahead.

Juliette grinned and Henri felt a thrill go through him. But his confidence was short-lived. A horde of fairies appeared, swarming in the air above them. These were no harmless pixies with brightly colored hair and delicate wings. They were fierce creatures with sharp teeth and excellent aim. One reached over and bit Juliette's ear. She yelped and tried to swat them away, but they were persistent; they covered her eyes with their tiny palms and aimed small kicks to her nose.

"What now?" Henri asked, but she didn't respond. One of the fairies was perched on her lower lip, trying to pry her mouth open.

Henri looked behind him—Maura's distraction had worked. The other teams were catching up. Maura's chariot pulled up alongside them.

"Juliette!" Henri shouted.

Finally, she seemed to register his voice, and she slapped the fairies away from her face "Defend with fire!" she said.

Henri nodded. Their dragon swung his head around, and with one breath set the fairies ablaze. But they were too late to preserve their lead. Maura shot them a smug look as she pulled ahead.

Juliette's expression went murderous. "Jam their wheels," she whispered, jerking her head toward their dragon's hindquarters.

Henri gave her an approving look. It was a smart move.

He focused his magic and their dragon sped up. They pulled even with Maura's chariot, and the dragon swished his tail and thrust it into the spoke of their wheel. The wheel began to wobble and the chariot slowed.

"No!" Maura's teammate cried. He dug his fingers into the hair at his temples as he stared at the wheel in dismay.

The finish line was in sight.

"I think we're going to win," Juliette said, her cheeks flushed with pleasure.

The words had no sooner left her mouth than the dragon let out a plaintive wail. Both Henri and Juliette spun around.

Juliette paled. "Oh no! He's hurt." She put a hand over her mouth.

Henri's heart sank as he followed her gaze. Blood oozed from a gaping wound on the dragon's tail. Maura was playing dirty.

"He'll be all right," Henri said. "We're almost there."

"We have to stop and help him." The dragon let out another whimper, and Juliette's lower lip trembled. "This is all my fault."

A stab of irritation went through Henri. He couldn't reassure Juliette that it was only an illusion without breaking the spell for her. And yet, he'd seem heartless if he insisted they continue. Maura had used Juliette's gentle nature against her. The last thing he needed was for her to leave unhappy.

He scrambled for a way to save the race.

"Look at him," Henri said, "he wants to keep going." He sent of wave of magic across the chariot, and the dragon swung his head around and looked back with what Henri could only hope was an eager expression.

Juliette looked dubious. "Do you think so?"

"I think he wants to win."

"All right," Juliette said, patting the dragon's haunches affectionately. "Let's win, buddy."

"What's next?"

Juliette eyed Maura's chariot. "They fixed one broken wheel awfully quickly. What if they lost all four?"

Henri lifted an appreciative eyebrow and waited for instructions.

"Our dragon can set things on fire," Juliette said, "but can he freeze them too?"

"He can if you say he can."

She nodded, resolute. "He can."

Henri directed a stream of magic toward the front of the chariot. The dragon opened his mouth and blew a gust of icy air in the direction of the leading chariot. All four wheels froze instantly, and then—a moment later—they shattered, spilling Maura and her teammate onto the ground among the glittering shards.

Henri and Juliette sailed past the broken chariot to the finish line.

The crowd roared.

Juliette bounced on her toes. "We did it! We won!"

She pumped her fist in the air and then turned and threw her arms around his neck. Henri's cheeks went hot. He hugged her back.

He'd been trying to create a sense of camaraderie for her, but he was surprised how satisfying the win had been for him.

It felt good to work together, and her creativity impressed him.

"Congratulations," he told her.

She grinned. "You too."

Warmth spread through him, followed by a nagging kernel of worry. Had he fulfilled Juliette's fantasy or had he only indulged in his own?

CHAPTER NINE

JULIETTE

J ULIETTE FELT INVINCIBLE. THE WIN IN THE ARENA HAD been incredible—wielding magic like it was second nature, the roar of appreciation from the crowd, the rush of delight when she and Henri crossed the finish line together.

She was so energized, she was certain she wouldn't be able to sleep. But as she made her way back toward her suite, her feet sinking into the plush carpeting, a feeling of calm settled over her. She was so happy to be here.

Caleigh was waiting at the door to her suite. "Welcome back. How was it?"

Juliette let out a small sigh. "Amazing. We won."

"Yes, I heard." Caleigh moved aside so Juliette could pass. The room looked every bit as inviting as it had last night. A platter of bread and cheese rested between the two chairs by the fire. Around the corner, the bathtub was again brimming with steaming hot water.

It looked like something out of a dream.

A lump formed in her throat. She still couldn't believe she was really here. She thought of the children's home—how much she used to dread the quick shivery baths in the galvanized iron tub. The children were allowed to bathe once a week, and they would line up outside the washroom to wait their turn. Miss Durand—the headmistress of the children's home—heated the water on the cookstove before filling the tub, but she only replaced it once, halfway through the queue. With a dozen or more orphans waiting for a turn, Juliette rarely got lucky enough for clean, warm water, though it was a regular wish. But even in her wildest dreams, she'd never imagined a bath like this—with delicately scented, perpetually hot water. If only Clare could see this.

Clare. The name landed in her mind like a bolt of lightning. Clare was the reason she came here in the first place, but Juliette had barely thought of her since she arrived. She scrambled to remember the last time her sister had even crossed her mind. On the dance floor she'd told Henri that Clare had raised her. But even then, she'd struggled for just a moment to remember her sister's name. And that was more than a day ago. She hadn't thought of Clare even once since. It was as if her sister had fallen out of her memory. A sinister feeling slid down her spine.

She spun around to face Caleigh, whose eyes went wide with alarm.

"Is something wrong?"

"I—" Juliette felt light-headed, and she sat heavily in one of the velvet chairs. "I don't know."

"Here," Caleigh said, holding up the platter, "you're probably just hungry."

Juliette took a slice of cheese and nibbled on the corner. The flavor was amazing—just the right amount of bite and it was just the right temperature to melt in her mouth.

She'd been about to say something. Or perhaps to do something? But now it was lost. Not alarmingly so. Not like the sudden, startled fright of a thief snatching a handbag from her shoulder. More like the thought drifting lazily away. A boat floating out to sea, slowly receding until one forgot it had ever been there in the first place.

"So, you and Henri got the win? Tell me everything."

Juliette smiled, the rush of adrenaline from earlier resurfacing as if she'd just crossed the finish line. She told Caleigh all about her idea to make the chariot a dragon. She recounted the race moment by moment. Caleigh was an appreciative audience, her eyes widening in all the right places.

"It sounds like you and Henri definitely deserved first place," Caleigh said.

"Speaking of Henri." Juliette tugged on her earlobe. "What's his story?"

Caleigh pulled her hair over one shoulder and twisted it around her palm. "Hmmm. Well, I don't know him well. He's quiet. Keeps to himself. Stella finds him indispensable."

"Stella?"

"She owns the hotel. Along with her husband, Theo."

"And they're Henri's guardians?"

A spasm of surprise crossed Caleigh's face. "He told you that?"

"It's not true?"

"Of course, it's true. Henri is just . . ." She let go of her hair and it unraveled down her back. "He likes his privacy. He doesn't usually advertise that he's an orphan."

Orphan. Her mind snagged on the word.

Henri's eyes had filled with sympathy when she'd told him about her childhood. About Clare.

Clare.

Juliette stood. The chair was too comfortable. The food too delicious. She kept losing track of her thoughts.

Caleigh hopped up and laid a palm on Juliette's arm. "Is everything all right?"

"Yes." Juliette rolled her shoulders. "Yes, I'm fine. But I think I'll take that bath now."

"Of course," Caleigh said. "I'm surprised you were able to resist this long. If you need anything at all"—she tipped her head toward the bell that still rested on the bedside table— "you know how to find me."

As soon as Caleigh left, Juliette let out a long breath and pressed her palms flat against her stomach. Finally, she was alone.

It didn't feel as good as she expected.

She peeled off her shoes and paced back and forth across the length of the room. The carpet was even softer than she remembered. But it wasn't enough to distract her anymore.

Loneliness rushed into the space Caleigh left, reminding Juliette of all she'd lost. Memories of Clare swarmed in her mind, buzzing against each other like a bunch of bees trapped in a glass jar. She'd spent the last few minutes desperately trying to hold on to her thoughts of Clare, but now that she had them, pain crept into her heart and something inside her gaped wide—a wound reopened with double the ache.

Clare didn't care about her anymore. It was why Juliette came here in the first place.

The Splendor had a reputation for giving you things you didn't even know you wanted. Maybe some part of her *wanted* to be free from thoughts of Clare. Her eyes flicked to the tub and the oblivion she knew waited for her there.

The Splendor kept giving her the chance to forget, presenting it over and over like a handful of jewels. She'd been pushing it away because it was alarming to have something so valuable offered so freely. It was too good to be true, probably a trick. But maybe it was exactly what she needed. Maybe the hotel was simply providing her the distraction she craved.

What was the point of trying to remember when remembering hurt so fiercely?

She quickly undressed and lowered herself into the water. The relief was instant and all-encompassing. Heat surrounded her, cradled her like a babe in a mother's arms. Fragrant steam blurred her vision. The tension unwound from her muscles and left her whole body feeling boneless and pleasantly heavy.

She closed her eyes and let her worries melt away.

Time ambled forward, seeming to slow to a luxurious pace.

When Juliette next blinked, it took her a few moments to realize she'd drifted off. The water was still hot, but the shadows in the room had deepened and Juliette's thoughts were muzzy and disjointed.

She'd definitely been asleep.

On a small table next to the tub was a fluffy white towel, a set of neatly folded silk pajamas, and a fluted glass filled with bubbly liquid. Had they been there at the beginning of the evening? Or had Caleigh slipped in and left them behind? The thought made Juliette shiver.

She stepped out of the tub and pulled the robe around her shoulders, cinching it tight at the waist. Then she drained the glass in one swallow.

A strange sensation came over her. Even though the beverage was chilled, she warmed pleasantly as it slipped down her throat.

It felt at once refreshing and like curling up for a nap in a patch of sunlight.

Juliette suddenly longed for sleep. She changed into the pajamas. The sapphire fabric was sumptuous and glided over her skin, barely making contact.

Juliette padded over to the dais and pulled back the curtain. She folded the covers down and climbed into bed.

A sigh escaped her lips.

She felt weightless. The mattress perfectly conformed to her every curve, relieving pressure so effectively she felt as if her body had disappeared entirely, and now she was simply a consciousness floating comfortably in space. It was complete and total release.

Within moments, Juliette fell asleep.

The next morning, breakfast arrived in waves.

Juliette was still swimming up through the gauzy layers of sleep when she heard a knock at the door. It took her a moment to remember where she was. Another knock. And then the door swung open and Caleigh's voice chirped out a hello.

Juliette parted the curtains around her bed. Caleigh was striding toward the table holding a tray piled with blueberry tarts. The flaky golden-brown pastries were studded with large crystals of sugar and topped with creamy sweet-cheese and ripe blueberries that oozed purple juices.

Juliette's stomach grumbled in appreciation. She swung her legs over the side of the bed.

"I trust you slept well?" Caleigh set the tray on the table.

Juliette settled into a chair and curled her legs beneath her. "I did, thanks."

The truth was, she hadn't felt this well-rested in years. Her whole body was loose and relaxed.

"I'm glad the night went well." Caleigh placed a napkin folded into the shape of a butterfly beside the tray.

"I'll be right back with the rest."

The rest? Juliette eyed the pastries. This was enough food to keep her full for two days. She couldn't imagine what else she'd need.

Caleigh returned with several more trays—one laden with baked eggs nestled in a bed of ragout made with tomato, spices, and spinach; another boasted tiny sandwiches of ham and brie between slices of thick fried bread.

"I'll never be able to eat all this," Juliette said.

Caleigh laughed. "Of course not. But you should have options."

Options. The concept was unfamiliar to Juliette, who had been raised to accept whatever meager scraps life had to offer. She couldn't imagine living in a world where a variety of choices were displayed before her, all of them beautifully presented with the promise to be equally satisfying.

Juliette swallowed the lump in her throat. It was what she wanted when she came here—options, or at least the illusion of them. But the contented feeling she'd had earlier vanished, and something restless twisted inside her. She couldn't quite put her finger on what it was.

Caleigh's eyebrows pinched together. "If nothing looks good, I can get you something else."

"No, that's not it. I'm sure it's all delicious. But I don't know what to choose."

Caleigh grinned. "Choose it all. Taste everything."

Juliette took the advice. She sampled the flaky tarts, the slightly tangy blueberry exploding across her tongue in a burst of flavor. She cut into the eggs with the edge of her spoon, and liquid gold yolk spilled over the savory sauce. She took a bite and closed her eyes. Divine. Juliette nibbled on sandwiches and dipped sliced oranges in melted chocolate. She ate until she felt stuffed.

Finally, she groaned and laid her head on the table. "That's it. I can't eat another thing."

Caleigh laughed and started gathering trays. "I'll get this out of your way and let you get dressed. You have an exciting day ahead."

Juliette lifted her head and raised her eyebrows in a question. "Exciting how?" She wasn't sure she could move, let alone leave the suite.

Caleigh ignored the question. "Dress for comfort." She dipped her head toward the closet. "You should have no problem finding something."

Once Juliette was alone, the restless feeling inside her unfolded again, expanding like a poisonous bloom. Why was she so unsettled?

She gazed longingly at the bed. She wished she could crawl back under the covers and go back to sleep. She'd felt so happy when she'd first woken.

And then she remembered her dreams—another night full of simple joys and small pleasures. Her lips curved in a smile. For a moment, she was swathed in warmth. And then—in the way of dreams—the images and feelings dissipated, leaving an ache behind. The contentment she'd felt earlier had come from the images floating through her mind while she was asleep.

It wasn't real.

Her gaze swept over the room. And neither was this. It was all temporary.

A void opened inside her—a space so vast it couldn't be filled with delicious food and pretty things. It was an emptiness that cried out for people to love.

A Clare-shaped hollow.

Even though she'd decided to surrender to the magic that kept vanishing Clare from her thoughts, her sister stubbornly refused to leave. Was escape hopeless? If even the magic of The Splendor couldn't fill her up—not for long anyway—how would she ever be whole again?

Juliette blinked back tears as she went to the closet—an enormous room that looked more like an upscale clothing shop than anything else. Floor-to-ceiling shelves were filled with hundreds of shoes displayed like sweets in a candy store; a wall of hooks held bright scarves and handbags in every imaginable size. There were ball gowns and trays of perfume. Boxes of jewelry and shelves lined with fancy hats.

Yesterday, Juliette might have been taken with the boundless luxury. But now she was distracted, barely registering the sumptuous fabrics as she rifled through the drawers, searching for something to wear. Two versions of Clare jostled for position in Juliette's mind: the Clare she'd always known—responsible, kind, prone to worry, but quick to laugh, and then the Clare she met last week, who eyed her with cool disregard. Even if staying at The Splendor had given Clare a taste for a different kind of life, even if she'd decided Juliette was too much a burden, shouldn't she show some sign the decision hurt her? Why didn't Clare have a Juliette-shaped hole in her heart?

Juliette dressed in a pair of soft black pants and a cozy gray top. She grabbed a pair of knee-high boots made from supple black leather and tried them on. Impossibly, they were a perfect fit.

She examined her reflection in the full-length mirror on the back of the door. Just like when Armond had dressed her for the ball, she looked radiant. Her hair fell around her shoulders in soft waves, her skin was lit with a healthy glow, and roses bloomed in her cheeks. She'd never looked better. She searched for some sign of her own fragility in the glass, but her eyes showed no hint of the sadness tugging at her edges. Instead, she appeared confident and self-possessed. A spark of wonder flared inside her, but her heavy thoughts fell over the flame and snuffed it out.

Had she been wrong about how much Clare loved her? Or was the magic of The Splendor really *that* powerful— strong enough to break a bond forged at Juliette's birth and strengthened through shared experiences of abandonment, loneliness, and hunger? She let these two ideas roll around her mind, bumping into one another, careening in opposite directions before colliding again. They were loud inside her mind, but she didn't try to quiet them. She simply listened.

Finally, the two thoughts settled and went still.

In the echoing silence, certainty settled over Juliette like a cloak of iron. She knew her sister as well as she knew herself. Clare would never leave her on purpose.

The Splendor must have changed her somehow.

Dread stole over Juliette. Maybe she had been wrong last night when she'd decided the hotel was giving her what she wanted. What she *needed*. Maybe her first instincts were right—something more than fantasy fulfillment was at play. But what?

"Are you dressed and ready for a magical day?" Caleigh's voice rang through the room and a ping of alarm went through Juliette. She needed answers. But she was unlikely to get them unless she pretended she was still as enchanted and delighted by The Splendor as any other guest. She'd had the same thought last night, but the magic had swept it away. She couldn't let that happen again.

"Just a moment," Juliette said. She took a deep breath and straightened her spine. She would use the rest of her time here to find out what happened to Clare.

And then figure out how to fix it.

She stepped around the corner and offered Caleigh a smile

she hoped was both excited and sincere. "Let's go. I can't wait to see what's in store."

Holding on to her focus was even more difficult than Juliette anticipated. Decadence called to her like a siren song as Caleigh led her through different sections of the hotel, pointing out all of the options for how Juliette could choose to spend her day. There were apothecaries with custom blends of herbs to let you experience any imaginable emotion, feasting rooms where a personal chef whipped up made-to-order delicacies, a fragrance bar with custom scents—everything from traditional smells like cinnamon and vanilla to more unique aromas like cut-green grass and freshly blown-out candles—all available to dab on your wrist or inhale from a jar.

"This is the repose area," Caleigh said as they turned a corner and stepped into an open-air oasis with soaring trees and blooming botanicals. "You can get a massage that will make you more relaxed than you ever thought possible. Or"— she pointed to a vine-draped pergola with a cushioned table in the center—"visit the tree house for a steam treatment. We also have heated soaking pools and cool waterfall showers. But the tranquility rooms are my favorite."

These, as it turned out, were mini private retreats—small rooms made of glass and furnished with cushioned lounge chairs so one could simply sit back and enjoy the view.

The temptation to forget everything and spend the day here was almost overwhelming. Maybe she could. Maybe one day of relaxation wouldn't hurt anything. Maybe it would even make her *more* focused for tomorrow. She could figure out what happened to Clare then.

Caleigh cleared her throat. "If you prefer something less laid-back, I can show you the adventure wing instead."

" Yes, let's do that!" Juliette blurted out the answer before she could change her mind. It was exactly the escape route she needed. If she stayed here one more moment, she knew she'd never leave.

"I like a woman who knows her own mind," Caleigh said with a smile in her voice.

But that was just it—this place seemed intent on producing the opposite result. Determined to make Juliette's thoughts spongy and malleable, until all she cared about was the next pleasure and she had no sense of her own mind at all. It was as if the hotel were designed to make her forget. It took so much energy to resist the allure of getting blissed out by a massage or letting a steam treatment leach the worry from her pores and make her forget her troubles.

As Caleigh led her back inside the hotel, they passed a courtyard with a garden in the center. At first glance, Juliette thought it was a small fruit grove—berry bushes and small trees heavy with apples. But on closer inspection, she realized the greenery was studded with sweets. Bright jelly beans grew on vines. Guests plucked sweet, soft balls of caramel from trees. Colorful chocolate truffles sprouted from plants.

"We could stop," Caleigh offered. "Indulge in a little snack before continuing?"

Again, Juliette pushed aside the temptation. "No thanks. I'm still full from breakfast."

But Juliette couldn't pull her gaze away. Were those flowers actually lollipops?

"Are you sure?"

Would it really hurt to try a little something? Juliette pressed her lips together and nodded.

"I'm sure."

"If you say so." Caleigh threaded her arm through Juliette's and they turned down another corridor.

Henri.

Juliette spotted him before he saw her. He walked toward them, both hands fisted and shoved in his pockets. His expression was unfocused and distracted, as if he were lost in thought. Dark hair fell across his forehead.

A bright spark went through Juliette; her mind suddenly felt sharp and very much her own.

She made a small noise at the back of her throat and Henri lifted his head and met her gaze.

His face changed instantly. He was happy to see her. But the moment the thought drifted through her mind, she swatted it away, her cheeks heating with embarrassment. What if it wasn't real any more than her dreams had been real last night? Henri was trained in the art of illusion, skilled at presenting a fantasy. And then this panicked-spiked question: Could he read her thoughts? Did he suspect she *wanted* him to be happy to see her?

"Juliette," Henri said warmly, "I was hoping to bump into you."

"Why?" she asked bluntly.

Beside her, Caleigh stifled a laugh, and Juliette's stomach squirmed uncomfortably. The question sounded harsh—even to her own ears—and her tone was infused with an edge she hadn't intended. She folded her arms across her stomach and shifted her weight from one foot to the other.

But Henri only laughed. "Because I enjoyed our time together yesterday. We make a good team. I thought you might let me tag along for whatever you're doing today?" As the silence stretched between them, his expression faltered. It made him seem younger somehow. "I mean, if you don't mind?"

She eyed him warily. "Don't you have work to do?"

A shadow darted through his eyes, gone so quickly she might have imagined it. "I'm done working for now."

Juliette fidgeted with the edge of her sleeve. "Well, I haven't decided what to do yet."

"We were headed to the adventure wing," Caleigh inserted helpfully. Her voice was overly cheerful, as if she took pleasure in watching the awkward exchange and intended to prolong it if she could. Juliette resisted the urge to turn and glare at her.

"I love the adventure wing," Henri said. "I could walk with you if you like? Advise you on the best activities?" He put his hand over his heart. "I promise to leave you alone if you get tired of me."

Caleigh squeezed her arm. "Perfect, I'll catch up with you later." She acted as if Juliette had already agreed to this plan. Which she had not. But she didn't even have time to protest before Caleigh spun on her heel and sauntered away, leaving Juliette alone with Henri.

"I think she enjoyed that entirely too much," Henri said.

The comment echoed her thoughts so precisely that a laugh spilled from her lips, chasing away the tension between them. "Yes, I think you're right."

They walked in companionable silence, and a deep sense of relaxation came over her. She shouldn't have been nervous. Being with Henri felt easy. Like strolling through a park on a sunny day.

"The adventure wing has a lot of options," Henri told her. "We can travel deep beneath the sea, where every creature glows with neon light. Or we can ride on a giant bird and see the most amazing views of Belle Fontaine from the air." He grinned. "If you're feeling especially brave, we can jump off a mountain and let the magic catch us."

Juliette's eyes went wide. "I'll never be feeling that brave."

They both laughed. A warm feeling spilled through Juliette. She had the sudden, ridiculous urge to reach for

Henri's hand. To thread her fingers through his. To be more connected to him.

And then a horrible thought sliced through her. Maybe her feelings weren't her own. Maybe Henri was controlling her somehow. She moved a bit farther away from him.

She could have sworn she saw him flinch.

"You're not enjoying The Splendor much, are you?"

She felt as if he'd reached into her mind, plucked out the thought, and then presented it on his outstretched palm so the two of them could examine it together.

"I don't . . ." Juliette trailed off, flustered. She swallowed and started again. "Why would you say that?"

"You seem . . ." Henri looked up as if he might find the word he was searching for written in the sky. But when it failed to materialize, he shrugged. "Sad, I guess."

"I *am* a little sad." The words slipped out before she was aware she would say them. Henri stopped walking and led her to a bench overlooking a wall of windows with a view of a small lake. They sat and watched a paddling of ducks swim in lazy circles on the glassy surface.

"Do you want to talk about it?" Henri asked.

Juliette tucked a strand of hair behind her ear. "Not really."

She didn't know if she could trust him. What if he was just another bit of magic meant to distract her? But then she thought of dancing with him, and hearing about his childhood. Of Caleigh's surprise that he was competing in the chariot races. Of the way his eyes met hers when they won their race—his joy wasn't feigned; she was sure of it.

And then she thought of Caleigh's surprised expression when she'd realized Henri had told Juliette about being an orphan. *He likes his privacy.* He'd confided in her. Maybe she could trust him enough to do the same. Her burdens were heavy, and it would be a relief to set them down for a moment.

She'd only meant to tell him a little, but the story tumbled out of her like a dropped ball of yarn—unspooling as it rolled, so it was impossible to stop before the whole of her life was displayed in one long line. She told him about growing up with Clare, about their mother getting sick and leaving them—for just a little while, she said—in the care of the children's home. About nights spent dreaming about a reunion that never seemed to happen. About slowly losing hope it ever would. She described the joy of finally moving out on their own. Of saving money for a special gift for Clare. She told him about Clare's visit to The Splendor and everything that came after.

Once she finished talking, Henri sat quietly for the longest time. Finally, he raked his fingers through his hair. "I'm so sorry."

"It's not your fault."

Henri went still. A muscle jumped in his jaw. "If The Splendor was the cause of so much heartache, why did you come?"

Juliette sighed. "I was furious with Clare. I wanted to punish her. And I wanted to forget." A shiver went through her. Maybe this was her fault. Maybe the hotel had misinterpreted her desire to forget her *pain* with a desire to actually forget Clare herself.

"Is it working?"

"A little. It's hard to hold on to the anger and the grief in the midst of so much luxury. But it's also impossible to be happy when I've lost everything."

Henri covered Juliette's hand with his own. His skin was warm, and his fingers wrapped around hers. "I'm sorry Clare hurt you."

"But that's just the thing. I'm starting to wonder if maybe she didn't. At least, not on purpose." The story had escaped from Juliette unwittingly, but this was different. This was carefully calculated to guage his reaction. If she was ever going to find out the truth about what happened to Clare, she'd need an ally on the inside. And for reasons she couldn't explain, she trusted him more than she trusted Caleigh.

"I don't understand. What do you mean?"

"I think The Splendor changed her somehow," Juliette explained. Henri shifted in his seat. Plucked an invisible piece of lint from his sleeve. "Clare would never intentionally destroy our relationship."

His careful expression dissolved into something different, something familiar. It was identical to the expression Miss Durand wore every time Juliette asked about her mother.

It was the expression of someone who had bad news they'd rather not share.

When Henri spoke, his voice was gentle. "Are you sure she wouldn't? People can be complicated."

"Of course, I'm sure." But the question planted a seed of doubt in Juliette's heart and it wriggled down into the fertile soil of her insecurity and took root. *Was* she sure? Could anyone ever be certain of someone else's motivations?

Was it possible she never really knew Clare at all?

CHAPTER TEN

HENRI WAS GOOD AT UNTANGLING THINGS.
Sometimes Stella would thrust a handful of necklaces at him—a knotted mass of silver and gold plucked from the belly of her hopelessly disorganized jewelry box—and beg him for help. She lacked the stamina to stay with a problem until she solved it, and Theo couldn't be bothered with such pedestrian requests.

But Henri's fingers were deft and patient.

He found the task satisfying, the slow separation of one unusable clump of metal into several distinct beautiful pieces. In a way, it was the reverse of illusion work—instead of weaving disparate bits into one cohesive whole, he was disconnecting things that should never have joined together.

And yet, even though he was good at pulling things apart in order to restore them to whatever they were meant to be, he couldn't manage to untangle Juliette. After the chariot race, he'd hoped he'd solved the mystery and that a week of friendship would be just what she needed to leave happy.

But he was wrong.

He lay on his bed, eyes fixed on the wood beams above him. The last drops of indigo light had drained from the sky hours ago. Henri had intended to catch a bit of rest before he made his nighttime rounds, but his thoughts wouldn't quiet enough for sleep.

He and Juliette had spent the afternoon in the menagerie. Henri had never been there with a guest before, and he marveled at how good the illusions were. Where Henri saw a pair of bored bullfrogs lazily catching flies with their tongues, Juliette saw two fierce fire-breathing dragons. The sedate parakeet in a small cage appeared to Juliette as a phoenix bursting into flame and then rising triumphant from the ashes. A swarm of moths became oversized butterflies—as big as dinner plates—with shimmering wings that caught the light like well-cut diamonds. Juliette was transfixed. He could feel the wonder rolling off her in waves.

But it wasn't enough.

He could tell that every illusion was like a sugar-dipped delicacy—delicious, but powerless to abate her hunger. Henri tried all afternoon, showing her one marvel after another, asking her questions about her life, her childhood. But every road eventually led to Clare. Juliette's own wishes were hopelessly tangled around her sister. It was a knot he couldn't unravel. When he left her at the door of her suite, she seemed even sadder than before.

He was failing.

He massaged his temples with the heels of his hands. If Juliette continued to believe her sister had been tricked into forgetting her, she'd never open up enough to share who she really was or what she really wanted. Right now, it seemed her only dream was to recapture what she had with Clare. But that was impossible.

Everyone lies, Stella always said, *even to themselves. Our job is to give our guests the truth beneath their fiction.*

What was Juliette's truth? What did she really want?

He thought of her first night at The Splendor. Of holding her in his arms as he questioned her. *Everyone comes looking for something. Adventure. Fame. Love. So what are you looking for?*

Her reply had been both simple and inscrutable. *Answers.*

Usually it was Stella's advice that floated through Henri's mind at odd moments. But this time he thought of Theo, whose counsel was often a mirror image of his wife's. *When someone tells you what they want, believe them.*

The solution kept circling Henri's mind like a vulture waiting for a wounded animal to die. But he kept looking away, repulsed. Unwilling to see. Then finally, in one last gasping breath, his hope perished. He knew what he had to do. It came into clear focus, as undeniable as it was unpleasant.

Henri had to tell Juliette the truth.

Talking to guests never made Henri nervous. It was part of his job to chat and flatter and put people at ease, and it came as naturally as breathing. So, it took him a moment, as he stood outside Juliette's door the next morning, to place the feeling that had wedged like a knot beneath his breastbone.

What if he was making a mistake?

Stella and Theo had given their staff twin imperatives. First, that the secrets of The Splendor were to be jealously guarded. The hotel was shrouded in mystery, which was precisely the way they liked it. *Magic ceases to be magical when the source is revealed*, Stella had lectured on more than one occasion.

But the second imperative was equally emphasized: Each guest must leave supremely satisfied with their experience. At The Splendor ordinary days didn't exist—let alone bad ones. No meal was anything short of delicious. No luxurious detail too small. There were no awkward conversations, no chance of failure. The hotel promised perfection, and Stella and Theo expected the staff to deliver it. Every guest. Every time.

In this case, Henri could only fulfill one of the priorities. Unless Juliette got answers, she would leave supremely unsatisfied. But if she learned the truth, he risked ruining the magic. Either option was a risk.

But he had the feeling Juliette was the sort of person who preferred an ugly truth over a beautiful lie.

He raised his fist and knocked on the door.

She didn't answer right away and for a breathless span, he worried she wouldn't. But then finally, the door swung wide. Juliette was dressed simply—in a navy-blue cotton dress and sandals. Her hair hung loosely around her shoulders. Not a single illusion clung to her—she must not have looked in a mirror yet this morning—and Henri marveled at her simple, unadorned loveliness. Her slightly crooked nose sprinkled with freckles. The tiny pearl-white scar on her chin. The pale pink ovals of her fingernails that had been chewed to the quick.

Juliette studied him, her lips pursed. "You look tired." With a start, Henri realized he'd failed to cloak himself in illusions before leaving his room. Between a long night of work and worrying over Juliette, he'd hardly slept at all. He must look a mess. Oddly, he found he didn't really care.

"Do I? Well, we make a good pair then because you look exceptionally well-rested and alert." Instead of sending dreams into her room last night, he'd instilled a deep sense of relaxation and allowed her to sink into the healing bliss of oblivion. He hoped it had worked.

She offered a rare smile. "Actually, I am. So, what delights do you have in store for me today?"

Henri opened his mouth and then snapped it closed again.

Juliette seemed so relaxed, so upbeat, it made doubt squirm in Henri's chest. Maybe she had finally given in to the magic. Maybe he should take her on some grand new adventure and postpone this entire plan until he was more certain.

Her face turned serious. "What is it? What's wrong?"

Henri suddenly missed the privacy his illusions afforded. He resisted the urge to disappear into an artifice of careful composure. Instead he answered her question with one of his own.

"Do you still want answers?"

She tilted her head to one side, as if searching her memory for the reference. Her expression darkened. Brightened. Darkened again. When she spoke, her voice was soft.

"Yes, I do."

"Follow me."

They were silent as they walked. He could have drawn her attention to the Four Enchanted Gardens—one for each season. Guests could throw snowballs in a wintry landscape where the sun was bright enough to glisten off the rolling white hills but never hot enough to melt the snow; or pluck a ripe, crisp apple and eat it while hiking through a forest of warmly colored trees whose leaves trembled on their branches and crunched pleasantly underfoot. Those who preferred spring could picnic near a burbling brook, where pastel flowers were perpetually in bloom, while others could choose to sit in the sand and bake under the sun of a forever summer. But he had a feeling such enchantments wouldn't impress Juliette for long. And so he pressed on without saying a word.

He led her through the maze of corridors until they reached the northwest corner of the main building. From there, they rounded a bend where a narrow staircase was tucked behind a wall, hidden from the gaze of curious guests. Henri ascended with the speed and ease of someone whose feet had traveled this path many times before, but the climb was steep, and behind him, Juliette grew winded. He stopped several times to let her catch her breath before continuing on.

Finally, they spilled out onto a landing and stopped in front of a set of tall wooden doors. Henri pushed them open and moved aside.

Juliette let out a gasp as she stepped over the threshold. The space was huge and sun drenched with floor-to-ceiling windows on two sides. Thick wood beams supported a vaulted ceiling, and the floor was a mosaic of tiles in intricate patterns. But Juliette's gaze was trained on the rows and rows of shelves that marched along the entire width of the room, stretching back farther than the eye could see. Shelves that were lined with thousands of vessels in all shapes and colors. Deep emerald containers the size and form of large onions, slender vases in bright tangerine, bottles the impossible blue of a postcard ocean. No two vessels were exactly alike.

The sunlight streaming through the window bounced off the rows of colored glass, making the space look like an old-world cathedral.

The metallic tang of magic hung in the air; Henri could taste it on his tongue and feel it thrumming through his veins.

"What is this place?" Juliette asked, her voice an odd mixture of awe and trepidation.

"I call it the Hall of Memories," Henri said.

"Memories?" Juliette echoed. The question in her voice indicated she wanted him to explain the illusion. But this room didn't have one. The only magic here were the thousands of memories swirling in glass. It was one of Henri's favorite spots. Sometimes, when he was especially lonely, he came here and gobbled up memories like a child sneaking treats from a cookie jar—ingesting dozens at a time until he was so stuffed with nostalgia, he felt both warmly satisfied and vaguely regretful.

Something about Henri's expression altered Juliette's own. She laid a palm on his forearm. "*Whose* memories?"

Henri readied himself. This was the hard part.

"They belong to The Splendor," he said carefully. "Until they're sold to a guest."

She leveled him with a steady gaze, clearly unsatisfied with his answer. "But where did they come from?"

Henri scrubbed a palm over his face and had the sudden image of erasing a blackboard after failing to solve a math problem. He'd gone about this wrong. He needed a fresh start. A new chance.

"Let me try again," he said. "When you first met me, do you remember asking about my role at the hotel?"

"You told me you were an illusionist."

"Yes," he said. "And I am. Most of what you see at The Splendor is illusion. It's all art and artifice—making things appear more marvelous than they really are. It's small magic. Easily taught and quickly learned. But along with all the luxury, each guest gets a Signature Experience—some grand adventure that makes a dream come true. Something real and lasting that will survive long after they go back home. Creating those encounters . . . *that* is my role at the hotel."

Juliette pressed a hand to her chest as if trying to hold her heart in place. "I don't understand. Those experiences come from here?"

"Yes."

"And they're not illusions? They're . . ." She trailed off as if she couldn't bear to say the rest of the sentence.

He raked his fingers through his hair. "Sometimes a guest arrives wanting to forget something. Maybe a relationship has soured, and the memory now only brings pain. But another guest might come to The Splendor longing for romance. We give them the option to exchange one memory for another. I can remove the experience of falling in love from a guest who no longer wants it and sell it to someone who does. Both guests leave satisfied."

"Why would anyone pay for a memory that didn't belong to them? If you wanted to witness two strangers falling in love, you could read a book."

"That's where the illusion comes in. I can weave a memory into someone's mind with enough personal detail to make it feel like it belongs to them." He paused for a beat, waiting for her to fill in the spaces he'd left. To come to the truth on her own. But when she stayed silent, he pushed on.

"Or maybe someone has a recurring nightmare, one that traumatizes them again and again. They'd rather get rid of the memory forever. But another guest might see the dream entirely differently. They might love the thrill of being frightened. Do you see?"

Juliette had turned away from him. She was studying the glass containers, running her fingers along the shelves where the memories were catalogued and stored. He wished he knew what she was thinking.

He traced the contours of a long-necked bottle in deep violet. "Has anything ever happened to you that you'd rather forget?"

The question froze her in place. She lifted her eyes to meet his. Her gaze was steely.

"I'd rather not remember how you ruined my sister.

Is there someone who might be clamoring for the experience of feeling gutted?" She didn't wait for a response before spinning on her heel and striding toward the far side of the room.

Henri's fingers twitched at his sides. He'd done this all wrong. He followed her down the aisle, reached for her fingers. "Wait. You don't understand."

She yanked away and whirled to face him. "No, Henri, I don't. So, explain it to me. What memory did you give Clare that changed her?"

A sinking feeling settled in his stomach. He'd tried to leave enough room in his explanation for her to draw her own conclusions, but now he realized his mistake: He'd left too much space and she'd drawn the wrong ones.

"I didn't give Clare a new memory," he said softly. "I harvested her memories of you. She wanted to trade them for a different experience."

All the color drained from Juliette's face. "Harvested?" Her voice had an alarming note of hysteria. She took a step away from him.

Henri resisted the urge to move closer, and instead anchored his feet in place. "I'm so sorry. I thought you deserved the truth."

"You're lying. Clare would *never* have sold me." The anger in her voice didn't surprise him—he saw the heat of it ripple through her, knitting her brows together, curling her hands into fists at her sides, making her whole body tremble—but he hadn't expected it to be directed at him. Not when it was Clare who betrayed her.

He shook his head. "I wouldn't lie to you."

Juliette gave a brittle laugh. "You specialize in deceit. You do nothing but tell lies."

The accusation hit him like a slap. He'd spent his whole

life—what he could remember of it—yearning for authenticity. For something real and unvarnished. But now that he'd laid this cold, stark reality on the table like a gambler revealing a winning hand, he wondered if his longing for truth had been misguided. The truth was clumsy and messy and complicated. And he hated the way Juliette was looking at him now. As if he made nightmares come true instead of dreams.

"I wish I were lying," he said, "but I'm not."

"Show me."

He raised his eyebrows in a question.

"Show me the memories you took from Clare."

It was a reasonable request, but something inside Henri recoiled. He'd only meant to give her a glimpse of the hall, not let her go exploring. He suspected seeing Clare's betrayal up close would only hurt her more.

But he was so tired of hiding things from her, and after promising her the truth, how could he refuse to give her all of it?

Even if it would break her heart.

CHAPTER ELEVEN

J ULIETTE TASTED SALT.
It wasn't until a trail of moisture hit the corner of
her mouth and inched between her lips that she realized
she'd been crying at all. Her limbs were numb. Her mind felt
slow and sticky.

She stood in front of an entire row of colorful glass
containers—dozens of them—her sister's name printed in neat
block letters on the shelf they occupied, as if it were perfectly
normal for a person to be labeled, catalogued, and beautifully
displayed.

Juliette was dimly aware of Henri beside her, crackling
with nervous energy. Was it because he was worried about
her reaction? Or was it because he was lying?

He *had* to be lying. Clare would never . . . but what if she
did?

A chasm cracked open in Juliette's chest. She trailed a single
finger along a pale pink vessel shaped like a seashell. The glass
was warm. Was the Clare she knew trapped in there? Could

Juliette release her like a genie in a children's story?

"I want to see what's inside."

Henri startled as if surprised she'd spoken, and Juliette wondered how long she'd been standing there, wordlessly weeping.

"I don't think . . ." He dried his palms on the front of his jacket. "Are you sure it's a good idea?"

"No," Juliette said flatly. "I'm not. But I want to see it anyway."

Henri nodded once, seeming to realize she wouldn't leave until he'd granted her request, however ill-advised it might be. He lifted the vessel and removed a stopper at the top.

"Hold out your hands."

She obeyed, cupping her palms in front of her in supplication. Henri tipped the container, and a milky white cloud floated out, twisting around her fingers like a small tornado.

And then she disappeared into Clare's memory.

⊖—✳ MOMMA SAT IN A WOODEN ROCKING CHAIR NEAR A window, slices of pale light falling across her lap. Her dark hair was pulled away from her face in a messy bun and she was dressed simply in a yellow cotton shift. She was young— perhaps in her early twenties—and she cradled a baby in her arms. At least Clare *assumed* it was a baby—it was impossible to tell for sure, swaddled as it was in a thin ivory blanket embroidered with bumblebees.

"Clare Bear," the woman said. "Come meet your sister."

Clare hung back. She'd rather not. She was still shaken from the events of last night. A strange woman—much older than her mother—had arrived late in the afternoon with a basket tucked under her arm. Momma introduced the woman simply as "the midwife," as if she had been given a title instead of a name at birth. The woman had a kind smile and a plump, doughy face. She'd presented Clare with a new rag doll and a set of building blocks and given her strict instructions to take them to her bedroom and stay there no matter what she heard. Clare had promised, only because the midwife was holding the toys just out of reach and seemed to require an agreement before turning them over.

At first it wasn't hard to obey. She absentmindedly listened to the indistinct garble of conversation, the heavy footsteps above her head, the sound of water being drawn for a bath. But later, her mother began to whimper.

And then she heard a scream.

Clare crept up the stairs and peeked around the corner. Her mother lay on the bed, back arched in pain, fists curled around a handful of sheets. Her nightgown had grown damp and it stuck to her as if it were coated in glue. The veins in her temples protruded from her skin, blue green and angry. Her face was flushed, and it glistened with a sheen of sweat.

Fear closed around Clare's heart like a fist. She scurried back downstairs and spent the rest of the day with her knees curled to her chest, wondering if her mother was dying. Wondering if the rag doll and building blocks were supposed to be some kind of consolation, like the fresh-baked pies neighbors brought to funerals.

But her mother didn't die. The midwife came down the steps the next morning humming a happy tune, her arms wrapped around a bundle of blood-soaked sheets.

When she saw Clare, her lips curved in a gentle smile. "Everything is fine, love. You have a new sister."

After last night, Clare was quite sure she didn't want a

new sister and all the trouble she brought.

But now her mother looked like herself again—though a more tired version. She beckoned again, her expression full of hope. "Come see, sweetheart."

Clare inched forward, stood on her tiptoes, and peered at the bundle. The baby's face was squishy, and her scalp was covered with a thin fuzz of hair that couldn't seem to decide if it wanted to be blonde or red. She studied the baby for a moment before dropping her heels to the floor and folding her arms over her chest.

"You said she was pretty. She's not."

Her mother's eyes widened, and she covered her mouth with one hand as if suppressing a laugh. Once she composed herself, she said, "Well, all babies look a little . . ."

"Mushed?" Clare supplied.

This time her mother laughed outright—a high, bell-like sound. She touched the tip of Clare's nose affectionately. "*Mushed* is a good way to describe it. But she'll grow to be a great beauty, you'll see. Now, come sit on my lap, darling. There's room enough for both of you."

The memory dissipated and the room slowly came back into focus. Juliette's heart thundered in her chest. She remembered that house. It had been small and drafty, with threadbare rugs that sat atop creaky, sun-bleached plank floors. And her mother. She was younger than Juliette's hazy recollections, but she had the same dark eyes. The same button nose. The barely noticeable lines around her mouth when she smiled.

Juliette didn't know how Henri had done it—replicated the details so accurately—but this was only an illusion.

Relief unfurled inside her with a decisive snap.

"This isn't Clare's memory," she told him.

A concerned expression flitted over Henri's face, vanishing as quickly as it appeared. When he spoke, his voice was measured. Careful. "What makes you say that?"

"Don't get me wrong, it's a good imitation. But Clare was only four years old when I was born. You've made her thoughts too complex. She wouldn't have known the word *consolation*."

"No, she probably wouldn't. But that's not how memory works." Henri's eyes were full of regret. Something about him made her want to trust him. But maybe she saw only what he intended her to see.

She swallowed. "I don't understand. Is this Clare's memory or not?"

"Memories are notoriously unreliable. And they're malleable too"—Henri tugged on the back of his neck—"that's part of why my magic is so effective. Each time we recall something, our mind alters it slightly—fills in new details, deletes old ones—even when we don't realize it's happening. Clare probably thought about that day many times over the years. But she was a different person with every recollection—she'd had more experiences, her perception of herself had changed, her feelings about *you* had evolved. So, each time she thought of the memory, it was in a new context, which would have made the details shift a bit. Four-year-old Clare might not have known the word *consolation*, but she definitely knew it at age twenty."

Juliette wrapped her arms around her stomach. The notion that her own mind might be unreliable made her feel as if the ground had shifted beneath her feet. Like she was standing on sand instead of stone. She couldn't accept it.

"This doesn't make any sense," she said. She meant both

his explanation of how the mind worked and his claim that Clare traded her memories away.

He sighed. "I know. But it doesn't mean it's not true." Juliette watched his face move from regret to resignation and back again. It was clear he meant both too.

Everything inside Juliette went still and silent. Like the desolate absence of sound after an explosion.

She had known the truth all along. She knew it when she stole the "someday money," knew it when she climbed into the carriage, knew it when she walked through the doors of The Splendor. Clare left her, just like Juliette always knew she would.

It was a truth Juliette understood deep in her bones: Everyone always leaves. Her father, who left before Juliette ever formed a memory of his face. Her mother, who promised to come back but never did.

And now Clare.

Juliette had spent her whole childhood dodging the ugly reality, much the way one avoids the gaze of a snarling dog in the hopes it will move along without attacking. But still the worry gnawed at her, unrelenting: What if Clare left too?

Now Juliette's worst fears had been realized. She was utterly alone.

Her ears began to ring.

"I'd like to go to my room now." Her voice was wooden, hollow.

"Yes, of course." Henri grabbed her elbow as if he suspected she might faint. Maybe she would.

The walk back was a blur. Juliette allowed herself to be led, stumbling through the corridors, unseeing. For once, the allures of The Splendor held no appeal; she trained her full attention on putting one foot in front of the other. Several times Henri cleared his throat, as if he wanted to say something, but then seemed to change his mind. So, they walked in silence. Juliette's thoughts wandered listlessly and without direction. She felt detached from her own body; idly she wondered if—when Henri let go of her elbow—she might float away.

But eventually, when they finally reached the doors to her suite, he did let go, and she was disappointed to remain heavily anchored to the floor.

Henri nudged the baseboard with the toe of his shoe. "I'm sorry. I thought the truth would help."

Juliette stared at him. "Help with what?"

Henri's expression faltered. He lifted one shoulder in a shrug. "I hoped it would help you figure out what you want. Help you be happy."

A spark of anger flared in her chest and her vision shimmered like the air above a fire. She'd forgotten how anger—if properly fed—would expand inside her, leaving space for nothing else. It was a greedy, hungry beast that shoved the despair out of her heart. Rage was the force that propelled her to the hotel in the first place, and somewhere along the way, she'd forgotten to feed it, and she started to nurture ridiculous hope instead—hope that The Splendor had changed Clare, and maybe Clare hadn't discarded her after all. But now she remembered how to nourish her rage.

It should frighten her, how the anger engulfed her so suddenly, it consumed everything else and left her gasping. But it didn't. The sensation was like cool water sliding down her throat on a hot day.

It felt like relief.

Henri was studying her, his expression so sincere she was tempted—for just a moment—to starve the anger. To deprive it of food and oxygen so it would shrivel and die. But she couldn't bear the thought of leaving a vacancy in her heart for something softer and more painful. So, she laughed at him, a derisive, cruel sound. He flinched and she was glad.

"You thought telling me my sister didn't love me enough to keep her memories of me would make me *happy?*" Her voice was brittle. Shrill.

"No, of course not." Henri's hair had fallen across his forehead and he shoved it out of his eyes. "But I thought knowing the truth would help you be happy. Eventually."

She fixed him with a withering glare. "Look around, Henri. No one comes here for the truth."

He gaped at her, wordless, seeming to gather his thoughts for a response. But Juliette didn't wait. She didn't want to hear anything he had to say. She flung open the door to her suite, slipped inside, and slammed the door behind her.

Juliette couldn't sleep.

Rage, as it turned out, was energizing. After Henri gave up knocking and pleading with her to open the door, she'd spent the rest of the day pacing the length of the room, ignoring Caleigh's offers of food and entertainment and resisting the urge to check out of The Splendor early and never return. She didn't feel like staying, but she didn't want to leave either. Her thoughts chased each other around and around, like a dog convinced it can catch its own tail if it only tries hard enough.

By the time night fell, she felt like an empty husk. Exhaustion ached in her limbs and she craved the blissful oblivion of sleep. She climbed into bed with all the eagerness of a puppy offered a bit of liver. But even the custom-molded comfort of the mattress couldn't lull her unconscious. Clare's memory kept appearing on the stage of her mind, replaying over and over.

Did Juliette's birth ruin Clare's life?

The notion shivered inside her. And then another thought made her bolt upright. When Clare came home from The Splendor, she recognized Juliette. She was cold and distant, but she *knew* her. So, clearly not every memory was gone. The realization slid under her skin like a sliver. Suddenly she was desperate to know which memories were in the other vessels, which memories Clare had selected to sell and why. She should have stayed in the Hall of Memories longer. She should have made Henri show her the contents of every single container that belonged to Clare.

Juliette slid out of bed and found a robe and a pair of slippers. She felt certain Henri would never let her enter the hall again after her reaction today. But she didn't need his permission. She remembered the way. She eased the door open and padded into the corridor.

Absent daylight, The Splendor was transformed.

Glimmers of pale moonlight trickled through the windows and cast the corridors in a cold, eerie glow. Shadows puddled in the corners and crawled up the walls like spiders. Trepidation slid down Juliette's spine and she nearly turned around.

But then torches on the walls flickered to life and bathed her in warm, welcoming light. On the landing at the top of the stairs a small table had appeared. Several mugs of steaming hot cocoa were presented alongside bowls of tiny marshmallows, dishes of crushed peppermint candy, and small carafes of flavored syrups. She couldn't help but think the treat was an enticement designed to nudge her back to her room. For a moment, she considered giving in to the temptation. Sipping hot chocolate in front of a crackling fire might be just the thing to relax her enough to fall asleep. But thoughts of

Clare flitted across Juliette's mind again—the mystery of the remaining glass containers were an insistent plea she couldn't ignore—so she skirted past the table. Hopefully, it would still be there when she returned.

Juliette crept down the stairs and wound through the corridors to the same northwest corner of the main building where Henri had taken her this morning.

But then something familiar caught her eye—a pair of leather wingback chairs cozied up to a shelf filled with books. The seating faced a waterfall that tumbled over glass boulders before landing in a small pool where two swans slept as they floated on the surface.

She passed this tableau a few minutes ago, though one of the swans had still been awake and had given a muffled grunt as she walked by.

Juliette had been so sure of her path, but somehow, she'd circled back.

Maybe she was just tired.

She took off in the correct direction, more careful this time. And yet, after several minutes she passed the waterfall again.

No matter how many times she tried, she couldn't find the hidden stairway.

When Henri had led her to the Hall of Memories, there had been no gates to pass through, no bolts on the door. She assumed she'd be able to easily retrace their steps and gain access to Clare's memories. But now she understood she was facing a challenge more daunting than picking locks.

In a hotel bursting with illusion, how could she ever find her way?

CHAPTER TWELVE

H ENRI WAS DISTRACTED.
  Usually he loved memory work—the exhilaration of gathering the discarded, unwanted bits of straw taken from one mind and spinning them into a shimmering gold treasure in the mind of another. But tonight he couldn't focus. Juliette's pained face—wounded and utterly bled of hope—kept floating to the top of his mind. He'd been so sure telling her the truth was the right move; so certain it would help her gain peace. He knew finding out about Clare's betrayal would hurt her—he would have been a fool to think otherwise—but he'd been convinced it would also set her free.

Once again, he'd made everything worse.

Even an extended soak in the hot springs did nothing to center him. His thoughts were at once sluggish and racing, as if his mind had divided itself precisely down the middle, one half frantically searching for answers, while the other languished in despair.

His bare feet left wet prints on the stone floors as he

moved absentmindedly from one room to another, dispensing half-hearted illusions into the dreams of the sleeping guests. He filled their minds with generic pleasures—holidays and food and relaxation. He didn't have the energy for anything more tailored.

And in between rooms, his mind kept circling back to Juliette. How had he convinced himself he understood her? Why did he assume they were the same, and that, like him, she would prefer reality to fantasy? It was as if he thought he had a winning hand, until his cards were snatched away, shuffled, and redealt. He no longer understood the rules. He didn't even know what game he was playing.

Juliette's words echoed in his mind. *No one comes here for the truth.* It was so opposite of what he expected from her, and he was surprised how it sent grief spiraling inside him to be wrong.

It sounded exactly like something Stella would say.

Stella. A bolt of panic went through him. She would be furious.

But he couldn't worry about that right now. He still had hours of work ahead. The night's labor stretched out before him in a dull gray line of obligation. He had many more rooms to visit and one particularly difficult Signature Experience to perform. He raked his fingers through his hair and decided to get it over with. He made his way to room 278: the suite of Arthur Charles.

Henri hefted a container from his satchel—bulbous and dark gray. Empty vessels were all the same—crystal clear, each a uniform shape and size. But the moment a memory was placed inside, the glass began to warp and change color. Happy memories tended to produce pleasing shapes and cheerful colors.

But this container was shaped like a bomb, and the

memory swirling inside had ominously darkened the glass.

Arthur Charles craved adventure and his greatest wish was to charge heroically into battle. Henri dreaded the task ahead. Usually creating a Signature Experience was rewarding—full of the kind of colorful images and intense emotions so lacking in Henri's own memories.

But this was different. It would take an unusual amount of focus to impart all of the adrenaline and exhilaration of war without passing on any of the trauma and despair that caused the donor to want to rid himself of the memory in the first place.

Unfortunately—after everything that had happened with Juliette—Henri's focus was in short supply at the moment.

Then again, the work matched his dark mood.

He took a deep breath and built walls around his heart, too tall to be breached by something as pedestrian as worry. He summoned a reserve of strength from somewhere deep in his gut and then removed the stopper from the vessel and let the memory pool in his fingers.

A flood of sensations and images assaulted him: the clash of metal on metal, the sharp copper smell of blood, the certainty of being willing to die for a cause. Carefully, he guided the memory through the small opening of suite 278 and let it gently rest on Arthur's temples. And then he began weaving.

He filtered out more than he saved, discarding the injured whine of horses, the sulfur stench of gunpowder, the sickening sight of a fallen friend.

The fear.

He carefully threaded what was left into Arthur's mind, interlacing it with the fantasies the man had nurtured since childhood. He let Arthur ride bravely into battle. Allowed him to feel the weight of the sword in his hand and the rise and fall of the horse beneath him. Henri gave Arthur camaraderie, honor, and eventual victory just as the man had imagined it, but now imbued with the carefully curated sensations from actual memory.

By the time he was finished, the experience was perfect—a memory Arthur would relive again and again, displaying the details in his own mind like a trophy on a shelf. It was a story he would someday tell his family while bouncing a grandchild on his knee. The man smiled in his sleep.

And Henri felt like a liar.

Henri avoided Stella as long as he could. He went about his work the next day with single-minded efficiency. He checked in with the ambiancers to make sure each guest's room was brimming with the kind of relaxation, charm, and magic The Splendor was famous for. He stopped by the clothier's to see how the costumes were coming along for the upcoming masquerade ball. And then he went to the kitchen to consult with Amella on the evening meals. For room 117 he requested a rich pasta dish infused with comfort; for room 397, a smoked salmon dish laced with the precise wonder of enjoying the reflection of the sunset as it falls in a tangerine wedge on the surface of a mountain lake; for room 123, a pot roast that tasted like coming home.

"That all sounds delicious," Stella said, coming into the kitchen and putting an arm loosely around Amella's shoulders. "I wish I could taste every dish."

Henri's stomach twisted at the sight of her. He had hoped to postpone a conversation about Juliette for as long as possible. Stella's gaze touched on Henri briefly, her expression unreadable, before flicking back to Amella. "I was hoping to borrow Henri for a bit. Unless . . . do you still need to speak with him?"

Henri hoped against hope the chef would say: *Yes, as a matter of fact, we still have dozens of guests to discuss.* But the staff rarely refused Stella, and this was no exception.

Amella smiled warmly. "No, of course not. We can finish talking later. He's all yours."

Henri followed Stella out of the kitchen and she threaded her arm through his. "Let's take a stroll through the gardens, shall we?"

"Of course," Henri said, "whatever you'd like."

Stella led him out a side door and they entered a perfectly manicured hedge maze. Or, at least to the guests it looked like a maze. To Henri and Stella, it was simply a straight path leading to a small rose garden with a stone bench in the center. They both sat, and Stella turned to face him, her professional facade giving way to a serious expression.

"I've been anxiously awaiting an update on our surprise guest."

Henri sighed with an exhaustion that had nothing to do with his lack of sleep. "There's been a small complication."

Her lips pursed slightly. "What sort of complication?"

"Juliette's sister was a recent guest." He stared at the ground. Nudged a pebble with his toe. "And a donor."

Stella sucked in a sharp breath, and Henri's gaze snapped up. Her face had drained of color, and she was slowly shaking her head. "No. How did this happen? Why didn't you come find me right away before your work last night?"

Henri gripped the edge of the bench so hard his knuckles turned white. He didn't have an easy answer. How could he explain that he'd known about Clare since the first night? And worse, how was he going to tell Stella about taking Juliette to the Hall of Memories? If he could just—

"Henri!" Stella's voice was sharp and commanding. "Answer me."

"I don't know how it happened," he said, answering only the first question and ignoring the other. "She was a late arrival. We had no chance to vet her."

"Remind me which memory you harvested from her sister."

The words stuck in his throat. "Not just one memory. Many. She was the guest who didn't want a sister anymore." As Henri said the words a cold sense of wrongness came over him, and he realized with sudden clarity the source of his discomfort earlier. He'd painstakingly removed nearly every memory of Juliette from Clare's mind. The result was that he felt as if he'd known Juliette his whole life. And he hated Clare for what she'd done.

Stella shot to her feet. She kneaded her forehead as she paced. "We have to get her out of here. This a disaster."

That same protective instinct rose within Henri, and he wondered if it was a remnant of the affection Clare used to feel for Juliette. But whether the feeling truly belonged to him or not, he had the urge to temper whatever Stella was planning.

"It's not a disaster," Henri said carefully. "I'm still working on finding out what she wants."

"What could she want except to ruin everything I've spent my life building?" Stella's eyes were wild, and her rib cage moved in and out in quick, gasping motions. Henri had a sudden image of a panicked bird trapped inside her, desperate for escape.

Henri stood and laid a palm gently on Stella's arm. "Her heart has been broken. She probably just wants a little time to heal."

"We don't have time," Stella snapped. "The buyer of those memories is already here, and if this girl interferes with the transfer, she'll ruin everything."

"She won't interfere," Henri said, trying to sound calm, even though his pulse had spiked. "I've got it under control."

Something shifted in Stella's expression. "Do you, though? I worry about you, Henri. I would hate for this stress to cause another episode."

Henri flinched. Though he was intimately familiar with memories—the soft patina of old experiences, and the way recent events seemed to vibrate with newness—his own memories were slippery things. Memory magic was both a blessing and a curse: He could help others, but it made his own memories unstable. Occasionally, he lost them altogether. It was a horrible feeling, knowing he'd forgotten something, but not quite able to figure out what. It was similar to the sensation of walking into a room and then not remembering why he was there. Except far more unsettling.

Even his recollections of his childhood were blurred and indistinct. As if someone had accidentally rested a palm on his mind before the ink was dry. But one thing he'd never forget: how Stella and Theo had taken him in after he'd been abandoned. His parents hadn't been able to cope with his eccentricities—neither his forgetfulness nor his tendency to access their memories and recount them later in vivid detail. Henri had a vague recollection of them packing a small box of his things, of taking him to the children's home, and speaking in hushed tones with the caregiver. He remembered begging them not to go, and the way his heart ripped open when they did. But as hard as he tried, he couldn't picture their faces, couldn't recall their names.

A few months later, Theo and Stella took him in. They brought him to The Splendor and treated him like the son they'd never had. They helped him understand his magic and how to control it. He shuddered to imagine what might have happened to him without them. If he didn't have his work at the hotel, his life would have been empty and without purpose. And who would want to adopt a boy who couldn't hold on to his own memories, a boy who might forget them one day?

Stella and Theo had saved him, and his loyalty to the two of them was absolute. He'd never let anyone hurt them. Not even someone he liked as much as he liked Juliette.

Henri swallowed the lump in his throat. Stella was studying him with a worried expression.

"I feel fine," he told her. "I'll figure out a way to handle this, I promise."

She laid a palm on his cheek. Her hand was cool against his warm skin. "You're a good boy, Henri."

A wave of affection washed over him.

The only thing Stella loved as much as she loved Theo and Henri was The Splendor.

Once—while recovering from a particularly bad episode—he recalled her sitting by the side of his bed and placing a cool cloth on his forehead. As she spooned warm broth between his lips she spoke softly, almost absentmindedly, as if she might well be talking to herself instead of him.

"I only ever had two dreams as a child. I wanted to be a mother and I wanted to create something spectacular, something so impossible it would seem as if fantasies could come alive. The day we purchased this land was one of the happiest of my life." She paused, the spoon hovering over the bowl. "Did you know this was once the site of an ancient temple?"

"No, I didn't." Though as he thought about the network of geothermal lakes in the crypt, he wasn't surprised. He couldn't imagine a holier experience than the restful healing they provided.

Stella pressed the spoon to his lips. "It had fallen into a horrible state of disrepair, but I saw past the illusion. I had a vision of what it could be."

Her expression—the dreaminess of it, the reverence as she talked about The Splendor—stuck in his memory the way little else did.

She set the bowl down on the bedside table. "Having you here made my first dream come true," she said. She took the cloth from his forehead, flipped it to the cooler side, and gently dabbed his temples. "I hope you'll help keep the second dream alive too. The Splendor could be yours one day."

The memory made him smile, and when his gaze met Stella's she was smiling too, as if they had traveled back to the past together. As if she'd only just nursed him back to health.

Henri squeezed her fingers. "Don't worry. I'd never let anything happen to your legacy."

"Not just *my* legacy. It's important for your future too. I'm counting on you to protect The Splendor for all of us."

CHAPTER THIRTEEN

JULIETTE

JULIETTE WASTED THE ENTIRE MORNING STARING AT herself in the mirror.

After her failed attempt at finding the Hall of Memories last night, she'd returned to her suite and spent several sleepless hours looking up at the ceiling. She was desperate to get to Clare, and yet no amount of wandering through the corridors had gotten her any closer.

The staircase hadn't actually moved—she was confident about that much—so there must be something about the magic that made certain things invisible to her. Something the staff of The Splendor must be immune to, either by nature or by training. And there were so many people who worked at the hotel, she decided it had to be the latter. If they could learn, she could too; she needed to teach herself how to see past illusions and find her way back to Clare's memories.

The idea felt dangerous and thrilling. She let it ricochet around her mind until the pale blue light of dawn seeped in at the edges of the curtains.

Even though she was convinced she'd correctly identified the problem, she didn't have the first clue how to solve it. Maybe it was simply a matter of convincing herself that the fantasies around her were just that—magic meant to conceal reality. If she could spot the trick, maybe she could see things as they really were.

She took a deep breath and squeezed her eyes shut. Before she opened them again, she counted to ten and willed herself to see the truth. The room came slowly into focus: the same plush white carpet, the same fluted marble columns, the same green walls studded with small pink rosebuds. Juliette gathered a handful of the bedsheets in her fist; the satin material slid across her skin, every bit as sumptuous as before. Was the luxury real then? Or had she failed? A frustrated sigh escaped her lips. Without having any kind of benchmark, she had no idea. She thought of her first night here, how everything had seemed so magical and breathtaking. And now those very marvels were obstacles in her path.

Juliette was no match for a magic powerful enough to convince her she was flawless. The thought crackled inside her, crystallizing into an idea. Maybe she did have a benchmark. She jumped out of bed and rushed to the mirror. She brought one thing with her to The Splendor that had since been magicked beyond recognition: her reflection. She could be her *own* benchmark.

She pulled a tufted ivory bench to the mirror and studied her reflection. Her long hair flowed over her shoulders in soft copper waves, her skin was as smooth as polished marble, and her cheeks were flushed with the barest hint of pink. She concentrated and tried to find her freckles. She ran her fingers through her hair to feel for the frizz she constantly battled, but to no avail; her tresses felt every bit as silky as they looked.

No matter how she searched, she couldn't find a blemish

or a bump. Her nose remained stubbornly straight.

Despair pushed against her rib cage. She could feel her skin heating and the tears prickling behind her eyelids. Yet, her reflection remained serene.

Juliette lifted her hand and laid her palm flat against her cheek, and she watched her reflection do the same. The mirror reproduced the facts, but it refused to reflect the truth.

It wasn't simply a lovely bit of magic that made the best of what was already there.

It was a lie.

The thought sunk inside her like a stone dropped in a lake. And as it did, something at the edge of her vision wavered. She saw—for just a moment—her true reflection flicker in the glass. A smattering of freckles, a blemish on her chin, her hair bed-rumpled and frizzy. But just as quickly it was gone, replaced by a bright-eyed, rosy-cheeked imposter with a waist several sizes too small.

Juliette was still sitting in front of the mirror, testing the limits of the illusions, when she was startled by a knock at the door. A moment later, Caleigh poked her head into the room.

"Hello? Anyone here?"

Juliette came around the corner. "Oh. Good morning."

"Is it still morning?" Caleigh asked, her voice light and playful. Her gaze flicked to the window. "I suppose it is, but just barely. I hope you're hungry. I brought brunch."

Juliette's gaze dropped to the silver tray Caleigh held, laden with flaky bread, a bowl of fruit, and a golden-brown soufflé. And as she stared, the tray began to—she searched her mind for the correct word—sputter. It winked in and out of focus several times before solidifying again. Her vision swam. She blinked.

Caleigh's brows knit together, and Juliette gave herself a firm shake. She couldn't afford to seem suspicious.

She smiled. "I'm starving."

Both of them moved to the table, where Caleigh set the tray down. Juliette stared at the food and tried to spot the lie. But nothing happened. The bowl of gleaming fruit—succulent purple grapes, perfectly ripe strawberries, slices of tart green apple—looked as appetizing as ever, the butter-glazed breads just as tempting, and the soufflé smelled divine.

She popped a grape in her mouth and tried to concentrate. The flavor burst against her tongue, perfect and delicious. But grapes were familiar—she knew what they should taste like—so perhaps an illusion would be easier to achieve. She picked up her spoon and tried the soufflé. The flavors were a symphony of smoked Gouda, diced ham, salty Parmesan cheese all wrapped in a shell of puff pastry. Just like every other meal at the hotel, it was one of the best things she'd ever eaten.

Maybe the food wasn't enchanted. She and Clare had longingly pressed their noses against enough bakery windows—watching customers close their eyes as they bit into desserts that looked as much like art as food—to know that culinary magic was as real as any other. Perhaps The Splendor didn't need illusion if they had skilled chefs.

But the tray had flickered.

Just as her false reflection had wavered before she saw her true self. She dipped her spoon back into the dish. *It's a lie. It's a lie. It's a lie.* As she lifted another bite of soufflé to her lips, it suddenly blinked out of existence, leaving a mound of oatmeal in its place.

Juliette dropped the spoon.

Caleigh gasped as bits of egg and pastry splattered across the table and onto the floor.

"I'm so sorry," Juliette said. "I . . . my fingers must be slippery."

"Don't apologize." Caleigh was already rushing to dab up the mess with a napkin. "It's no trouble at all."

Juliette's heart sped. She'd done it. She'd managed to see past the illusion. But she needed to keep it to herself if she had any hope of finding the Hall of Memories.

Caleigh went to the trash can to shake out the napkin, and Juliette used the moment of distraction to take a deep breath and school her expression into submission. She needed to find out as much as she could about how the hotel operated. By the time Caleigh returned to the table, Juliette was sitting calmly with what she hoped was a relaxed smile.

"So how long have you worked here?"

"Hmm . . ." Caleigh twisted a lock of hair around her fingers. "It's been about a year, I think."

"Was the training difficult?"

She shrugged. "Not particularly. I had concierge experience from another hotel. It's not so different."

Juliette chewed on her bottom lip as she struggled to formulate a question that would give her more information than the bland answers Caleigh kept providing. She mentally sifted through a dozen or more possibilities: *Is the entire staff trained in magic or just a select few? How well do you know Henri? Has he ever explained exactly what he does?* But in the end, she couldn't think of a single question that wouldn't arouse suspicion. An awkward silence stretched between them.

Finally, Juliette cleared her throat. "Are you happy here?"

Caleigh's eyes narrowed and she sat forward in her chair. "Why do you ask?"

Panic fluttered in Juliette's chest. Had she gone too far? She decided to try a different tack, one that hopefully would draw Caleigh out of her shell instead of making her suspicious.

"I've thought of working here," Juliette said.

"Ohhh." Caleigh's eyes sparked with interest. "Well, it's hard not to be happy in a place like this." She plucked a strawberry from the tray. "The food alone is amazing." She popped the fruit in her mouth and closed her eyes as she chewed. Did she not see through the illusions after all? Or was she that good of a liar?

Or maybe she was just engaging in a bit of misdirection.

"So, what is it like to be on the staff?" Juliette asked, careful to keep her voice light and casual, even though the desire for more information was practically trembling inside her.

Caleigh stood abruptly. "Do you like stories?"

The question took Juliette off guard. "Yes, I do."

Caleigh pressed her hands together and bounced lightly on her toes. "Then I have the perfect activity for today."

Before Juliette knew what was happening, Caleigh pulled her to her feet and out the door.

"Wait," Juliette protested, "I haven't even changed out of my nightclothes."

Caleigh waved a dismissive hand in the air. "You're dressed perfectly for where we're going."

"Where are we going?"

"You'll see." Caleigh's voice was full of excitement, and Juliette hoped she might be taking her to some behind-the-scenes area of The Splendor in response to Juliette's curiosity about the hotel staff.

But instead, Caleigh led her to a cozy, dimly lit room where a dozen people covered in soft fleece blankets and leaning against oversized pillows lounged on the floor. A woman sat on a large leather chair with her bare feet tucked beneath her. Nearby, a stone hearth crackled with fire.

The scene was charming but lacked the otherworldly, luxuriant magic Juliette had grown to expect from The Splendor. Everyone looked relaxed but quietly expectant, as if they were waiting for some event to begin. Was this a staff meeting?

"What are we doing here?" Juliette whispered.

Caleigh nodded toward the woman sitting in the chair by the fire. "Cadence is a weaver."

Juliette stared at Caleigh, confused. "She works with fabric?"

"No, silly. She weaves *stories*."

Oh. Juliette's tentative hope blew away like a dried leaf in a strong wind. She was being redirected. Distracted. Deprived of the knowledge she was desperate to obtain. She nearly stood and stalked out of the room, but then Cadence began to speak.

"Once upon a time, in a land not so very far from here . . ."

Everything went quiet and still as if the earth itself were holding its breath to see what would happen next. Cadence's words seemed to be made of moonglow and starlight, and she used them to weave a shimmering tapestry that was both intricate and achingly beautiful. She spoke sentences delicious enough to eat.

Juliette forgot where she was. She forgot *who* she was. She became a pirate sailing the high seas. An adventurer searching for treasure. A dragon-wrangler riding on the back of a giant winged beast, the wind in her hair.

Cadence's voice spilled over her like a lullaby, coaxing Juliette into another world. One where she was always the hero, and her quests—however difficult—always succeeded in the end. When Cadence's voice finally trailed away, Juliette felt weightless, like a dust mote dancing in a shaft of sunlight. But slowly the room woke from the trance. People shifted. Stood. Stretched. The spell was broken, and Juliette was filled with a yearning emptiness.

When Juliette was a child, she had fallen out of a tree. Time seemed to slow as she tumbled from the branch where she'd been perched before losing her balance, the moments passing like honey dripping from a spoon, stretching, but never landing. Until they did, and she hit the ground with a force that knocked the breath from her lungs. The sickening crunch of bone hit her ear like a bad omen and from the corner of her eye, she saw her arm twisted at an odd angle.

Her scream brought Miss Durand running from the children's home, her face as pale as freshly fallen snow. Despite the woman's gentle touch and calming assurances, Juliette had been hysterical with panic and pain.

When the healer arrived, he forced her to swallow a spoonful of foul-tasting liquid that made her gag as it slid unpleasantly down her throat. But once she choked it down, the medicine seemed to coat her insides and dull her pain, making her feel disconnected and muzzy until eventually it gently lowered her into an untroubled sleep.

But when she woke, her arm screamed in an agony made worse by the peace that had come before.

The same feeling settled over her now. As a child, she'd begged the healer for more of the bitter syrup to numb the pain, and she now had the urge to rush to Cadence and plead with her for more delectable words, more tales of adventure and bravery. More medicine to quell her discomfort.

Since yesterday, she'd been trying to throw off the blinders of fantasy and let her gaze fall on the reality, no matter how difficult it might be.

But now that she'd spent the last several hours cocooned in the soft oblivion of a dreamworld, it was even harder to return to the cold, unfeeling truth: Fantasy was better than reality. Especially the kind of fantasy the weaver had presented— the kind made more believable because it wasn't trying to be something it wasn't. This wasn't oatmeal masquerading as a soufflé. It was medicine for the soul, the kind that dulled pain and let you slip away from reality without artifice or trickery. But the consequences of waking up were just as jarring.

Caleigh looped an arm through hers. "Wasn't that wonderful?"

Tears prickled at the backs of Juliette's eyes, but she couldn't risk letting them fall in front of Caleigh. She was certain now—the visit to the weaver had been intended as a distraction from her line of questioning, and she had to let Caleigh believe it had worked. As much as she hated her real life, she couldn't forsake finding the Hall of Memories and getting answers about why Clare wanted to get rid of her. Not for any amount of mindless pleasure, no matter how decadent.

Juliette smiled—a beaming grin completely disconnected from the reality of what she was feeling. "Yes," she said, "it was."

"I knew you'd love it!"

Juliette felt a small, mean stab of satisfaction.

Apparently Caleigh was terrible at seeing through illusions too.

CHAPTER FOURTEEN

HENRI RATTLED AROUND THE HOTEL LIKE A RESIDENT ghost. The guests tended to disregard those who worked at The Splendor unless they needed something, and the other staff occasionally acknowledged Henri with a quick hello or a brief nod, but he couldn't help but notice how they tended to speed up a little as they passed. And sometimes they pretended not to see him entirely.

Maybe it was all in his head.

Two clothiers about his age were coming toward him from the opposite end of the corridor, each rolling a large rack full of clothes, shoes, and silk masks—items clearly being prepared for the upcoming masquerade ball. Henri lifted his hand to wave, when the men turned toward each other in unison and began talking, as if they'd been in the middle of an engrossing conversation.

His arm dropped to his side. It wasn't in his head. The staff had always kept their distance. He had professional, polite relationships with some of them, like Amella, but mostly he worked alone.

A familiar ache stirred in his chest. It was the same feeling that drove him so often to the Hall of Memories to gorge himself on other people's connections—the sensation of having siblings who knew your secrets well enough to tease you, parents who watched you grow, friends who would revel in your joy and sit with you in sorrow. Henri had none of it. His only stable connections were to Stella and Theo.

And now he'd put even that at risk.

His conversation with Stella earlier left him unsettled. He thought of the heat that had infused her voice. *How did this happen?*

He'd only scratched the surface of the truth, and she'd reacted so strongly, he hadn't dared tell her everything. But she'd find out eventually. He needed to fix this, and quickly. There must be a way to make sure Juliette had a positive experience at The Splendor; if she left happy, the reputation of the hotel would be secure, and Stella would be satisfied.

But he wasn't sure how to make it happen. It was as if his mind were full of a list of numbers, but each time he'd almost calculated the sum, his attention wandered, and he had to begin all over again.

Henri had started walking to clear his head, and he'd been wandering aimlessly through the corridors with no particular destination. But now he stopped at the base of the staircase that led to the penthouse. He hadn't intended to come here, but perhaps his feet knew he was craving family even when his head didn't. Stella would be away working—she rarely returned before nightfall—but maybe Theo was home. If anyone had insight on how to get back in Stella's good graces, it would be him. The thought cheered him and he took the stairs two at a time.

As he stepped onto the landing one flight below the

penthouse, he heard voices. Maybe Stella was home after all. And then he heard his own name and froze.

". . . no longer confident Henri can handle it." Stella's voice floated down the stairwell.

Henri's pulse roared in his ears. He flattened himself against the wall.

"I'm keeping a close eye on things." The voice belonged to Caleigh. "She's been asking a lot of questions, but so far I've been able to redirect her."

Stella made a noncommittal noise. "We can't afford any risks. How does Juliette feel about Henri?"

"She seems fond of him," Caleigh said, "but I was more optimistic at the beginning of the week. So far, she hasn't shown any particular interest in having a romance. Do you want me to keep him away from her?"

"No. Henri is——" Stella paused, as if searching for the right word, and Henri held his breath against what she might say. But when she spoke again, the blow landed harder than he thought possible. "He's fragile. I don't want to discourage him. And who knows? Maybe he'll have a breakthrough. But keep me updated. If she becomes a liability, we may have to take more drastic measures."

"Hopefully, that won't be necessary. But you'll be the first to know when I have any new information."

"Thank you, Caleigh. I'm relieved I can count on you."

"Of course."

The sound of footsteps sent Henri scurrying down the stairs. He hurried through the hallways, no longer concerned with connecting with anyone. His vision had gone white. Fire burned in his veins.

He's fragile.

Hot shame licked up his neck as he thought of his promise to Stella to protect her legacy. To protect The Splendor.

And all the while she hadn't considered him capable of protecting anything; she thought he was weak.

Even though sunset wasn't for hours yet, Henri decided against retreating to his attic bedroom and headed directly for the crypt. He felt like a stuffed animal ripped apart at the seams, and only magic could stitch him back together.

Henri didn't bother to undress before slipping into Lobster Lake and sinking into the warm, healing water. Steam curled around his head and made his vision go pleasantly hazy. He inhaled deeply as he tried to untangle the emotions that had twisted into a hard, heavy knot against his breastbone that made it hard to breathe. But he couldn't quite explain his feelings, even to himself.

Stella had never pretended to be his mother. She viewed him through the lens of what he could do for The Splendor. Henri had always been clear about his role in her life, and in Theo's. So why did her comments feel like a paper cut across his heart? Swift and surprising. Slow to bleed, but also slow to clot.

He sank deeper in the water. It was, he decided, that she'd made him feel special. Irreplaceable. And her faith in him was something he kept folded close to his heart, like a secret written on pages with creases made soft from being opened and read so often. To hear her speaking about him so callously . . . it was as if she'd snatched the pages away and laughed as she read them aloud. It made him feel small and naive, as if he really were nothing but a lonely orphan boy with no one to love him.

For the first time since he came to the hotel as a child, he wondered what it would be like to leave. He'd seen a good portion of the world in the minds of others, so he had some idea what paradise might look like. He often dreamed of cool mountain air, pine trees, and burbling streams.

Meadows full of flowers and serene lakes teeming with fish. But in the end, it wouldn't fix anything. Because whether he was in the mountains or at The Splendor, Henri was all alone.

He ran a wet hand over his face. He needed to stop pitying himself and start problem solving.

When he was young, he often complained that his world was too small. *Why can't we go somewhere new?* he once asked Stella.

She had given him a reproachful frown. *Not every orphan ends up with a roof over their head—especially not one as grand as this. And with magic as breathtaking as yours, you can go anywhere. See anything. You should be more grateful, Henri.*

Stella was right. He had a charmed life, and it was greedy to want more.

She was always right. Her words echoed painfully in his mind. *No longer confident Henri can handle it. . . He's fragile.*

But then he remembered the rest of her conversation with Caleigh—about Juliette becoming a liability. About having to take more drastic measures. What did she mean?

Henri scrambled out of the water. As much as he wanted to please Stella, he didn't want Juliette to be forced to leave the hotel. There must be some way to fix this. Maybe he could use her dreams to reshape her experience in the Hall of Memories. The unconscious mind was a powerful tool. If he could send her healing dreams—ones where she saw Clare in a new light—perhaps she could grieve the betrayal and move on to things that brought her joy.

But before he could make his way to Juliette's room, he had work to do.

The first Signature Experience of the night was one of Henri's favorite kinds. Suite 153: a man named Leon, whose greatest wish was to revisit his own past. He didn't want fame greatest wish was to revisit his own past. He didn't want fame or fortune or the quick rush of thrill seeking, but he would give anything for one more day with lost loved ones.

Though Henri had never met the man, never even seen him, he felt an immediate kinship with Leon. Henri hoped— when his hair had grayed and his skin had folded in to soft, worn wrinkles—that he'd lived a life so happy it begged to be repeated again and again. He ran his fingers over the cool stone on the wall as he walked along the hidden passageway, stopping when he reached suite 153. This time he didn't need a glass vessel. He only needed to find Leon's precious faded memories and bring them vividly to the forefront of his consciousness.

Henri released his magic and let it sink gently into Leon's mind like water slowly disappearing into warm sand.

On the surface, Leon's memories were fuzzy and forgetful. Full of half-remembered grocery lists and forgotten names. For a moment, Henri worried he wouldn't find anything useful.

But he dove deeper in Leon's mind. Images rushed past: a walk through the park where Leon stopped to admire a sparrow with a gray head and a rich black bib; a perfectly cooked egg on toast—the golden yolk spilling over crisp bread; falling asleep to the sound of rain pattering on the roof. Henri kept going and the melody of a lullaby floated past. It seemed so insignificant, he almost moved on, but then he realized it was a thread that wove into the deep recesses of Leon's mind. And so, Henri followed it. He found the lullaby over and over again—a song hummed to a baby, a music box given to a chubby toddler, a piece played at a piano recital. It was as if an entire childhood had floated on the wings of this one tune.

Henri was going to give Leon his daughter back—

from the glossy black pigtails she wore at age three to the strong, confident woman she became as an adult. One who gave Leon a proud, achy feeling in his chest each time he looked at her. Old memories were in sepia—faded by time and the failing of age. But Henri could make them new again. Full of life and color. The process was like sanding down a hardwood floor and applying fresh varnish to make it look as new as the day it was installed.

The lullaby seemed to be an anchor point to so many of the memories of—Henri searched for her name—Vivienne. So, Henri started there. He played the melody over and over, weaving it firmly into Leon's mind. And then he began to let the other recollections of Vivi float to the surface and he attached them to the notes of the tune. Vivi eating her first bite of chocolate, her eyes wide with delighted surprise. Vivi curled up next to her mother, listening to a bedtime story. Vivi dressed in white with a bouquet of yellow roses in her hand. He restored memory after memory until he was confident Leon would wake tomorrow morning bursting with nostalgia and love for his daughter.

Henri could have stopped there. He knew Stella would say he *should* stop there. *Give a guest everything they paid for, but don't give them two visits for the price of one.*

Leon would leave The Splendor supremely satisfied with his experience, and likely would return again and again to reclaim more memories.

But Henri was still stung by Stella's comments earlier and was disinclined to care whether she made a single additional penny from Leon. Besides, the nostalgia felt like balm to his wounded heart. He needed it almost as much as Leon did. So he kept going. He searched for other memories to restore.

He reached farther back into Leon's past. A warm summer night under a canopy of stars. Leon and his brother Jack sitting in a cool patch of grass with a jar of strawberry jam they'd pilfered from their grandmother's pantry. They felt like rebels as they ate directly from the container—dipping their spoons into the sticky concoction and licking them clean, certain that nothing tasted as sweet or captured the magic of summertime quite as well.

Henri searched loose threads of long-forgotten memories—some of them big moments, some small—but woven together, they were the kind of memories that made up a life.

And he restored them all.

By the time he was finished, his worries had been washed away and he felt as clear as the air after a spring storm. He could instill Juliette with the same sense of calm. He climbed to room 718 and sent a thread of magic through the opening. But it never landed. Despite the late hour, the room was empty.

Juliette was missing.

CHAPTER FIFTEEN

JULIETTE SHIVERED AS SHE CREPT DOWN THE STAIRCASE, the marble chilly beneath her bare feet. She'd gotten better about spotting illusions and then holding on to the glimpse long enough to peel back the filmy layer of magic and reveal the reality beneath. She'd practiced all evening—staring at the clothes in the closet of her suite until the ball gowns turned to simple cotton tunics and the fancy sequined shoes transformed into plain leather flats; running her fingers along the fabrics on her bed and feeling them roughen in her hands to something no more luxurious than anything she'd had at the children's home; and watching her own appearance in the mirror until the perfect reflection wavered and she became as ordinary as the day she walked through the front doors of The Splendor.

It was disappointing.

Even though she knew the magic of the hotel was powered by illusion, she'd still clung to the hope that some of it would last.

She tried to focus on the things she knew were real: the breath moving in and out of her lungs; her heart thudding in her chest; the smooth stone of the railing beneath her hand.

A sharp pain stabbed her palm. Startled, she lifted her hand to her face. A small jagged sliver was embedded in the fleshy skin beneath her thumb. She pulled out the splinter and a slender line of blood trickled toward her wrist. How did this happen?

She blinked and the illusion flickered. Beneath the beautiful marble banister was a handrail of dilapidated wood. She glanced down. Her feet rested on planks of pine. Her throat went tight. The illusion had been so convincing. The stone had been so cold, hurrying her steps as she descended. Fear gripped her heart. If she couldn't even count on the ground beneath her feet to be real, what else was a deception? A terrifying thought floated through her mind: What if she was dead? Maybe nothing was real, and Juliette was only a consciousness floating through oblivion, her mind creating and destroying fantasies in some vain attempt to replicate life.

Was she truly still breathing in and out? Was her heartbeat real or only an illusion?

At the bottom of the staircase she stopped—palm pressed to her chest—and waited for the world to right itself. She concentrated on her pulse—faster than normal, but it didn't flicker as she focused on it. With practice, she could find what was real.

And her love for Clare was real; she knew that much was true.

Juliette kept walking. She retraced the steps she'd taken with Henri and this time the staircase was precisely where it had been before.

A jab of triumph went through her, and she scrambled up the steps, worried her attention would wander and the steps would vanish beneath her feet.

Her breath was jagged when she finally pushed open the tall double doors and stepped over the threshold.

Juliette was primed to spot deception, convinced she'd find a ramshackle room with memories stored in old tin cans. But the hall was every bit as breathtaking as before. Oil lamps on the wall lit the room in a soft glow, illuminating rows of shelves filled with colorful glass jars in every size and shape imaginable.

She found the shelf marked with her sister's name and ran her fingers along the collection of glass vessels. She stopped on a tall container—cobalt blue with diamond shapes etched on the surface. She sat on the floor, removed the stopper, and tipped the cloudlike substance into her palm.

Juliette was plunged into a memory.

IT WAS SUMMERTIME, A DAY OF BUTTERY SUNLIGHT AND an azure sky. Clare stood at the end of a dirt road with her hands on her hips. "You really think you can beat me?"

"Yes, I'm fastest." Juliette plopped down in the dirt and shoved her nose into her kneecap, imitating the pre-race stretching she'd seen from the competitors of the footrace at the autumn festival a few weeks ago. But she moved her chubby toddler leg toward her face instead of the other way around.

Clare suppressed a giggle. "I don't know, Jules. I'm pretty fast too."

Juliette hopped to her feet. "Weddy. Set. Go."

She took off running before Clare realized what happened. Even so, Clare was able to catch and then pass her in a few strides. She glanced behind her. Juliette's cheeks were bright pink, and her face was pinched in concentration. She shoved a lock of copper hair out of her eyes. Her tiny bowed legs looked like they were pumping as fast as they could go.

Clare grinned and slowed enough for Juliette to catch up. Clare let her pass.

Juliette gave her a sidelong glance that was equal parts exhaustion and glee. "I'm"—heavy breath—"fastest."

Clare loved her sister, but she couldn't let that kind of arrogance go unchallenged. She took off at full speed, laughing at Juliette's outraged expression.

When she made it to the end of the lane, she spun around to watch her small sister struggling to catch up. Juliette was so focused on speed, she didn't see the dip in the path. The toe of her shoe caught the lip of the depression and Clare felt like she saw the next few seconds in slow motion. Juliette pitching forward, her eyes saucer-wide, her small body sailing through the air a few inches above the ground, and then a hard thud as she landed face-first.

Clare rushed to Juliette and knelt beside her. "Are you all right?"

Juliette whimpered as she crawled into a sitting position. Her face was smeared with dirt. Clare pressed a hand to her forehead because she didn't know what else to do, and it was what Momma always did when either of the girls was hurt or sick.

"My knee hurts," Juliette said, turning her leg so Clare could see that it was scraped and very slightly bleeding.

"Here." Clare used the bottom edge of her shirt to dab at the scratch, wiping away the dirt. "Is that better?"

Juliette seemed satisfied with Clare's caretaking abilities and nodded through a sniffle. "I would have won," she said, "if I hadn't tripped."

Clare didn't point out that she'd already made it to the

end of the path long before her sister fell. Instead, she decided to give her this one. They could race another day, and Clare would put her in her place then.

"You probably would have, Jules." She pulled her sister to her feet. "Now, c'mon, let's go home." ⚞—❂

Juliette came out of the memory breathless.

As a little girl, she used to extend her arms and spin as fast as she could until she was so dizzy she couldn't stand anymore and fell to the ground in a giggling heap. The sensation of watching herself from Clare's point of view was the same. She was disoriented, and the only thing she could do was put the memory back in the vessel, lie on the ground, and wait for the world to stop moving.

Eventually it did.

She climbed to her feet and plucked another container from the shelf. This one was ruby red and shaped with jagged edges, like a maple leaf. She pulled out the stopper and tipped the contents into her fingers.

❂—⚞ CLARE WOKE TO THE SOUND OF COUGHING. IT WAS A soupy, rattling sound and she crept to her mother's bedside.

"Momma?"

No response.

Clare gave her mother a little shake. Momma's sweat-slicked nightgown clung to her skin. She moaned. Opened her eyes. Startled.

"What's wrong?" She laid a palm on Clare's cheek. Her skin was unusually hot against Clare's face. "Are you all right?"

"I'm fine," Clare's voice trembled. "But *you're* sick."

"Oh, love. I'm sorry. Did I wake you?"

"Yes." Clare wanted to say more, but she didn't have words for the growing discomfort in her stomach that made her feel as if she'd swallowed something spiky.

"I'll be fine with a little rest. Go back to bed, sweetheart." And then her eyes drifted closed before she could make sure Clare obeyed. So, Clare didn't.

She watched her mother's forehead crinkle in her sleep against some unseen pain. Someone should watch over her until morning.

Clare sat on the floor by her mother's bed and tried to keep guard. But she must have drifted off, because the next thing she knew, golden-pink light was falling across her face, coaxing her eyes open. And her mother was in the middle of a coughing fit—loud, wheezy, panicked. Clare scrambled to her feet. Her mother sat up, legs dangling over the side of the bed. Her skin was pale; her hair was damp and hung limply around her face. She covered her mouth and coughed.

When she pulled her hand away, it was speckled with blood.

Clare's chest went tight. "Momma?"

Her mother wiped her palm against her nightgown, leaving bright red streaks behind. "I need you to wake your sister and get her dressed. And then pack a bag for each of you. Can you do that?" Her voice was raspy, but urgent. She sucked in a breath and winced.

The sharp thing in Clare's gut stabbed her. "Why? What's wrong?"

Her mother gave her a sad, haunted smile. "Everything will

be fine, love. But I need to take you and Juliette somewhere safe so I can visit a healer. Be a good girl and help your sister." ⚷

Juliette slid the memory back into its bloodred container and pressed the heels of her hands against her eyes. She didn't know if she could keep going. Clare had never told her this story, and seeing it now felt at once like a violation and a revelation. She'd always thought her pain and Clare's were the same. They'd both been left at the children's home at the same time. They'd both waited with unwavering faith that their mother would return. And when she didn't, they both suffered the same crushing disappointment that was made so much worse by the hope that came before.

But she realized now that Clare's burden had been greater. Juliette had only been required to nurse her own grief, but Clare had shouldered the burden of pain for both of them—comforting Juliette when she woke up crying in the night, patiently holding her sister's hand every waking moment for months because Juliette was so worried Clare would leave too, and telling stories of their mother over and over at Juliette's request even though it must have hurt her to do so. *Be a good girl and help your sister.* How those words must have echoed in Clare's mind over the years. Is that why she sold these memories? Were they simply too painful? And did it work? Did forgetting Juliette give her the relief she craved?

Juliette rolled her shoulders against the tension gathering in her muscles. She wished she knew which of these vessels would give her the answers she needed. She studied them one by one and then plucked a small lemon-yellow container from the shelf.

Ⓞ—🔑 CLARE DRUMMED HER FINGERS ALONG THE DESK IN Miss Durand's study. She tried to keep her face bored and impassive, but her heart was trying to escape from her chest. It flung itself against her rib cage in a mindless panic.

"Do you understand what I'm saying, darling?" Miss Durand leaned forward, peering at Clare over the spectacles perched on the bridge of her nose. "Someone wants to adopt Juliette. She'll have a new home."

"But I won't go with her?"

Miss Durand's expression went soft and a little sad, like a candle left burning too long. "We try to keep siblings together when possible, but this couple only wants one child."

"Maybe they won't like her," Clare said hopefully.

"I think that's unlikely. They came to the children's home a few days ago and watched her play. They found her utterly charming."

Stupid Jules with her stupid freckles and chubby cheeks and infectious laugh. Why did she have to go around making people like her? Clare was so angry she wanted to grab her sister by the shoulders and shake her until she promised never to speak around an adult again. Not until Clare was old enough to get them out of here.

Miss Durand reached behind her and retrieved a bundle wrapped in brown paper and tied with twine.

"I've purchased a new dress for your sister. Will you help her get ready?" She held out the package with an eager smile, as if it were a holiday. As if this would be a treat for Clare—to outfit her sister like a doll so she would be more appealing for the family who would come to take her away.

Something feral and ugly reared up inside Clare, and she

had to lace her fingers together behind her back to restrain them. She wanted to rip the bundle from Miss Durand's hands and toss it to the ground. A wrinkle appeared between Miss Durand's eyebrows and Clare could almost see the thoughts swirling around her head.

Clare had to show she was compliant. Now, before it was too late.

She released her hands and carefully took the package. She tried her best to smile. "Yes, Miss Durand. I'll make sure she's ready."

"Thank you, darling. This is for the best. You'll see."

Clare counted her steps as she left the office. One. Two. Three. She must not run. Four. Five. Six. She must not seem disobedient. Seven. Eight. Nine. But she wouldn't let them take her sister. Ten. Clare made it to the stairs and took them two at a time. She threw open the door to the girls' room. Juliette was lying on her stomach, playing with a paper doll whose head had been crumpled and smoothed out again. Clare knelt beside her.

"Jules, do you want to play a game?"

"What kind of game?" Juliette gently kicked her feet back and forth, like a little duck paddling on the water. It gave Clare an idea.

"Who do you think is stronger? Me or you?"

Juliette's eyes lit up and she pushed herself into a sitting position. "Me! I know it's me!"

Juliette gasped as the memory faded. She *remembered* that day. Clare had convinced her to kick a pair of strangers in the shins as hard as she could, promising they'd give her a new dress if she proved she was the strongest girl they'd ever seen. She also taught Juliette a few choice curse words to whisper in their ears if they got close enough. Which they did.

The couple left in a huff and Miss Durand had been *so* angry. Juliette wasn't allowed to eat sweets or play outside for a month.

She'd been furious with Clare. She'd screamed at her that night before bed: *You tricked me and I hate you!* But Clare had been trying to protect her, just like always.

And she'd been the obnoxious little sister who never returned the favor.

A band of sorrow tightened around her throat, and she slid to the ground and sobbed.

CHAPTER SIXTEEN

HENRI

ENRI FOUND JULIETTE IN THE HALL OF MEMORIES.
She sat on the floor, brightly colored glass vessels
scattered around her like empty candy wrappers.

Her face was streaked with tears.

He'd rushed here with fire in his belly, ready to evict her
from the hotel himself. She was going to ruin everything. But
now the sight of her—surrounded by her sister's memories,
looking unmoored and haunted—made something warm and
sympathetic wind through him. How did she even get here?
The entrance was protected by illusions. If they were failing—
or worse, if she could see through them—his problems were
even bigger than he thought.

He cleared his throat and Juliette lifted her eyes to his.
She didn't seem surprised to see him, and she had no trace of
panic in her expression at having been caught in a restricted
area of the hotel. He wasn't sure whether to be impressed or
annoyed.

"She loved me."

"Yes." Henri sat across from her, his legs folded in front of him. "But I suspect you already knew that."

"I knew. But I didn't *understand.*"

"Did this . . ." Henri gestured to the memory containers strewn around her. "Did it help?"

"No," Juliette said, and now there was an edge in her voice. "I still don't get why she would do this."

"Neither do I." Henri had been mulling over the same question for days. He remembered wondering about it, briefly, when he'd harvested Clare's memories. He was surprised that she'd want to deprive herself of so many lovely experiences with her sister, even if they were sometimes laced with obligation and pain.

He often felt that way about extractions, though. He understood the impulse to remove the parts of one's heart that ached and stung and were so hollow they could never be filled. But it didn't seem worth the sacrifice to him. A broken heart was evidence of having loved deeply. And he knew better than anyone that a life empty of memories—good or bad—was its own kind of misery. However, it wasn't his life, wasn't his choice. So even though he disagreed with Clare's decision, he'd done his job and carefully excised Juliette from her memory.

At least he knew someone else would cherish the experience of having a sister to love.

He never imagined the next person to see the memories would be Juliette herself. He wished he had some comfort to offer her besides explaining that he thought Clare was a snake. That she didn't deserve Juliette. But the words stuck in his throat—he doubted they'd be helpful—and a tense silence stretched between them.

"You can't be in here," Henri said finally.

Juliette shrugged, her fingers idly tracing the patterns on the strawberry-colored container in her lap. "Apparently, I can."

He heard the challenge in her voice. She'd found a way around the security of the carefully placed illusions. This was a disaster. He couldn't both protect Stella's legacy *and* find a way for Juliette to stay.

Henri sighed. "Maybe Stella is right. Maybe it's time for you to go home."

Juliette looked up sharply. "Stella? As in your guardian?"

Some part of him was touched she remembered their conversation from the first night. "Yes."

"She wants me to go home?"

"Yes."

"Why?"

Henri squirmed. It was likely a bad idea to be honest with Juliette. But he didn't know what else to do. Things with her tended to go sideways no matter what he did.

"She's worried about the reputation of the hotel."

"Exactly!" Juliette slapped a palm on her knee. "Because she's hiding something."

"No. She just doesn't want . . ." Henri trailed off, unsure how to explain.

"What?" Juliette pressed. When Henri didn't answer right away, she fixed him with an icy stare. "She doesn't want *what*?"

"You could make trouble."

"Oh, I intend to make trouble." Juliette stood and began picking up vessels, gathering them in her arms like they were bags from the market. As if she thought she could waltz out of here and take them home.

"Those don't belong to you," Henri said softly.

"They don't *belong* to me?" Juliette's voice went high and reedy. "I'm in every. Single. Memory."

"I know. But they were Clare's, and she sold them to The Splendor."

She raised her chin. "Fine. I'll buy them back."

Henri winced. "Someone else already purchased them."

Juliette's face drained of color. She shook her head. "No. You can't do that."

"I don't have a choice. This was Clare's decision."

Juliette's eyes were glistening, and when she spoke, her voice came out quiet and small. "Just because she wanted to get rid of me doesn't mean I should have to lose her."

Her arms were trembling, the glass containers rattling against one another, and Henri was worried she'd drop them, and they'd shatter. He began to take the vessels from her— one by one—and place them back on the shelf. He spoke as he worked. "You don't have to buy these memories for them to belong to you. Now that you've seen them, they're your memories too. No one can take that away from you."

"Well, apparently *someone* can."

The words stung, but maybe he deserved them. "I can't. Not without your permission." He took the last container from her and set it on the shelf.

"What did Clare *say* exactly when she gave her permission?"

"I don't know."

"What do you mean you don't know?"

"I don't have direct contact with the guests . . ." He paused, realizing how this must sound to Juliette, since he'd seen her nearly every day. Stella's voice rang through his mind: *You better manage her yourself.* "You're an exception, of course," he added lamely. But Juliette didn't seem to be thinking about herself, or how much time she'd spent with Henri. A slow horror was spreading over her face like spilled ink trickling across a blank page.

"You never spoke to Clare?" Her voice was low and strained. "Then how do you know what she wanted?"

Henri raked his fingers through his hair. "Stella and Theo handle harvesting requests."

Her eyes narrowed. "Stella . . . who wants me gone."

He understood her skepticism. He'd be doubtful himself if he hadn't seen the moment of decision in so many of the guests' minds as he went searching for the memories he was tasked with removing.

He'd seen the same scene dozens of times—a guest sitting across from either Stella or Theo, explaining why they had no use for whatever experience they wanted to sell. Sometimes he understood the decision. Other times it filled him with a kind of bittersweet grief.

Henri remembered the first time he saw the negotiation. It was a woman who had gone cliff jumping. She'd been talked into it by a new friend she was trying to impress, and she'd been reluctant at first, but in the end she'd agreed. The experience had been adrenaline soaked—equal parts thrilling and terrifying. She felt weightless as she fell, but she hit the cold water with so much force it knocked the air from her lungs. Terror crawled up her throat as she struggled to resurface. Her vision went black and she wasn't sure if it was the murky water or if her body refused to obey her order to open her eyes. She grew disoriented, unsure which way was up and which way was down. Eventually she made it to the surface, and her friend pulled her gasping from the water, but the incident gave her nightmares for weeks afterward.

Stella instructed Henri to remove the memory entirely from the woman's mind, along with all the nightmares it had caused. She had no use for them anymore, and there were customers who would pay handsomely for such an adventure. Later that evening, Henri had worked backward in the woman's mind in order the find the memory in question, and he'd found her conversation with Stella.

"Are you certain it's what you want?" Stella asked, her elbows resting on the desk, her expression soft and concerned. "Removing memories is a drastic step. It shouldn't be taken lightly."

The woman sat across from Stella, her back ramrod straight, her hands clenched tightly in her lap. "I'm sure." Her voice was steady, resolute. "I won't be at peace until it's gone."

Stella nodded as she unfolded a contract, plucked a pen from the drawer, and slid both toward the woman. "I completely understand. Just sign here and we'll take care of everything."

Henri couldn't remember if he'd seen this same negotiation in Clare's memories, but thinking about all the ones he had seen gave him an idea. He touched Juliette's wrist lightly.

"What if I could prove to you that Clare agreed to this? That she knew what she was doing?"

Juliette's eyes held his. "It would break my heart."

But when he left the room, she followed.

Oil sconces burned at evenly spaced intervals along the walls of the main corridor, bathing The Splendor in soft yellow light. Henri's muscles began to unwind. The hotel never felt more like home than it did at night, when everything was still and silent.

But it was clear Juliette didn't feel the same. She chewed her bottom lip as they walked. Fidgeted with the slender silver ring on her index finger.

"Where are we going?" she asked finally.

"The records room." Henri examined her from the corner

of his eye. Her red hair gleamed in the lamplight, and her cheeks were stained bright pink. He could hear the jagged sound of her breath. She was agitated.

Guilt squirmed in his gut. He should probably escort her from the hotel and wish her the best. This plan probably wouldn't work any better than anything else he'd tried. Juliette had been remarkably resistant to accepting the truth, and he wasn't sure if seeing hard evidence would finally convince her or if she'd continue to believe Clare incapable of betrayal. Was it a kindness to keep trying to prove that her loyalty was misplaced? Or was he only hurting her more?

Something else simmered at the back of his mind. A small part of him still hoped he could succeed. If he could help Juliette see reality and help her accept the truth, maybe there was still time to make her dreams come true. Maybe there was still a flicker of hope she could leave The Splendor happy, and Henri could prove he wasn't fragile, that Stella's trust in him hadn't been misplaced. Maybe he could still make Stella proud. He shrunk away from the train of thought. It made him feel young and naive to crave her approval so desperately.

Henri was so distracted, he nearly missed the small nondescript door. He stopped abruptly and Juliette stumbled into him.

She let out a startled gasp, and Henri grabbed her arm to keep her from falling.

"Sorry," he said. "I almost—" But then he noticed Juliette had gone rigid. Henri released her and let his gaze slide away. "Sorry," he repeated. "We're here."

Henri turned the knob and slowly pushed the door open, cringing as the groaning hinges pierced the silence. He held his breath and waited several long moments, half expecting the rush of footsteps. But none came. The hotel was as still as ever.

He darted a glance in both directions, and then stepped over the threshold, motioning for Juliette to follow.

She didn't.

He looked back to find her frozen in place, trembling. "What's wrong?"

She didn't move. Didn't even acknowledge him. Then it dawned on him. The records room was protected by magic. He'd been so focused on making as little noise as possible, he'd barely noticed the thick film of illusions clinging to the room. And whatever Juliette was seeing clearly terrified her.

"It's not real," he told her.

"I hate spiders." She spoke through clenched teeth.

"So do I. But there aren't any spiders here. It's an illusion." He offered her a hand, but she ignored it.

"Juliette," he tried again, "you saw through the illusions protecting the Hall of Memories. Can you do that again?"

She shook her head. "It's not the same."

"What do you mean?" He wished he could see what she saw so he could help her through it. The illusions protecting the threshold were general ones—fears, phobias—and they relied on the guest's imagination to fill in whatever details would terrify them the most. But since he couldn't tell the extent of what Juliette was seeing and where, it was hard to convince her it wasn't real.

The irony wasn't lost on him. It was the same problem that had brought them here in the first place—his attempt to convince Juliette to accept reality instead of fantasy. And now the same problem would prevent her from even getting through the door.

His hands balled into fists at his sides. He was so tired of illusions.

"What's different?" he asked. "Tell me."

Juliette swallowed and took a step back, her gaze still

fixed somewhere near the ground. "Before, I just got lost. Or saw things that made me feel good. This . . ." She shuddered. "It feels more real."

What was it about people that their fears felt more solid than their dreams?

Henri could dismantle the illusions, but since he hadn't placed them, they'd be impossible to replicate. Stella and Theo would know someone had been here.

But maybe he could make the illusions less real for Juliette.

"Take my hand," he told her.

This time she listened to him and intertwined her fingers with his. She buried her head against his shoulder as he guided her over the threshold and into the room. A feeling wound through him—equal parts warm and magical—that reminded him of sitting in the hot springs.

"Is it safe now?" Juliette asked.

"I think so." Henri's voice felt rough. He needed to pull himself together. He let go of Juliette's hands and went to the large wooden file cabinet in the corner of the room. He yanked open the top drawer and began sorting through folders. They were organized by surname, each name printed in neat block letters. Acord. Aguillard. Ansel. Bardes. Bastien. Belcourt.

There. Berton, Clare.

He plucked the folder from the drawer, set it on the desk, and flipped it open. A single page stared up at him and his chest went tight.

As Juliette scanned the document, her expression changed. She gently brushed a thumb along her sister's name—as if the words were Clare herself. As if Juliette were wiping away a tear. Henri's throat went thick.

They shouldn't have come.

CHAPTER SEVENTEEN

JULIETTE

J ULIETTE WISHED THE SPIDERS WERE BACK.
Anything would be better than the ragged chasm that had split her heart in two.

The words seemed to float above the page—all sharp angles and cruelty. *Hereby agree to the harvesting of the aforementioned set of memories . . . leaving only enough remnants to avoid confusion . . . the undersigned no longer wishes to have a sister.*

And at the bottom was Clare's familiar slanted signature, as if her name were perpetually climbing a hill.

Miss Durand once said everyone grieves in stages—first denying reality, next desperately wishing it would change, and finally accepting that it won't. She had meant it to be a comfort when, one afternoon, Juliette had tugged at her skirt and asked the question that had itched beneath her skin for months. "My momma isn't coming back, is she?"

Miss Durand had been folding a stack of towels. She stopped and crouched down so she was eye level with Juliette.

"No, dear, I'm afraid she's not."

And then Miss Durand explained about grief. About how the different stages were like towns you could visit down a long, straight stretch of highway. But even when you'd finally traveled to the end of the road, to the town called Acceptance, you might turn around the next very day, retrace your steps, and end up right back in the one called Denial.

Juliette had spent the last few weeks bouncing back and forth between believing Clare would never abandon her to realizing it was always inevitable she would leave someday. But now the truth stared up at her in black-and-white, creating a roadblock so tall, she was certain she couldn't ever go back to hoping it wasn't true. Her vision blurred with unshed tears.

"Juliette?"

She lifted her head to find Henri watching her, his expression tight and inscrutable. He opened his mouth. Closed it again. Kneaded his forehead with his thumb and forefinger. Why was he acting so strange when this was precisely what he was expecting to find? Shouldn't he be reminding her that he told her so? She blinked and her eyes spilled over. She furiously wiped her tears away with the corner of her sleeve.

Suddenly, Henri's eyes went wide. "Someone is coming."

He grabbed the file from the desk and shoved it back into the cabinet. And then he rushed to the door and peered into the hallway.

"Go," he said, motioning her forward and practically shoving her through the door.

The alarm on his face shook her. Henri—who moved around The Splendor with the casual confidence of someone who had been raised here—looked as if he'd seen a ghost.

"What's going on?"

"Go back to your suite. Don't stop for anyone or anything."

"Henri—"

He circled her wrist with his fingers. "I'll find you tomorrow and explain everything, but for now, you have to go. Please." His voice was low, urgent.

She could hear the footsteps growing closer. She nodded and turned away.

"And, Juliette?"

She spun toward him. "Yes?"

"Don't trust Caleigh."

When Juliette first heard about the masquerade ball, she had envisioned a lavish event where guests would don beautiful masks made from papier-mâché, leather, or silk. But the moment she stepped into the clothier's the next morning, she realized her imagination had been severely lacking. The masquerade ball would be far more magical than anything she could have dreamed.

Hundreds of costumes were displayed in glass cases throughout the room—the silky black feathers and sharp beak of a raven, the spotted fur of a snow leopard, the emerald scales of a small dragon. Juliette let out an awed breath. If the costumes looked this realistic at the clothier's, how much more impressive would they be once they were animated by the hotel guests?

"What strikes your fancy?" Caleigh asked.

Juliette felt her skin prickle, even as she forced a smile. She was trying to act like nothing was wrong, but she couldn't get Henri's voice out of her head. *Don't trust Caleigh*. What did he mean? Don't trust her with what? It wasn't as if Juliette had confessed her late-night excursions to Caleigh. She hadn't really confided in the girl at all. So why would Henri say such a thing? Anxiety fell into her stomach like a brick.

Juliette laid a palm on a glass case displaying a mouse costume, realistic in every detail, from the speckled pink nose to the long black whiskers.

"This is interesting," she said absently.

Caleigh laughed. "We're not going for interesting. We want spectacular."

Juliette shrugged and allowed Caleigh to lead her away. In truth, she didn't care one bit what she wore to the ball. Her thoughts were occupied elsewhere. She couldn't stop wondering about Henri; he said he'd find her today and explain what had made the color drain from his face, but so far he hadn't kept his promise.

Even more important, she needed to get back to Clare's memories. Last night, she'd let Henri take them from her and put them back on the shelf, only because she had no other choice. But she had every intention of going back.

"Ohhh," Caleigh murmured, "this one is gorgeous."

And it was.

Caleigh had stopped in front of a glass case that boasted a stunning peacock costume. The soft body was the brilliant blue of lapis lazuli, and the tail feathers—vibrant metallic green dotted with eyespots that looked like jewels—were fanned out in a breathtaking display. It was a work of art.

"It's beautiful," Juliette said.

"And distinctive." Caleigh gently nudged Juliette's hip with her own. "I won't lose you in the crowd."

Juliette's blood went cold. Caleigh's tone suggested she was teasing, but what if she wasn't? What if she had actually been tasked with keeping Juliette in her sight at all times? Maybe Henri told his guardians about Juliette finding her way to the Hall of Memories, and they wanted to make sure she didn't have the chance to do it again. But then, why would Henri bother to report her if he was only going to turn around and warn her not to trust Caleigh?

None of it made sense. But she'd have to figure it out later. Caleigh was still watching her with an expectant expression.

"Should I have Armond reserve it for you?" Caleigh asked.

"Yes, I'd love that." Juliette forced a pleasant expression to fall over her face like a curtain, but inside her lungs felt as if they'd been caught in an iron vice. If she didn't get back to Clare's memories and find some way to smuggle them out, they'd be lost to her forever.

Last night, as she'd lain awake, she thought the masquerade ball would be the perfect opportunity: With everyone in disguise, she could slip away from the ball and rescue Clare's memories before Henri had the chance to give them to another guest. But that was when she assumed everyone would be dressed in gowns, suits, and masks; if everyone looked relatively similar, she'd have an advantage. But now, how could she sneak away unseen if she was decked out in iridescent plumage meant to draw attention?

Caleigh left to go find Armond, and Juliette dug her fingernails into her palms, leaving crescent-shaped marks. She watched as a handful of people meandered through the clothier's. Some were with other guests—new acquaintances, old friends, lovers—but most were alone. Not a single other person arrived with a concierge. So why did Caleigh refuse to leave Juliette's side?

Something icy skittered down her spine. Caleigh had been with her nearly every waking moment since she stepped foot on the grounds.

A woman sidled up beside Juliette. Her lips were ruby red and strings of jewels had been braided into her dark hair.

She gave a low whistle as she admired the peacock costume. "This is exquisite. Have you already claimed it?"

Juliette shrugged. "It seems so."

The woman gave her a curious look. "You don't seem excited."

"Just wondering if I should have gone with something less flashy."

"Never." She stuck out her hand. "I'm Emilie, by the way."

"Juliette." She nodded toward the box tucked on the woman's arm. "What did you choose?"

Emilie grinned. "I'm going as a fairy. A good pair of shimmery wings always makes me weak in the knees."

"See, and I love whiskers." Juliette waggled her fingers toward a nearby case. "I should have chosen the mouse."

Emilie gave a deep belly laugh. "Well, you shouldn't second-guess yourself. You're going to be a vision in this costume. I'd trade you in a heartbeat."

An idea unfolded inside Juliette and her pulse quickened. "Really?" She tried to keep her tone light. Playful. "Maybe I'll take you up on that." She leaned forward and lowered her voice to a whisper. "We could create a little mischief."

Emilie's eyes widened in delight, but before she could respond, Calcigh returned.

"All set," she said, threading her arm through Juliette's. "Armond will have the costume delivered to your room by tonight." Juliette stiffened and it took every ounce of her will not to pull away.

"I'm sorry," Caleigh said, her gaze skipping between the two women. "Am I interrupting something?"

"Not at all." Emilie nodded toward the peacock. "I was just admiring her excellent taste."

"It's a beautiful costume, isn't it?" Caleigh said, mollified.

Emilie made an appreciative noise. "Yes, it really is." When Caleigh looked away, Juliette shot Emilie a grateful look and she was rewarded with a conspiratorial grin. "It was nice to meet you, Juliette. I hope we'll run into each other again soon."

"Yes," Juliette said. "You can count on it."

Juliette didn't recognize herself.

The masquerade ball was starting soon, but she couldn't tear herself away from the mirror. This was more than illusion, more than some clever bit of magic that erased a handful of freckles. This was astonishing.

The costume fit like a glove—she'd expected no less—but it was how her face disappeared beneath the mask, how she wouldn't know her own reflection from a stranger's that kept her gaze glued to the image in the glass. She wasn't dressed as a peacock; she'd become one.

"You're going to miss all the fun if you don't get moving," Caleigh called from the doorway. When Juliette didn't answer, Caleigh came around the corner.

"Wow. You look incredible."

"Thank you." Juliette fanned out her jewel-colored train.

"Technically, the colorful bird is male," Caleigh said, tracing her fingertip along one of the blue, gold, and green eyespots on Juliette's tail feathers, "but the peahen costume is terribly drab. No one ever selects it."

"I can't imagine choosing anything else," Juliette said, turning her body to the side, to get a better view.

"You look amazing," Caleigh said. "You'll be impossible to miss."

The words hit Juliette like a bucket of ice water. She'd been so absorbed with admiring the costume, she'd momentarily forgotten what was at stake. Forgotten that Caleigh was more a jailer than an attendant, even if she was acting like the latter.

Juliette blinked her bird eyes. The stiff crest on her head vibrated. But she couldn't make her face look annoyed.

"I'm ready," she said. "Let's go."

Caleigh walked with her as far as the main staircase and then lightly touched her shoulder. "Enjoy yourself. I'll check in with you in a bit."

Juliette heard: *I can watch you from a distance because you're easier to spot than a lighthouse.*

She sighed and made her way down the stairs. At the bottom, her breath caught.

The entire first floor of The Splendor had been transformed into a glamorous ballroom.

Juliette stood motionless as she tried to take it all in.

A silver-and-gold-checkered dance floor stretched from wall to wall in every direction. Dozens of servers—who no longer looked like people, but human sized cats dressed in tuxedos—carried trays of canapés, hors d'oeuvres, and drinks, their tails swishing jauntily as they circulated through the crowd.

A pair of burbling bronze fountains sat in the center of the south quadrant. Every few minutes a chime sounded, and a burst of water jetted from each fountain and formed into a pair of animated figures: a couple who joined hands and then waltzed around the room; two jousting knights on horseback; a cat chasing a mouse.

Above was a midnight-blue sky full of frequently shifting constellations and a low-slung moon that felt close enough to touch.

But most breathtaking of all were the other guests.

Her own costume was more magnificent than she could have imagined. But seeing everyone else's—the spectacular corkscrew horns of a markhor, the speckled blue of a hatching robin's egg, the coppery-green scales of a lizard—left her awestruck. It was a feast for the eyes, and Juliette couldn't get enough. She wanted to stay here forever, drinking it in.

And she did. She stood for the longest time, transfixed, feeling like she was observing something marvelous from outside her own body.

And then a pirate bumped into her from behind, his drink sloshing onto the floor.

"Pardon me," he said, "I'm so sorry."

Juliette noticed he had a live parrot on his shoulder. It watched her curiously, as if puzzling out if she were human or bird.

"It's no problem," Juliette said, moving so the man could pass. In truth, she should be thanking him for snapping her out of her reverie. She couldn't afford to get sidetracked.

She had a fairy to locate.

Juliette wound her way through the room, her eyes scanning the crowd for a pair of translucent wings. But distractions were everywhere. She stopped to watch a group of contortionists folding themselves into such strange shapes that five of them were able to wedge inside a giant champagne glass like a handful of pretzels in a small crystal bowl.

She passed by a cluster of topiary trees that began to move, and it took her a moment to realize they were guests in costume. An entertainer juggled inside a giant glass bubble hovering in the air. Everywhere she looked was another wonder—stilt walkers in suits made of light, aerial dancers who seemed to swing from the stars, fire blowers who breathed out huge circles of flame and then sucked them back in again.

Juliette forced herself to focus on the task at hand.

She kept walking as she searched. She spotted the bold orange and black wings of a monarch butterfly, a set of delicate, filmy dragonfly wings, the bony wings of a bat.

But she couldn't find a fairy.

A frustrated sigh escaped her lips. If she could find Emilie, she hoped to be able to convince her to switch costumes. Juliette had already hatched a plan. A line was forming for the illustration booth—a curtained cubicle guests could enter, alone or with a friend, to have their likeness magically drawn. She and Emilie could go in together and swap costumes behind the curtain. If Caleigh was watching, she'd see a peacock and a fairy enter, then a peacock and a fairy leave. As long as Caleigh was observing from a distance, she'd never know the difference. After the trade, Caleigh would start watching the wrong woman, and Juliette should be able to slip away and get to the Hall of Memories unnoticed.

But the whole plan would fall apart if she couldn't find Emilie.

She made her way to a wrought iron table at the edge of the room and sunk into a chair. A human-sized cat sauntered over and offered Juliette a tray of desserts. She considered waving the server away but decided it would look suspicious if she appeared to be sulking. Even though she was.

She chose a tart filled with soft orange cream and topped with a sugared daisy and a slice of glazed fruit. She took a bite and the sweet citrus flavor burst on her tongue.

A hand fell on Juliette's shoulder and she spun around to see a spiky head of bright pink hair framed by a pair of gossamer wings.

Her heart leaped in her chest.

Emilie gave her a wide grin. "I believe I was promised a bit of mischief?"

CHAPTER EIGHTEEN

H ENRI SPENT THE NIGHT AT STELLA AND THEO'S
penthouse, tucked into the same bed he'd slept in as a
boy.

Stella had framed it as concern when she found him last
night slinking out of the records room like a thief. But he
recognized the gesture for what it was: She was punishing
him. She hadn't even asked what he was doing there. She'd
simply given him a disappointed frown. "You're working too
hard. Come, you'll stay with me and Theo tonight."

It wasn't a question.

But he'd followed her up to the penthouse because he was
just as ready for a conversation as she was, and if he was going
to scream at her in the middle of the night, he should probably
do it far removed from the guest quarters. He bit his tongue as
he trudged up the stairs behind her. His fingers were restless
and sparking; he kept tapping them against each other as if
trying to extinguish a flame. Stella was walking too slowly.

Finally, she opened the door to the penthouse and Henri

took a deep breath. But Theo was still awake, and when he saw Henri, his whole expression lit up.

"Well, isn't this a nice surprise?" The genuine pleasure on his face stole the wind from Henri's sails. He looked helplessly at Stella, who smiled.

It wasn't a terribly kind smile.

Stella made a pot of chamomile tea, and Henri sat by the fire with Theo, sipping and making small talk. The entire time, he kept waiting for Stella to ask him what he was doing in the records room. But soon he realized, for some reason, Stella didn't want to have this conversation in front of Theo. And Henri couldn't seem to force himself to bring it up either, even though he was desperate to confront her about what he'd seen.

Clare's file had been cloaked in illusions. They clung to the page like a spiderweb of lies, and seeing the reality beneath had been like trying to see the horizon through fog. But he *had* seen it, and he could never go back. It wasn't a page with a signature. It was a standard research sheet like the hundreds he had prepared over the years. *Indications show guest wants to remember her mother better.*

Juliette had been right. Clare didn't want to lose her sister.

It should have been a moment of vindication for Juliette. Of relief. And instead, her expression was devastated. The illusion on the page was too strong for her to resist, and watching her take it in made him feel ill. Clare's signature in large, sloping script, above words that tied his stomach in a tight knot: *The undersigned no longer wishes to have a sister.*

He was still grappling with what it all meant when he heard footsteps and sent her away with no explanation.

Guilt ate at him. He'd needlessly hurt Juliette. She thought her sister didn't love her anymore; had sold all of their experiences together like they were worth nothing more than a basket of vegetables at the market.

Thinking about it agitated him again and he stood to stoke the fire. He stabbed a log and watched sparks fly. He opened his mouth to speak, but Stella caught his eye and gave him a silencing look.

She cleared her throat. "It's late."

Theo, who had been gazing at the fire, mesmerized, glanced up.

"I suppose it is." He drained the rest of his cup and set it on the side table. Then he stood and stretched. "I'm going to turn in." He clapped Henri on the shoulder. "It was good to spend some time with you, Bear."

Henri froze. Theo hadn't called him Bear in years. It was a childhood term of endearment, abandoned a long time ago.

Henri shifted uncomfortably. "You too."

Theo left the room and Henri spun to face Stella. "What's going on?"

She lifted both hands, palms up in surrender. "Not tonight, Henri. Get some rest. We'll talk tomorrow."

"No. You lied to me. I want answers."

"*Tomorrow.*" Her voice caught on the word. She sounded raw and vulnerable, yet her tone left no room for argument. Now that he looked at her more closely, he saw the blue smudges underneath her eyes. Her slightly ashen skin.

Henri became aware of his own exhaustion. It dropped over him like an iron cloak around his shoulders, and he slumped under its weight. Tomorrow. Maybe this could wait until then. Maybe his head would be clearer with a few hours of sleep.

"Fine. But I'm not leaving in the morning until I get some answers."

"I'll tell you everything you want to know," Stella said. "I promise."

Sunlight was pouring in through the wrong window.

Henri rubbed his eyes, disoriented. He blinked. It took him a moment to remember where he was, and then the events of yesterday came flooding back, and his anger along with them.

A shaft of bright sunlight fell across his face, but it was coming from the west. He hadn't . . . could he have slept that long? Was it afternoon already?

Henri bolted upright and groaned. He'd slept most of the day away.

The masquerade ball would be starting soon, and he still needed to talk to Juliette before it started. He couldn't bear for her to believe a lie one more moment than necessary.

And he still needed to confront Stella.

He scrambled out of bed and hurriedly dressed.

Stella was waiting for him, her hands neatly folded on her lap as if she'd been there for hours. When she saw him, she stood.

"You need to harvest Juliette Berton's memories."

Whatever Henri had been intending to say flew out of his head like a flock of startled birds. "What are you talking about?"

"You've gotten too attached to her and you've made a mess. Time to clean it up."

His anger from last night reignited into a roaring flame.

"*I've* made a mess? You lied to me. You lied to her." His hands curled into fists. "And I don't harvest memories from guests who don't request it."

"Don't you?" Stella's voice was low and dangerous. It made Henri's blood turn to ice.

"What are you talking about?"

But she didn't answer. She didn't need to. The chill in her eyes said everything her mouth didn't. He had harvested memories without permission.

He backed away from her. "Who *are* you?"

"Henri—"

"No. Explain yourself. How could you do this? How could you let me believe I was doing something good, when all along—"

"Henri—" Stella's voice was pleading.

"Why would you—?"

"BECAUSE I HAD NO CHOICE!" Stella's voice thundered through the room. Bright red spots had erupted on each of her cheeks, and her eyes were wild.

Henri stared at her, speechless.

"Theo is sick," Stella said softly.

Her words hung in the air. Henri felt as if he could see them—gathering like a poisonous cloud—ready to injure him if he breathed them in.

And so, he didn't.

He held his breath, waiting for her to take it back, to explain that she'd misspoken. But she just stood there, waiting. Henri exhaled. He fell into a chair, defeated.

Stella sat next to him. "I'm sorry. I should have told you before now."

"What's wrong with him?"

"His memory has been slipping."

A bright spark of terror went through Henri. "He's been having episodes too?" Had Henri done something to cause this? What if he was contagious in some way? He'd never forgive himself if he'd done something to hurt Theo.

"Oh no." She touched his wrist lightly. "Nothing like that. It's not like what happens to you. He doesn't seem to realize when his memories go missing. It's probably just age.

But it doesn't make it any less painful."

"How long?"

"I first noticed a few years ago. It's only gotten worse since then."

"A few years? But that's impossible. I would have noticed something. He's been fine."

Stella pinched the bridge of her nose. "He's been fine because I've been working—all night, every night—to make sure he's fine."

Realization washed over Henri. "You've been enhancing his memories." It was a common technique when a guest wanted to remember something more vividly—like Leon in room 153, whom Henri helped revisit his own past—but trying to hold on to every memory in an aging mind would be overwhelming. Especially since Stella was out of practice. She hadn't done much memory work since she'd trained Henri years ago. No wonder she looked exhausted.

"He's getting older, Stella. You can't prevent that, even with magic."

"I can try." They sat quietly for a moment, the futility of the sentiment stretching between them.

"What does any of this have to do with Juliette?"

Stella sighed. "I've told you the hotel was once the site of an ancient temple?"

"Yes." Henri's voice was impatient. He wished she'd get to the point.

"Do you know how the hot springs work?"

"They're filled with magic," he said simply.

Stella arched a single eyebrow, indicating she expected a more robust answer.

But he couldn't give her one. Magic was an integral part of Henri's life. He'd never questioned where it came from any more than he questioned why the sky was blue or why the sun rose in the east. It just was.

"Many years ago, when the temple was occupied by the priestesses of the old order, they would only leave the grounds to go help those in need—minister to the sick, feed the poor, lend a listening ear to those with burdens to unload. Ancient records say when they returned to the temple and soaked in the springs, their own burdens were lightened. The more they soaked, the stronger they felt. They began to realize the water had mystical properties.

"One winter, sickness swept through the temple and it closed its doors to the faithful for an extended length of time. And do you know what happened? The springs began to dry up. The priestesses realized they couldn't just use up magic without replenishing it. The magic only flourished if the springs were fed."

"Fed what?"

"Experiences," Stella said. "The magic thrives when the hotel is full of life, and vibrancy, and people experiencing new things. But if our guests were to suddenly dry up? If rumors began to circulate that our customers were unhappy, or worse, if we had a scandal? The Splendor would die, Henri. And all the magic with it."

Deep lines of worry etched a path across her forehead. The implication was clear: If the magic of The Splendor disappeared, Theo's memories would disappear too. The thought unsettled Henri. But so did Stella's request.

"Tell me the truth. Did I take memories from Clare Berton without her consent?"

Stella's gaze locked on his. "Yes."

"Why?"

"It was a misunderstanding. I've been so distracted with Theo." Her fingers twined together in her lap. "I mixed up two guests."

"It's easily fixed," Henri said. "We'll ask Clare to come back here and I'll restore her memories."

Stella's jaw went tight. "Don't be naive, Henri. It would cause a massive scandal that we can't afford right now. We can figure out how to make it right with Clare later. But it's urgent you execute a harvest on Juliette Berton. You've told her too much. Now you need to fix it by making sure she doesn't remember why she came here in the first place."

His stomach plunged, and he went hot with shame. How did Stella know what he'd told Juliette?

Stella's expression was sharp. She frowned. "Yes, I know about your little escapade to the Hall of Memories. I'm terribly disappointed. We've done so much for you, and I thought I could count on your loyalty if nothing else." It was a venom-tipped arrow aimed right at his heart.

And it found its mark.

"Of course, you can," Henri said past the lump in his throat. "I've always been loyal to you and Theo."

"No," she said, "not always."

Stella stood and ran her palm across the smooth mantel over the hearth. "Theo will be back from his walk soon. You should go."

"Stella—"

She turned toward him, but her expression was shuttered. As if he were just another member of the staff she'd lost faith in.

"I'm sorry," he said.

"I trust you to do the right thing tonight." She lifted her chin. "If you don't, I will."

The masquerade ball was already in full swing by the time Henri made it downstairs. He felt as if a net had been cast over his mind; every time his thoughts tried to change direction, they were hopelessly caught in place—spinning and turning without ever escaping.

He was worried about Theo, crushed at Stella's disappointment in him, but worst of all, horrified at the realization Juliette had been right. He had taken memories from Clare without her consent. Bile rose in the back of his throat as he remembered Juliette's question: *What did Clare say exactly when she gave her permission?*

He should have been more careful. He should have asked Stella to see the paperwork each time he executed a harvest. What if this wasn't an isolated incident? What if he'd done it before?

He wove through the crowds of guests in costume, pushed past the servers dressed as tuxedoed cats. The ballroom rang with noise—laughter and conversation and the awed gasping reactions from a dozen different performances all happening at once.

A group of acrobats swung over his head. Each was painted head to toe in a different bright color—blue, green, orange—and they shimmered as if they'd been dipped in diamond dust.

Henri's pulse skittered in his neck. He needed to find Juliette and fast. He knew Stella well enough to know she wasn't going to let this go. She wouldn't be satisfied until Juliette had no memory of learning why Clare came to The Splendor.

But no matter how he searched, he couldn't spot Juliette in the crowd. He had no way of knowing what costume she'd chosen. At this rate, he'd never find her.

Henri decided to change tactics. He took the stairs up to a mezzanine area, where staff could observe the festivities without interfering. As he suspected, Caleigh sat in one corner sipping a cup of cocoa, her gaze fastened to the crowd.

He headed in her direction and noticed the other members of the staff staring. A wave of irritation rose within him. Maybe they were surprised to see Stella's puppet out of the toy chest before playtime. Let them stare.

He sat on the bench next to Caleigh.

"Henri," she said, acknowledging him without looking in his direction.

"I spoke to Stella." Henri knew he had to tread carefully.

Caleigh's gaze slid to his and then quickly back to the ballroom floor. "And?"

"She told me she asked you to keep an eye on Juliette." It was a guess, but it was an educated one. Henri dipped his head toward the crowd. "So, where is she?"

Caleigh hesitated, and he could see her weighing the responsibility Stella had given her against who Henri was and the status he had at The Splendor. He knew she wanted to impress Stella, but he also knew she wouldn't risk offending him on the chance he had Stella's ear.

"She's the peacock," Caleigh said, pointing to a bright blue bird dipping a skewer threaded with strawberry slices into a chocolate waterfall.

Henri tried to act nonchalant as he watched Juliette, but he felt as if insects were crawling across his skin. The urge to squirm, to move, to run was overwhelming. He willed himself to stay still.

The last thing he needed was Caleigh getting suspicious and sabotaging his plans.

Finally, when he couldn't take it anymore, he stood and stretched. "My workday is starting soon." He hoped his voice was light and casual. "I'll let Stella know you've got things under control here."

"Thank you." Caleigh pressed her lips together and her expression went tight. He understood then, how she'd interpreted his surprise visit. She assumed Stella was using Henri to check up on her. Just as Stella had used her to check up on him. Good. That would work in his favor.

Henri walked at a measured pace until he turned the corner and then he ran. Once he made it to the ballroom floor, he slowed. He made his way toward Juliette while being careful to stay out of Caleigh's line of sight. He walked in step with one of the servers, keeping her between him and the mezzanine. When she broke away, Henri strategically positioned himself behind a cellist wearing a top hat until another server came along to give him cover. Finally, when he was close enough to reach Juliette, he tapped her shoulder and then ducked behind a tree blooming with caramel apples. She spun in a circle, peeked beneath the tree. Henri only had a moment. He leaned forward and grabbed her wrist.

"You're in danger," he said. "You have to get out of here right now."

She inhaled sharply. "What are you talking about? In danger from what?"

Her voice . . .

Two realizations struck Henri like twin cannonballs slamming into him at precisely the same moment. First, he'd startled her so much that her words were nearly hysterical with alarm. And second, her voice didn't belong to Juliette.

CHAPTER NINETEEN

JULIETTE

T HE HALL OF MEMORIES WAS EASIER TO FIND THE second time.

Juliette wondered if so much magic was concentrated on the masquerade ball, it rendered the illusions in the other areas of The Splendor as thin and worn as a threadbare rug. Or maybe she was just getting better at seeing through them.

Just like last time, the room was softly lit. Glass vessels in a hundred hues left prisms of color on the tile floors. This space felt different from every other part of the hotel—like there was a pressure in the air here. It made Juliette wonder if memories had weight. If they hung thickly in the atmosphere, demanding to be acknowledged.

She examined the shelf labeled with Clare's name. There were at least fifty containers here. She'd never be able to smuggle them out of the hotel tonight—not when the entire main floor was swarming with people. But she had to do something. Henri's words haunted her. Someone else already purchased them. It was only a matter of time until he took these memories for whichever guest wanted a sister made of a lie instead of one of flesh and blood. But Henri couldn't use them if he couldn't find them.

Juliette sifted through the possibilities. She could move the memories to another shelf, but that probably wouldn't buy her enough time. Once Henri realized they were missing, he could easily search the room and locate them. Besides, she didn't like the idea of putting Clare's memories above some other person's name. What if the vessels got mixed up and she had trouble finding them all again? She discarded that option and kept brainstorming.

She could try to move the memories to another room in The Splendor, but with so many containers, she'd have to make multiple trips and the chances of getting caught were too huge to make it a viable solution. Maybe she could find something to carry them in? A box or bag of some kind? But that still left the problem of getting through the hotel undetected. She wouldn't exactly blend in if she were carrying a large box full of glass vessels.

Whatever decision she made, she needed to hurry. It was only a matter of time before Caleigh realized she'd switched costumes with Emilie and came looking for her.

Juliette spotted a tall rolling library ladder mounted to the wall at the back of the room. There seemed to be a bit of space near the ceiling above the top shelf. Maybe she could hide the memories up there, where Henri wouldn't think to look right away. It was an option worth exploring.

She steadied the ladder and started to climb. The vaulted ceiling didn't seem to get any closer as she rose. The shelves hadn't appeared this tall from the ground. The ladder slid just a bit to one side, and Juliette let out a startled gasp. And then she made the mistake of looking down.

She was far higher than she realized.

Her vision went wobbly and her stomach turned over. She squeezed her eyes shut and took a deep breath. Clare was always better at handling heights.

Juliette remembered watching her sister scramble up a giant oak in a park near the children's home. Clare made it look easy, taking off at a sprint and pushing off the trunk to grab the nearest branch. Juliette wasn't nearly as athletic. She tried the running start several times, before giving up in favor of a less flashy beginning. She grabbed the lowest branch big enough to support her weight. But even then, it took considerable time and all her effort to finally hoist herself up and into the tree.

"You did it, Jules!" Clare couldn't have sounded prouder if Juliette had sprouted wings and flown onto the branch. "Now let's keep going."

They kept moving, and everything went fine until Juliette looked down. The ground was so far away. She let out a cry.

"You're all right," Clare said gently. "Just keep going."

But panic had frozen Juliette in place, and she couldn't convince her body to move. She clutched the tree trunk with both arms.

"We're too high up. I'm scared of falling."

"Would you be scared of falling if we were closer to the ground?"

"No."

"Then pretend."

"I can't pretend," Juliette wailed. "We're too close to the sky."

"Don't look at the sky and don't look at the ground. Just look at the next branch. Can you do that?"

The next branch was close. "Yes," Juliette said, "I can." She grabbed the branch and climbed a little higher. And then she found the branch after that was close too.

She followed Clare's voice, keeping her gaze fixed on one branch at a time until they made it all the way to the top of the tree.

The memory made Juliette smile, and she wondered if Clare's version of events was stored in one of the vessels below, and if the glass was the vibrant green of an oak leaf. She kept her eyes one the next rung and then the next until she reached the top of the ladder.

A little thrill of pride went through her, and she wished Clare were here to see her. And then reality fell like a blade, and a stab of pain punctured the moment. Clare didn't want Juliette in her life anymore. She wouldn't be proud to see her; she'd be relieved to finally be rid of her.

Juliette pushed the thought away and studied her surroundings. From the ground it had looked like a small alcove at the top of the shelving, but it was actually a deceptively deep ledge. Even for someone afraid of heights, it was plenty big enough to walk along without feeling insecure. At least as long as she didn't look down. Juliette lifted herself onto the ledge. She'd have to bring the vessels up a few at a time, but if she stored them near the back wall, they'd be invisible from the ground. As she searched for the perfect spot, something caught her eye: a small square door set into the wall—the kind that could only be accessed on hands and knees. It must be some kind of attic crawl space. If she was right, it could be the perfect place to stash Clare's memories until she came up with a plan to get them out of the hotel.

She murmured a quick prayer to any god who would listen and turned the knob. The door swung freely. She crouched down and crawled through the small opening.

Juliette expected to emerge into a cramped unfinished space, but instead the room opened up and she found herself in a larger-than-expected storage area. A small window spilled cool moonlight into the room, providing enough illumination to see several shelves filled with boxes and stacks of paper. This was perfect.

A stack of empty wooden crates sat in the corner. Juliette grabbed one and scrambled down the ladder, filling it with as many memory vessels as she thought she could safely carry. Climbing back up with a heavy load was awkward and slow, but she managed to get the crate to the storage room without falling or breaking any of the glass, so she counted it as a win. She nestled the crate at the back of one of the shelves near a stack of dusty picture frames. And then she repeated the entire process again, traveling up and down the ladder with Clare's memories clutched against her chest on the way up, and an empty crate dangling from her fingers on the way down.

After several trips her arms ached and her lower back had developed a spasm. She leaned against the wall in the storage room to catch her breath. Clare's shelf was nearly empty; Juliette should be able to bring up the rest of the memories in one final batch. But she'd used up the entire stack of crates. She'd need to unload one of the others and reuse it. The thought made her want to curl up and go to sleep. She was weary to all the way to her bones. Her gaze flicked to the myriad of boxes stacked on the shelves. Maybe one of them was empty.

It was worth a try. She peeked inside boxes full of candlesticks and cutting boards, serving platters, and silverware.

And then she opened one filled with memory vessels.

She blinked, confused. Had she filled a box instead of a crate on one of her trips? Was she that tired? But then she looked closer. None of these containers looked familiar. She scooped up a small aquamarine vessel shaped like a teardrop. And then a tall thin vase the deep purple of an eggplant.

These didn't belong to her sister.

Someone had stashed memories here before.

Maybe it wasn't such a good hiding place if Juliette hadn't been the first to think of it. The thought should have worried her, but she was too intrigued. A thousand questions swarmed her mind like a colony of bees. Who hid these memories here? Did they all belong to the same person? Did someone intend to retrieve them later, or had they been abandoned forever?

There was only one way to find out. Juliette pulled the box from the shelf and sat on the floor. She moved it in a slow circle and examined it from every angle.

When she gave the box a final turn, she froze.

She'd spotted a label written in the same block print used on the shelf that held Clare's memories. A chill skittered down her spine as she traced a fingertip over the letters.

H-E-N-R-I

She sat motionless, trying to collect her thoughts. What did the label mean? Were these memories Henri had taken for himself? Experiences purchased from guests that Henri wanted to claim?

Or—a dull pulse of dread went through her—were they memories that actually *belonged* to Henri?

Juliette knew she should put the box back on the shelf, hide the rest of Clare's memories, and get back to her suite before Caleigh realized she was missing. The contents of this box had nothing to do with her. And yet . . .

It wasn't as if she'd be invading anyone's privacy. Whoever lived these experiences didn't want them anymore, so would it really be so bad if she took a peek? Juliette lifted a soft blue container with the rounded shape of a ginger jar and removed the stopper.

A memory floated out of the vessel, and Juliette gathered it in her palm.

⊙—▪ Henri stood barefoot in the fountain in the courtyard of The Splendor, concealing himself behind the wall of water jetting toward the sky. His heart thudded against his rib cage. He was about to get caught. Steps approached from the other side of the fountain. If he was going to go down, he was going to go down fighting. Henri crouched and scooped a handful of water in his cupped palms, using his magic to shape it into an arrow.

"Ha!" said a voice behind him. "Got you!"

Henri spun around to see Clementine racing toward the fountain, her braids streaming behind her like two pale ropes in a stiff wind.

"Nope, I've got *you*." Henri aimed his water arrow at her chest.

Clementine's eyes went wide. "Don't. You. Dare."

But it was too late. Henri had already let the arrow fly and it slammed into her with a wet slap, soaking her from head to toe.

She sputtered for a moment before her eyes blazed. "I'm going to kill you," she said, stomping toward him. "I'm going to kill you so hard you'll die twice."

Henri couldn't help it; he erupted into a fit of laughter. She just looked so comical—dripping braids, wet dress, enraged expression.

"It's not funny," she said, hands on her hips. "Using magic is against the rules."

He shrugged. "It wasn't very *much* magic. Besides, it's only water. It's not like I made an actual weapon."

It was the wrong thing to say. Clementine reached him in two strides, put both hands on his chest, and shoved.

Henri lost his footing and fell backward into the jetting water, landing with a hard thud on the stone. Water shot up his nose and seeped through his pants. Coughing, he scrambled to his feet and climbed out of the fountain.

Clementine smirked. "I don't need magic to beat you."

Henri tried to school his expression into something menacing—or at the very least something annoyed—but he couldn't manage it. Laughter bubbled up his throat.

And Clementine wasn't having any luck staying angry either. The corner of her mouth twitched, and soon she was giggling too.

"My mother is going to pitch a fit when she sees this dress," Clementine said, sitting on the ground, her back resting against the fountain.

Henri sat beside her. "We could stop by the clothier's and see if they'll give us something fancy for dinner. My parents would be thrilled if they thought I was making an effort to look nice for once."

Clementine pursed her lips and looked pointedly at her dress. "I *was* trying to look nice, and you went and ruined it."

"Sorry," he said. "Is it new?"

"My parents bought it for my birthday last week. They said twelve is old enough to start dressing like a young lady." She sighed. "And acting like one too."

"Ah, so I'm guessing they wouldn't approve of our Splendor duels?"

Clementine shrugged. "Probably not, but who cares? Our parents get to come here once a year and live out their fantasies. Why shouldn't we get to live out ours?"

Henri gave her a look of mock outrage. "You're saying fancy parties and caviar aren't what you dream about all year long?"

Clementine wrinkled her nose. "Ew, hardly."

He laughed. "You have to admit, the chocolate mousse is pretty good though."

"Yeah, I do dream about the chocolate mousse. And the strawberry tarts."

"Are you thinking what I'm thinking?"

"Depends. Are you thinking we should go spoil our dinner?"

Henri grinned. He offered her his hand and pulled her to her feet. "That's exactly what I was thinking."

The memory faded and the room slowly came back into focus. The attic suddenly felt warm and claustrophobic. A bead of sweat slipped from Juliette's hairline and inched slowly down her spine.

What she'd just seen made no sense. The first night she met Henri, he'd told her he was an orphan.

And yet . . .

Henri's young voice still echoed in her head. *My parents would be thrilled if they thought I was making an effort to look nice for once.*

Juliette tried to think of every conversation she'd ever had with him. He'd told her Stella and Theo took him in when he was young. He'd given her the impression he'd never even met his parents, but obviously they were frequent guests at The Splendor when Henri was plenty old enough to remember them. So, what did this mean?

Moonlight puddled around her as she stared helplessly into the box of memories. Did Henri lie to her?

Or did someone lie to Henri?

CHAPTER TWENTY

HENRI

T HE MASQUERADE BALL WAS WINDING TO A CLOSE AND Henri was out of options.

Juliette had somehow managed to evade both him and Caleigh, and now he didn't have time to warn her.

He couldn't even find her.

He'd wandered through every public area of the hotel, roamed the corridors, stopped by her suite, all to no avail.

The only place left to check was the Hall of Memories. On any other day, it was the first place he would have tried, but Juliette would never be so bold as to go there with a celebration in full swing downstairs. Would she?

As he climbed the steps, he decided maybe she would. He thought of the despair on her face as she'd tried to gather the memory vessels in her arms. And the same despair doubled when she thought she saw Clare's signature disowning her. If he were Juliette—if he loved someone as much as she loved Clare—he'd want to soak up every possible experience together before the memories were gone forever.

Even if it came with risk.

By the time he made it to the top of the staircase and opened the double doors, he'd all but convinced himself he'd discover Juliette exactly as he'd found her last night: sitting on the floor, surrounded by colored glass.

But the Hall of Memories was empty.

It took Henri a moment to identify the sinking sensation in his stomach for what it was: disappointment. He'd wanted to Juliette to be here, and not just to warn her.

He went to the place she should be but wasn't. And he found himself standing in front of an empty shelf. A bright spark of alarm pinged through him. Every single one of Clare's vessels was missing.

Stella.

We don't have time, she'd told him in the rose garden. *The buyer of those memories is already here, and if this girl interferes with the transfer, she'll ruin everything.*

Had Stella lost so much faith in Henri that she thought the memories needed to be moved to protect them for the buyer? Had Stella decided to handle the implantation herself?

A shimmery bit of fabric caught his eye, and Henri bent down to examine it more closely. It was pale—nearly translucent—and it curved just a little on one side, as if it were the tip ripped from something larger. Something like a wing.

Sudden understanding waterfalled over him. Juliette had been here. In a costume that was decidedly *not* a peacock.

But how had she managed both to get in without being seen and get out again with Clare's memories?

He couldn't help but have a grudging respect for her tenacity and her loyalty. Juliette still thought Clare willingly sold her memories of their life together, yet she wouldn't give up her sister without a fight. He admired her devotion, but she'd just made all his problems so much worse. If Henri had been able to find her in time to warn her to leave, he might have been able to figure out a way to convince Stella not to sell Clare's memories.

Stella was worried about scandal. If he could tell her Juliette had already left the hotel, he'd have some leverage to change her mind. What better way to appease an unhappy guest than to give her what she wanted in the first place and restore her sister's memories? But once Stella found out Juliette had stolen the vessels, there would be no staying her rage. She'd have two unsatisfied guests on her hands: both Juliette and the buyer who had paid for Clare's memories but wasn't going to get them.

He raked his hands through his hair and let out a long breath. If only Juliette had just stayed at the masquerade ball instead of taking matters into her own hands. His frustration with her was only outweighed by a sense that he might do the same thing in her situation. Like so many times before, Henri felt an uncanny connection to Juliette. He understood why she was so doggedly fighting for her sister. So willing to forgive Clare even though—at least as far as Juliette knew—she'd done something terrible. Clare was her family. She'd been there for Juliette when no one else had.

Just like Stella and Theo had always been there for him. Bonds like that didn't break easily. Even though Stella had lied to him, it didn't erase all the good she'd done. She and Theo were the only family he had. He was loyal to them just like Juliette was loyal to Clare.

A rumble in the distance snapped Henri's focus back to the present—a steady stream of footsteps moving up the main staircase. The ball was over, and the guests were turning in for the night.

Henri was out of time.

He hoped Juliette had made it out of the hotel with her

sister's vessels in hand. Because, although Henri could delay following Stella's orders while he tried to find a different solution, he could never bring himself to betray her. If Juliette was still at The Splendor, he'd have no choice.

He'd have to harvest her memories.

The hotel was eerily quiet, but the remnants of illusion still hung in the air like ghosts. Acrobatic shadows balanced along the walls, hints of light flickered like a dying candle, a melody floated past too soft to hear, but Henri knew if any of the guests happened to pass by, they'd all be humming the same tune.

It reminded Henri of the way the smell of campfire smoke lingered long after the last embers had gone dark, clinging to skin and hair and clothes, as if desperate to grasp at some remaining bit of life.

Fantasy and reality were like jealous rivals. They both wanted to be the other.

And Henri wasn't happy with either of them right now.

Henri often wondered what his life would have been like if Stella and Theo hadn't taken him in. Would he have ever discovered his magic? If he'd grown up far from here, would the idea of The Splendor be appealing to him? Would he have some unfulfilled wish to swim with sharks or fly over the world on the back of a giant bird?

Henri yanked open the door to the crypt, and it slammed behind him with a ring of finality. The air was thick with steam.

He tried to breathe deeply and let the magic calm him, but it didn't work. Dread curdled in his stomach like soured milk. He skipped his usual soak in Lobster Lake and went directly to room 718, hoping to find it as empty as the Hall of Memories had been.

He let a tendril of magic slip through the opening, but before it landed, he heard voices and his heart sank.

". . . no need to drop it off yourself," Caleigh was saying. "I would have taken care of it in the morning." Her voice was tinged with worry.

"It was no problem. Besides, I couldn't wait until morning. It was a beautiful costume, but to be honest, it was a bit cumbersome. By the end of the night, I just wanted to be dressed in normal clothes, you know?"

"Sure," Caleigh said, and Henri wished he could see her expression. She must know Juliette had bested her, but she couldn't quite figure out how. "I just wish you'd let me know you were uncomfortable. We could have made alterations."

"But how would I have found you? It's not as if I could just go wandering through the hotel, right?"

Henri bit back a laugh.

"And it wasn't so much uncomfortable," Juliette continued, her tone light. "It just kept getting in the way. Have you ever tried to dance while wearing tail feathers?"

"No," Caleigh said. "I haven't."

"Well, I don't recommend it."

A warm feeling curled through Henri. He leaned against the wall and listened to the two of them verbally spar, each trying to get information from the other without giving anything away.

Juliette clearly had the upper hand. Caleigh sounded suspicious, but she couldn't very well run to Stella and confess that something had gone wrong if she didn't know what. And he doubted she wanted to admit she'd failed in her only task of the evening.

Henri's chest tightened as he realized he was rooting for Juliette. He'd been lying to himself earlier when he thought his loyalty for Stella trumped everything else. As much as he cared about Stella, he didn't want her to succeed in subduing Juliette into blind gluttonous oblivion. He had no desire to make her forget Clare. Or forget him.

There must be some way to buy more time. Maybe he could take the memories just long enough to convince Stella he'd solved the problem and then restore them before Juliette left. But then what would he do when she regained her memories and was furious at the betrayal?

And even if it worked, it still didn't fix his moral dilemma: Juliette had never given permission for her memories to be harvested.

And the thought of doing it anyway made his skin crawl.

His only choice was to get her out of the hotel before Caleigh had a chance to report back to Stella. An idea flickered at the back of his mind. Maybe Juliette didn't need to leave feeling like all her dreams had come true. Maybe Caleigh only needed to *think* she had. But then he dismissed the idea. He wasn't sure if Juliette could pull off the deception. His best option was to get her out of the hotel under the cover of darkness.

He had hours of work ahead before he could deal with the situation, but at least now he had a plan. A weight lifted from Henri as he went about his evening tasks. His first Signature Experience of the night was a surprisingly cozy one. The guest in room 392 wanted to visit a fantasy library that existed outside the confines of time, where she could read as long as she wanted without missing anything in her real life. He gave her a light-filled room full of comfortable furniture, bookshelves stretching all the way from the floor to the top of the soaring ceiling, and a side table where her favorite snacks appeared at regular intervals.

Henri moved on to room 658, to a man who had never been socially confident and longed to be well regarded. So Henri created a dinner party filled with friends who hung on to the man's every word, laughed at every joke, listened with their chins cradled in their palms as he told stories about his life. The man's mind buzzed with animated joy, and Henri's chest expanded with satisfaction. Moments like these reminded him what he loved about The Splendor.

Room by room, Henri fulfilled fantasies, provided restful sleep, sent good dreams seeping into the minds of every guest—every guest except Juliette. He needed her to stay awake if he was going to help her sneak out of the hotel.

After Henri was finished, he slipped out of the crypt and into the main part of The Splendor. He took one look at the grandfather clock in the corridor and felt a pang of anxiety. It was nearly morning. If he didn't talk to Juliette soon, it would be too late.

And she wasn't going to like what he had to say.

CHAPTER TWENTY-ONE

JULIETTE

T HE KNOCK ON JULIETTE'S DOOR IN THE EARLY MORNING
hours didn't wake her.

She'd lain awake all night thinking about Henri.
Finding the box filled with his memories left her unsettled, but
she still didn't know what to do about it. On the one hand,
she felt like it would be a betrayal not to tell him, but on the
other hand, if she *did* tell him, she'd have to reveal where
she'd hidden Clare's memories.

And she didn't want to do that.

Even when Juliette begged him to let her have the vessels,
he wouldn't agree. He was willing to sell them to another
guest whether she liked it or not.

But if she was right—if someone lied to him about where
he came from—maybe he'd be more likely to help her. She just
didn't know if trusting him was worth the risk.

The soft sound of knuckles against wood quieted her mind
for the first time in hours, and when she opened the door to
find Henri standing there, she felt as if she'd summoned him

with her thoughts. Perhaps it was a sign.

She hadn't seen him since the night before the masquerade ball, and he looked as if he hadn't slept, bathed, or eaten since then. His clothes were rumpled, and dark moons curved under his eyes.

"I need to talk to you," he said. "It's important."

She studied him warily. Something about the tone of his voice made her stomach tighten, like she was bracing for a punch. "I need to talk to you too. I—"

He shook his head sharply. "Not here. Get dressed."

She opened her mouth to ask him what was wrong with having a conversation at the threshold of her empty room, but the way his gaze kept flicking up and down the hallway made the question die on her lips.

Instead, she left him there and stepped around the corner to the closet, quickly changing out of her sleeping clothes and into a pair of soft knit pants and a long tunic-length sweater. When she looked in the mirror, her reflection flickered annoyingly between her true self with her sleep-tousled hair, full hips, and imperfect complexion and a polished, flawless version. She suddenly missed not being able to see through illusions.

She wriggled her fingers through her hair to loosen some of the tangles, but it was hopeless. Henri would see what he would see. He'd probably never perceived her as perfect anyway. The thought was oddly freeing.

Juliette slipped on a pair of flats and went back to the main area of the suite. Henri was slumped against the closed door as if it were the only thing holding him up.

"Are you all right?" she asked.

He straightened. "I'm fine." He wasn't fine, but she had the feeling he wouldn't tell her why until he was ready.

"So where are we going?" she asked.

"There's a lepidopterarium on the grounds."

She raised her eyebrows. "A what?"

He gave her a crooked half-hearted smile. "A butterfly house. We should have privacy there."

"I don't understand. We have privacy *here*."

Henri kneaded the muscles on the back of his neck. "For now. But if anyone were looking, they'd know where to find you."

"*Will* someone be looking?"

His gaze held hers. "I don't know."

She swallowed. "All right. I'll follow you."

Henri led her down the corridor and out a side door. They spilled out onto a narrow brick pathway that unraveled before them like a long red ribbon tumbling over the rolling hills in the distance. The rising sun had turned the sky pale pink. The butterfly house was just over the first dip on the path—a large glass structure shaped like a dome. Henri pulled open the door and a rush of warm air enveloped them as they stepped inside.

The space was brimming with life—plants with glossy green leaves, blooms of fragrant lavender, intensely pink coneflowers. Wrought iron benches were placed at regular intervals along the stone walkway that threaded through the atrium. Juliette followed Henri about halfway down the path before he chose a bench and sat. She settled beside him, and they both watched a monarch butterfly land nearby and sip from a butter-colored snapdragon. The silence grew into a heavy thing.

"So why are we here?" Juliette asked finally.

"This is one of the few truly beautiful places on the grounds," Henri said. "It's not enhanced by illusion at all."

"That's not what I was asking."

"I know." He sighed and turned his body so they were face-to-face. "You were right about Clare. She didn't want to lose you."

"What do you mean?"

"She never sold your memories."

All the air left Juliette's lungs. This was a cruel joke. She'd seen Clare's signature beneath those words. They had sliced through her like broken glass.

"You showed me what she signed," Juliette said. "I saw it with my own eyes."

"So did I," Henri said. "Only, my eyes didn't lie."

"It was an illusion?" Her pulse spiked. She felt like she couldn't breathe. "But why didn't you say so? Why did you let me believe—?"

"I didn't have time. Someone was coming and I was afraid . . ." He trailed off.

"Afraid of what?"

Henri stared at the ground. His hands were splayed over his knees. Juliette could hear the rise and fall of his breath.

"Afraid of what?" she asked again.

"Someone obviously went to the trouble of making sure Clare's record was covered in illusions."

"Someone knew I might come looking?"

"Yes."

The hair on the back of Juliette's neck prickled. "Stella?"

Henri's teeth caught on his lower lip. "She asked me to harvest your memories."

Juliette inhaled sharply. She went hot all over. Her heart was beating too fast. When she finally spoke, her voice trembled. "Of Clare?"

Henri laid a palm on her forearm. "No. No, nothing like that. She wanted me to remove the memory of you finding out about Clare. Of me taking you to the Hall of Memories."

"What did you tell her?" Juliette's muscles tensed. She wished she were closer to the door.

"I won't be able to hold her off much longer."

"What is that supposed to mean?" She inched to the far side of the bench.

Henri's eyes widened, and she saw him take in her ready-to-run posture. "I'm not going to do it. I would never—"

"But you didn't tell her no?" Juliette's fingers tightened on the edge of the bench. Her knuckles turned white. They were so far from the hotel. She wasn't sure she could outrun him.

"Listen to me," Henri said. "You need to leave the hotel. Today."

A swallowtail butterfly alighted on Juliette's arm. She felt as if she were standing outside her body, watching the soft flutter of pale yellow wings against freckled skin. Time expanded and contracted like a pair of lungs, and she wasn't sure if it had been hours or moments. Her heart felt torn in two—one half joy that Clare hadn't abandoned her after all, and another part fear that she'd be forced to give up her own memories of Clare. She couldn't lose her sister again.

Finally, Juliette found her way back to her own body. She inhaled and the butterfly flew away. "I'm not leaving without Clare's memories."

"I know," Henri said. "Tell me where you hid them, and I'll bring them to you."

Suspicion whistled through her like steam from a teakettle, curling around the vulnerable parts of her heart. She should have known he'd already found out the vessels were missing. Is that why he brought her here? To recover The Splendor's stolen merchandise?

"No," Juliette said. "I'm not leaving without them."

Henri raked his hand through his hair. "Are you listening to me? You can't stay here."

She didn't respond. Henri stood up and began to pace.

"If you won't leave now, I see only one other option.

You need to talk to Caleigh and tell her you want to have your memories of Clare harvested."

Juliette's hand flew to her mouth. "No! I'd never do that!"

"I know you wouldn't," Henri said. "I'm not asking you to *actually* do it. I'm asking you to make her believe it's what you want."

She stood up and backed away.

Henri was instantly on his feet, coming toward her. "Please wait. Let me explain." Juliette flicked a quick look at the door. She didn't want to hear his explanation. He took Clare's memories without her permission, and now he was threatening Juliette's memories too.

"I'm going back to my suite," she said, turning away from him. "Leave me alone."

His hand darted out, circled her wrist, and spun her around. "I wouldn't ask you to do this if I didn't think it was absolutely necessary."

She fixed him with an icy stare until he let his hand fall away. "What possible reason could you have for asking me to make Caleigh believe something so horrible?"

"Because I'm worried she suspects you switched costumes last night, and I think she's planning on reporting it to Stella. And unless Stella thinks you're going to let this go, she'll take matters into her own hands."

The words blazed through Juliette like a ribbon of flame. "So, she just takes whatever she wants whenever she wants, is that it?"

Henri scrubbed a hand over his jaw. "No, it's not like that. Stella made a mistake when she ordered me to remove Clare's memories—she mixed her up with another guest—and now that you know, she's worried you'll cause a scandal."

"She didn't make a mistake," Juliette said softly.

Henri cocked his head to one side as if he wasn't sure he'd heard her properly. "What?"

"A moment ago, you said Stella made a mistake. She didn't."

"Yes, she did. I spoke to her about it. I know she should have handled it differently. I told her we could just ask Clare to come back and I'd restore the memories, but she's concerned about the reputation of The Splendor. She's not thinking clearly."

Juliette was certain Henri was wrong—she thought Stella's thinking was crystal clear—but she could see his loyalty forced him to give her the benefit of the doubt. Still, she didn't think she could go along with his plan.

"I don't know if I can say I want to forget Clare," Juliette said. Even thinking of it made her feel as if she were coated in something sticky. "Caleigh will never believe me."

"She'll believe it if you make her believe it. She has no reason not to. I wish I had a better plan, but we're out of time. We have to pretend to bring her into the inner circle in order to keep her out."

Juliette swallowed. Henri needed to buy time, but so did she. She needed a plan for getting Clare's memories safely out of the hotel, and she wouldn't leave until she had one. If that meant lying to Caleigh, then so be it.

Even if it would make her feel like a traitor.

"Fine," she said. "I'll do it."

Relief washed over Henri's face. "Good." He looked at the ever-lightening sky and frowned. "We don't have much time. Let's get this over with."

Juliette wasn't confident that the small bell would actually work to summon Caleigh, and so she was both surprised and relieved when the concierge showed up at her door not long after she'd shaken it. Caleigh had clearly come straight from bed—her clothes were rumpled and her hair was disheveled.

"Oh no. I woke you." Juliette tried to infuse her voice with a regret she didn't feel. "I'm so sorry."

"It's no trouble at all." Caleigh attempted to untangle her hair with her fingers. "What can I do for you?"

"I've been awake all night," Juliette said. "I just—I needed to talk to someone."

Caleigh gave her a sympathetic frown. "Of course. Why don't you have a seat and I'll get us a cup of tea?"

Juliette sat at the table, her heart beating out a staccato rhythm as she waited for Caleigh to return. She didn't know if she could do this. How could she look Caleigh in the eye and say the very thing that had hurt her so deeply when she thought Clare said it about her? *I no longer wish to have a sister.* Even if it was a lie, it would feel like a betrayal.

A few minutes passed, and Caleigh returned with two steaming mugs of tea and set them on the table. She'd changed her clothes and her hair was now brushed and braided. She sat across from Juliette.

"I'm sorry you had such trouble sleeping. What's going on?"

Juliette's stomach felt like a writhing den of snakes. She took a deep breath and tried to remember Henri's advice. "Can I tell you a secret?" she asked, tracing the rim of her mug with her index finger.

Caleigh leaned forward. "Of course."

Juliette let the silence stretch between them Henri told her she needed to seem hesitant about opening up, since she'd never shared anything this personal with Caleigh before.

"My sister was a guest at The Splendor."

"When?"

"A few weeks ago." Another long pause. "She wished to never have a sister." Juliette didn't have to fabricate her strained voice or her bleak expression. The words still hurt to say.

Caleigh squeezed Juliette's hand. "I'm so sorry. How did you find out?"

"Henri told me. He *showed* me actually."

"Wow." Caleigh's eyes went wide, and Juliette could tell she was struggling to control her reaction. "I'm surprised Henri did that. I don't think he was supposed to—" She broke off and changed course. "I'm sure that was difficult to see."

"You can't imagine. But it gave me clarity. At least now I know what I want."

"That's good," she said lightly. "So, what is it?"

"Clare wanted me removed from her memory. And I don't think I'll be able to get over it. Not until she's removed from mine." Juliette's gaze met Caleigh's. The words tasted bitter coming out of her mouth, but she tried to make her expression resolute. "I'm going to ask Henri for an extraction."

A fleeting look of triumph crossed Caleigh's face, gone so quickly that Juliette might have missed it if she hadn't been watching carefully. Caleigh composed herself quickly, slipping into a concerned expression like it was a comfortable robe. "That's a big step. Are you sure?"

"I'm sure. I'm going to do my best to enjoy the rest of my time here, and then before I leave, I'll make sure Clare can never hurt me again."

Caleigh flinched, and Juliette wondered if was because she knew Stella wouldn't like the delay. "If you know what you want, why not get it over with and do it now?"

"I just want to hang on to her a little longer." Juliette

threaded her fingers together. Her gaze lifted to Caleigh's. "You probably think that sounds ridiculous."

"Of course not. I think it sounds wise. Whatever makes you happy makes me happy. Let's make the most of the next few days."

"Thank you," Juliette said. "Truly."

"So, what would you like to do today?"

"Can I be honest?"

Caleigh laughed. "Of course."

"I'm exhausted, and I'd love nothing more than to go back to sleep until at least midday."

"Can *I* be honest?" Caleigh's voice was conspiratorial. "Me too." She stretched as she stood. "Get some rest. I'll see you this afternoon."

Henri returned only moments after Caleigh left, slipping through the door without even knocking first. He must have been waiting close by. He paced as Juliette related the conversation.

"You did well," he said. "And it was a genius idea to tell her you wanted to sleep more. That should give us plenty of time. Gather your things and let's get you out of here."

Juliette's forehead creased. "I told you. I'm not leaving without Clare's memories."

"They're not here?" His gaze flicked around the room as if he might spot the vessels shoved under the bed or resting on top of the bureau. "But where else would they be?"

Juliette's thoughts slowly circled around the box in the attic labeled with Henri's name. She ignored his question and asked one of her own.

"Do you actually trust that Stella will let this go?"

"Yes," he said. "I do."

"You shouldn't."

"Look, I know Stella can be . . ." Henri trailed off and

then blew out a frustrated breath. He tugged on the back of his neck. "We need to go."

She dragged a toe through the plush carpet. "It won't matter. I won't be safe even if I leave."

"Of course, you will. Once Stella sees that you don't mean any harm—"

Juliette lightly touched his wrist. "I think there's something I need to show you."

Juliette had forgotten how beautiful the Hall of Memories was in daylight.

Broad squares of sunlight fell across the shelved vessels splashing colored light on every surface. She felt Henri relax beside her, and an ache built in her chest. What if she was making a huge mistake? Henri loved this place and she was about to either poison it for him or find out he'd been lying to her.

She didn't like either outcome.

"What are we doing here?" Henri asked. They'd been quiet the entire walk, both lost in thought.

Juliette had planned to climb up the ladder and thrust the box of memories at him. *Explain this*, she imagined herself saying. But now that they were here, her courage faltered.

"When we first met, you gave me the impression you were an orphan."

Henri's brows pulled together. "I *am* an orphan."

"What happened to your parents?"

A spasm of pain flashed over his expression that made Juliette doubt herself. "I don't remember them well." His voice was soft and raw. "Only that they didn't want me."

Her throat tightened and she had to force the next words out. "I think Stella lied to you. I think your parents were guests at The Splendor."

He gave a rough, humorless laugh. "They got rid of their kid and then just happened to come here for a little pampering?" His tone suggested he thought she was trying to hurt him.

Juliette bit the inside of her cheek. She wasn't explaining it right. "No, Henri. I think *you* were a guest here before Stella and Theo took you in."

She'd thought about the memory a hundred times since she'd first seen it and it was the only explanation that made any sense. Theo and Stella had kidnapped him for his magic and then taken his memories of his parents to cover their tracks. It was so evil it made her ill. But he should know the truth.

"If I'd suspected you wanted to play detective, I could have arranged that for your Signature Experience, but don't pretend you know anything about me."

Juliette tipped her head toward the rafters and closed her eyes. She'd wanted to soften the blow, but perhaps she was only prolonging the pain. She wouldn't be able to explain something she wasn't even sure she understood. Henri had to see for himself.

"Come on. I'll show you." She went to the back wall, rolled the library ladder into the correct position, and started to climb. At first, she thought Henri might not follow, but then she felt the weight of the ladder shift, and his breath warm against her neck.

Juliette pulled herself onto the ledge and ducked into the small room.

"So, this is where you hid Clare's memories." Henri stood, brushing the dust from his pants. His gaze swept over the room as if he'd never seen it before. Maybe he hadn't.

"You can't tell Stella," Juliette said. "Promise me, or I won't tell you what I found."

Henri was silent for a moment, as if weighing the trade. "I promise."

She pulled the box from the shelf and placed it on the floor between them. "This is labeled with your name."

Wordlessly, he sat.

He lifted an oddly shaped container. It was made from purple glass that bulged outward at even intervals, so it resembled a stack of donuts. Henri dragged his thumb down the length of the container, letting it bump over the warped glass before setting it on the floor beside the box. He picked up one vessel after another, turning them over in his hands.

Juliette watched the emotions play out on his face. Disbelief. Confusion. Betrayal.

"I don't understand," he said softly. "Where did these come from?"

Juliette opened her mouth to answer, and then realized he wasn't talking to her. She remembered seeing the shelves of Clare's memories for the first time—how curiosity and dread battled in her chest—and her heart went out to him.

She touched his knee. "Would it be easier if I just told you what I saw?"

"No." Henri took the stopper from a sage-green vase and tipped the cloudy substance into his palm. "I'm sure there's an explanation."

Juliette didn't say what she was thinking: Some things weren't made better by an explanation.

Some things were made much, much worse.

CHAPTER TWENTY-TWO

THE GIRL'S NAME WAS CLEMENTINE AND SHE HAD THE coloring of a summer day: eyes the shade of a cloudless sky, hair like gossamer sunshine. But she had the attitude of a thunderstorm, and the first time Henri saw her she was rolling through the lobby like a tiny but powerful rain cloud.

"You promised this would be fancy." Her small shoes echoed loudly on the marble, and she flicked a braid behind her shoulder, looking for all the world like a small but very demanding heiress. "And it's not fancy at all."

"*Clem-en-tine,*" her mother said between clenched teeth, as if emphasizing each syllable would make it more forceful, "hush."

Henri—who was hidden behind a tall plant near the front desk—chuckled softly.

Clementine swung around so quickly one of her braids slapped her in the face. Her eyes narrowed, until they landed on him. His pulse sped, waiting for her to loudly announce his presence and humiliate him in front of an entire lobby full of guests. But she didn't. She lifted her hand and waved.

He was so taken aback he just gaped at her through the glossy green leaves, dumbfounded. She flashed him a conspiratorial grin as if the two of them had come to some silent agreement he didn't understand.

The concierge arrived to help Clementine's parents with their bags, and Henri watched as the family walked away. But just before she disappeared around the corner, Clementine cast another quick look over her shoulder and caught him staring at her. His ears went hot and he glanced away.

He tried to shake off the embarrassment. He told himself it didn't matter. It was a big hotel, and he'd probably never see her again.

But just to be safe he decided to spend the afternoon outside.

At the very edge of The Splendor's sprawling grounds was a small meadow filled with tall trees and birdsong. A few days ago, Henri discovered a thick fallen log spanning a gushing stream. It was too tempting a challenge to pass up, and he'd been waiting for an opportunity to slip away from the hotel to see if he could cross without falling.

He started over the log, arms extended like a bird in flight, carefully placing one foot in front of the other. A surge of pride expanded in his belly. He was doing it. A breeze trembled through the trees, ruffling his shirt and lifting his hair, but Henri stayed steady. He was nearly to the center of the stream, water rushing beneath him, when he heard something moving through the meadow.

And then a voice. "Oh, good! I found you!"

Before he thought better of it, he glanced over his shoulder. Clementine stood at the edge of the stream, hands on her hips, her shoes nearly kissing the water. The movement threw him off balance and he slipped from the log, his arms pinwheeling through the air until he landed with a splash in the water.

He scrambled to his feet, slipping over stones and stumbling through bramble. His pants caught on a branch and tore at the knee. His elbow was bleeding.

He crawled out of the stream, hair and clothes dripping, and glared at Clementine. "You made me fall."

She looked affronted. "I did not."

"Yes," he said, "you did."

"Oh, really? I climbed up there and shoved you in the stream?"

His gaze slid away. "You shoved me with your voice."

Her eyes went buggy. "With my *voice*?"

He suddenly became obsessed with inspecting the rip in his pants. How old was this girl anyway? She couldn't be more than six—at least two years younger than he was—but she talked to him like she was his nanny. It made his stomach feel like a pot of boiling water.

"I'm sorry you got hurt," she said, sitting on a rock near the water. It seemed to be a concession of sorts. She wasn't admitting fault, but she wanted to prove she wasn't heartless either. He tried to decide if it was enough as he poked at his skinned knee.

"It's not so bad," he said. A concession of his own. He wanted her to know he still thought she was responsible for making him fall, but also that he was willing to let it go without holding a grudge. "So, what are you doing here?"

"Looking for you." She swung her feet restlessly, her shoes smacking against each other before bouncing apart again.

"But why?"

"This place is creepy," she said matter-of-factly, darting a glance back toward the hotel, "but it wouldn't be so bad if I had a friend." ✦

Henri emerged from the memory disoriented. His ears were ringing as if something had exploded nearby. Maybe it had.

Gentle pressure against his palm drew his gaze downward. Juliette's fingers were entwined with his, the memory twisting around their hands like a rope of mist binding them together. His first instinct was to pull away, to voice his objections to her being so close and witnessing something so personal. But the truth was he didn't mind the security of her hand in his. And the memory didn't feel personal. It didn't feel like his at all.

"Are you all right?"

He didn't know how to answer. Was he? His thoughts felt like a hopelessly tangled ball of yarn. He wasn't sure what he'd seen or what it meant. Had Stella used Henri's face in a Signature Experience for one of the guests? He'd resorted to similar measures in a pinch. Like earlier this week in room 124. Henri had used the likeness of Gemma Caron's childhood friend to be her partner in a trapeze routine.

But doubt wriggled in his gut. This felt different. If it was a Signature Experience, it wouldn't be here, hidden away in some far-flung dusty corner. It would be nestled in the mind of a former guest.

"Henri?" Juliette was still waiting for an answer. Her tone was careful, like he was a scared animal she didn't want to startle.

"I'm fine," he snapped.

Juliette let go of his hand. She tried to slide the memory back into the vessel, but it kept twisting toward Henri. Finally, she wrangled it back inside and replaced the stopper. "You were young."

He heard the question in her statement. She wanted to

know how old he was when Theo and Stella took him in.

But he couldn't remember.

He worried at the leather sole of his shoe with his thumbnail. "It might not have been me."

"Who else would it have been?" When he didn't answer, she frowned. "It *looked* just like you."

The truth was it *felt* just like him too. The memory had a particular timbre and rhythm he recognized from his own thoughts. His lungs clamped down so tight he couldn't pull in a full breath.

"Henri? Who else would it have been?"

"I don't know."

"What do you want to do?"

Two impulses wrested inside him. He wanted to devour every single memory in this box, but he also wanted to throw the box against the wall and watch the glass shatter and the memories dissipate into oblivion. He wanted to know everything. He wanted to know nothing at all.

Finally, it was Juliette who decided. She picked up a container made from frosted glass and removed the stopper. "It's better to know even if it hurts."

It was as if she had reached into his mind to feel the shape of his thoughts. He felt exposed and understood all at once and it shook something loose inside him. "I'm afraid to look."

Her hand closed over his knee. "You don't have to do it alone."

Didn't he? Even though Juliette was sitting beside him, he'd never felt so alone. But he couldn't avoid this forever. He took the vessel from her and tipped out the contents. The substance seemed to have a mind of its own as it tried to wriggle from his fingers, as if it wanted to return to where it came from. But Henri held fast so Juliette could see it too; and they were both pulled into another memory.

O—❈ THE SPLENDOR WAS COVERED IN SNOW.

Henri and Clementine hurried down the majestic front steps of the hotel, their mitten-clad hands wrapped around steaming mugs of apple cider, and metal baking sheets stolen from the kitchen tucked under their arms.

A line of horse-drawn sleighs waited to take guests on a scenic tour of the grounds, over the rolling hills of sparkling white and forests of sugar-dusted pines. In the distance, a crowd gathered around a bonfire.

The pool in the center of the courtyard was frozen—transformed into an enormous ice rink—and guests glided gracefully over the surface, leaping and pirouetting, as if each one of them had trained for years.

But Henri and Clementine weren't interested in feeling like highly trained athletes or touring grounds they already knew well. They wanted a little adventure.

They tried to remain nonchalant as they passed by hot cocoa stands, ice sculpture demonstrations, and cheery sing-alongs with bundled-up guests living out the fantasy of having perfect pitch. But once they got to the far edge of the grounds where the cobbled lane dipped toward Belle Fontaine, they tossed aside their mugs of cider and broke into a run.

"Are you ready?" Clementine asked, pulling the tray from beneath her arm and positioning it in front of her.

"The question is, are *you* ready?" In one smooth motion Henri threw the tray to the ground and leaped on top of it, his knees slamming into the metal and propelling him forward.

"Hey!" Clementine cried out in protest as she vaulted onto her own tray, and a moment later, he could sense her right behind him.

Henri grinned as the icy wind stole his breath and nibbled at the tips of his ears. The baking sheets worked even better than he hoped, and they flew down the hill with exhilarating speed.

Near the bottom of the lane, Henri's tray tipped over and dumped him into the snow.

"The universe has spoken," Clementine shouted as she sailed past him. "When you cheat, you lose."

Henri lay there for a few moments gazing up at the bright blue sky as the cold seeped through his coat. His heart was full to bursting, and he thought it must be impossible to feel happier than he did in this moment. This had all the makings of a perfect day. Adventure. Laughter. Clementine.

A pair of blonde braids dangled over his face. "Should we go again?"

"Absolutely." He scrambled to his feet and they hiked back up the path, warm breath curling from their lips.

They sledded down the hill over and over, until their legs ached from climbing and their cheeks were ruddy with cold. After sunset, they decided to warm up in front of one of the many campfires the staff had arranged on the grounds. They sat together on a log, mesmerized by the blaze.

"How is your stay going this time?" Henri asked. The two of them had been having so much fun over the last few days, they hadn't talked about anything serious, but he knew Clementine had something she wanted to say. He felt it between them, like a pressure in the air.

"I'd hate it here," she said quietly, "if it weren't for you."

He nudged her shoulder with his own. "Well, then thank goodness for me."

She turned toward him, the reflection of the flames dancing in her eyes. "I'm worried about Papa."

"Why?" Henri asked, surprised. They never really talked

about their parents. When he was with Clementine, it was as if they existed in a separate universe that only included the two of them. "What happened?"

"He changes when we come here. And not for the better."

"Changes how?"

Clementine shrugged. "It's hard to explain. But this place does something to him. He's always a little less himself when we leave." She absently fidgeted with the blanket on her lap. "Does that happen with your parents? Are they different here?"

Something heavy settled in his chest. He didn't want to answer questions about his parents, so he asked a question of his own instead.

"What do you mean he's less himself?"

"He promised to take me to the botanical gardens for my birthday this year; we planned it months ago. But when I mentioned it this morning, he acted like we'd never discussed it before."

"Maybe he forgot?"

She shook her head. "Not possible. We'd talked about it more than once and he was just as excited as I was. He loves the botanical gardens."

"Could he have changed his mind?"

"Maybe. It seems like every time we come here, something that used to be important to him isn't important anymore."

Henri couldn't make sense of the worry in her voice. "And you're worried this time it's the botanical gardens?"

Clementine gave him a reproachful look. "I'm worried this time it's *me*."

Firelight flickered over her face. Henri squeezed her fingers. They felt like ice. "That would never happen," he told her.

"How do you know?"

"Because—" His ears went hot. He shifted in his seat. "Because no one would ever think you're not important."

"Not unless someone made them think that."

"What do you mean? How would anyone *make* him think something?"

She blew out a frustrated breath. "I don't know. But something strange is going on at the hotel and I need you to help me figure out what it is."

His throat went tight. He struggled to swallow. "How am I supposed to do that?"

"I'm not sure yet. But promise me, Henri." This time her hand closed around his. He could feel his pulse in the tips of his fingers. "Promise you'll help?"

Her gaze was locked on his, earnest and pleading. What else could he do?

"Don't worry," he told her, "I promise."

Henri's limbs were numb as the memory slid from his fingers. He tried to drop it back into the vessel, but it flew straight to his temples instead like a messenger pigeon returning home. He let it sink into his mind and settle.

Juliette was right. Stella and Theo's story of finding him in the children's home was full of holes. They'd clearly known him before. His old self had nearly revealed the truth to him. He could feel it there at the edges of the memory: the vague panic when Clementine mentioned parents, the pressure of some secret he was trying to keep. But it had darted in and out too quickly to identify more than a hazy shape. He recognized the shame though. It was as familiar as it was irrational—as if not having parents was some kind of personal failing.

He heard the gentle rise and fall of Juliette's breath beside him, but she didn't speak. He turned his head and his eyes found hers. He blinked and her face blurred. A feeling melted through him; he tried to name it and failed. The irony nearly made him laugh. Because Henri collected feelings. It was one of the impulses that drove him to the Hall of Memories to satiate himself on the experiences of others. He hoarded the emotions like a dragon protecting treasure, pulling them out in quiet moments to examine and admire them.

Homesickness: a hollow feeling beneath the ribs that aches like only emptiness can. Jealousy: a hungry lion that can never be satisfied. Elation: a happiness so full it becomes weightless.

He used to wonder what was wrong with him that he felt most alive experiencing other people's emotions instead of his own.

But eventually he realized the truth: Some feelings require memories. And Henri didn't have many. He always thought his own memories were slippery things, impossible to hold.

But not all missing things are lost.

Sometimes they're stolen.

#

CHAPTER TWENTY-THREE

MAYBE THIS HAD BEEN A TERRIBLE MISTAKE.

Juliette waited for Henri to speak, but he didn't. His eyes were glazed over and instead of looking at her, he looked through her as if she were a clear pane of glass. She'd never seen an expression quite like the one he wore.

It made her feel cruel.

She thought of the first time he brought her to the Hall of Memories. *Has anything ever happened to you that you'd rather forget?* She'd only been thinking of herself at the time, and she hadn't considered the implications: that maybe Henri was speaking from experience. Not just as someone who harvested memories but as someone who'd had them harvested as well. What if she'd just forced him to remember something he *asked* to forget?

A wave of nausea rolled through her. She touched his elbow. "I'm so sorry. I should have never—"

"Yes," he said, "you should have."

Juliette blinked, unsure what to say.

They sat in silence for a moment, and then Henri sighed. "I spent my whole life wanting a friend like Clementine."

His wistful expression made her want to reach forward and push the hair off his forehead. She twisted her hands together in her lap.

"Do you want to tell me about her?"

"You know exactly as much as I do." Henri's gaze swept over the remaining vessels. "Maybe more."

"You don't remember her *at all?*"

"No." His expression was troubled, and Juliette couldn't imagine how disconcerting it would be to have an entire person disappear from your memory. "But I have a feeling I didn't keep my promise to her."

Henri began gathering the vessels and putting them back in the box.

"What are you doing? We have to find out what happened to her. What happened to *you*."

"We will. But we don't have time right now. The morning is nearly gone, and Caleigh will be awake soon. If you're not in your room when she gets there, she'll go straight to Stella."

Fear prickled at the base of Juliette's spine. Stella asked Henri to execute a harvest on her. The thought of her memories trapped behind colored glass made her shiver. "I don't want to go back to my room. I want to take Clare's memories and leave."

Henri's expression turned stony. "I can't let you do that."

"What do you mean you can't let me?"

He gave an exasperated sigh. "I *begged* you to leave last night and you refused." He threaded his fingers together behind his neck and touched his elbows together. "Juliette, if you go now, Stella will know I convinced you to lie to Caleigh."

Realization washed over her. "And you'll never find out

what happened in your past."

"Please," he said. "Just go back and keep pretending you're still on board with everything you told Caleigh this morning, and I promise I'll not only get you out of here but I'll also restore Clare's memories. It will be as if none of this ever happened. You'll have your sister back."

Her pulse skipped. "You can do that?"

"Yes."

"But then what? Even if I can convince Caleigh it's still what I want, eventually Stella will expect you to actually remove the memories."

"People usually stop fighting once they think they've won. This will buy us some time until we figure out a better plan."

"What if we don't figure out a better plan?"

"We will," Henri said. "I promise."

As soon as the words were out of his mouth, a curtain of dread fell over his expression. They'd both just watched him say the very same words to Clementine.

And his memories of her ended up in a box in the attic.

Juliette couldn't stop thinking of home.

The little flat she shared with Clare on Garden Street hadn't felt very welcoming when they first moved in a year ago. It was shabby and cramped and smelled like day-old fish. But Clare was determined to make it cozy, and she'd attacked the place with all the care of a mother bird preparing a nest—scrubbing the floors, sewing pretty curtains from old dresses, boiling cinnamon sticks over the fire so the whole flat smelled like a bakery.

Clare had more magic than anyone at The Splendor:

She'd transformed four run-down walls into a home. Juliette ached with how much she missed it. With how much she missed Clare.

Her sister didn't abandon her after all. The wonder of it was still fresh, and it made her heart feel raw—like a burn just beginning to heal.

She didn't want to keep pretending.

But the only alternative was to betray Henri. And she had no desire to do that either. A knock startled her from her thoughts. She went to the door to find Caleigh, who looked sleep-drunk and sheepish.

"I'm so embarrassed. I intended to be back hours ago." She was completely pulled together now—perfectly dressed, not a hair out of place—but she smoothed her palms along her scalp as she came into the room. It was a self-conscious gesture that made her seem younger than her years.

"I just woke up myself," Juliette lied. She hadn't slept a wink and she was sure it showed. But if Caleigh noticed, she didn't let on.

"How are you doing after last night?" Caleigh settled in a chair and tucked her legs beneath her.

A flutter of panic went through Juliette. She didn't know if she could do this. It was one thing to lie once when she thought she'd be leaving immediately afterward and never have to see Caleigh again. But this—continuing to pretend she'd decided to cut Clare out of her mind forever—it was even more painful than she'd imagined.

Juliette sunk onto the settee and drew swirling patterns in the velvet with her fingers. "I'm doing fine."

"Are you? Because like I told you before, giving up your memories of your sister is a huge step. No one would blame you if you'd had a change of heart."

Maybe this was her chance to find a way out of this

predicament. If she said she'd changed her mind, then no one would suspect Henri asked her to lie in the first place. But what would Stella do then? If she was convinced Juliette's disapproval would cause a scandal for the hotel, who knew what she'd do to protect it? If Juliette could just talk to Stella. Convince her she wanted nothing more than to leave with Clare's memories. Gooseflesh broke out over her arms. If Henri thought that would work, he would have suggested it himself.

"You've reconsidered," Caleigh said. "I knew it. Last night felt a little off. We both must have been too tired to think rationally."

Juliette thought of Henri's promise to restore Clare's memories. Even if she found a way to leave The Splendor, her relationship with Clare was still damaged. And nothing would fix that if her sister didn't remember her.

"I haven't changed my mind," she said softly.

Caleigh studied her skeptically. "You're certain?"

"Yes." Juliette forced resolve into her voice. "I wish there were another way, but I don't see it."

Just like this morning, a triumphant look flitted across Caleigh's expression, gone as quickly as it appeared. It sent a chill through Juliette. Caleigh stood and busied herself by smoothing invisible wrinkles on the front of her pants. When she looked up again, she was sober and composed. "All right then. I'll let Henri know."

"Could you tell him I'd like to see him?" Juliette tried to keep her voice casual. "I have a few questions about the process." It was the only way she could think to summon Henri without arousing suspicion.

Caleigh gave her a gentle smile. If Juliette didn't know better, she'd think it was sincere. "Yes, of course. I'll send him right away."

The door closed with a soft click and Juliette dropped her head into her hands. She thought of one of the bullies in the children's home—a boy named Warren—who used to find kids smaller than he was and pick on them until they made some small humiliating concession. He once held a girl's arms behind her back until she agreed Warren was smarter than her; another time he sat on a new arrival until the boy loudly announced he drank toilet water.

She'd always wondered why it took the other children so long to give in to Warren when everyone knew the results of his demands were always lies. She told herself if he ever came for her, she wouldn't even bother resisting. Everyone knew he was horrible, so why suffer for nothing? But now she understood. Being forced to say something untrue was a wound as real as any other. A lie— even when coerced—stole a bit of dignity.

She remembered Henri telling her that memory vessels all started out clear, but they changed color based on the kind of memory stored inside. If Henri were to remove the memory of her conversation with Caleigh, it would turn the glass the color of a bruise.

Juliette stood and paced across the suite. Questions bubbled inside her faster than she could find answers. What was taking Henri so long? What if she'd been wrong to trust him? What if at this very moment he was gathering Clare's vessels and moving them somewhere Juliette would never find them again?

She felt like a bird in a cage. Time seemed to grind to a halt. Finally, she couldn't stand it anymore; she had to get out of this room and get back to the Hall of Memories before she lost Clare forever.

She flung open the door just as Henri was lifting his fist to knock.

"Where have you *been?*" she asked.

He shot her a sharp silencing look and shifted his body slightly to one side. Caleigh stood right behind him.

"I understand you're anxious," Henri said clinically, as if the two of them were only casually acquainted. As if they hadn't spent the entire morning together exploring his forgotten childhood. "But I assure you there's nothing to worry about."

She gaped at him.

"Can we come in?"

Juliette didn't answer. She just opened the door wider so Henri and Caleigh could pass. Her gaze darted between them. She needed to talk to Henri alone if they were going to make a plan. So, why wasn't he asking Caleigh to leave?

"Should we sit?" Henri asked, indicating the chairs by the fire.

She eyed him warily. "I suppose?"

"Caleigh said you have some questions about the harvesting procedure."

Juliette shot a look at Caleigh, who made a little motion with her hand as if to say, *Go ahead, don't be shy.*

Juliette wanted to throttle them both.

"Yes," she said, her voice terse, "I'd like to know what the plan is."

But if Henri caught her meaning, he didn't show it. He leaned forward, his elbows resting on his knees.

"It's really very simple. I'll isolate the memories of your sister and remove them while preserving the integrity of the surrounding experiences. So, if you have fond memories of holidays, for example, you'll retain those experiences, but you'll no longer recall your sister attending. I'll leave just enough of a remnant behind that you won't feel disoriented if you should run into her again, but your attachment to her will be gone. Don't worry. It's completely painless. You won't feel a thing."

Horror pushed up Juliette's throat. Henri was describing what he'd done to Clare in the most bland, unfeeling tone imaginable. He'd plucked Juliette from her sister's mind and tossed her aside like she was a bit of eggshell in a bowl of cake batter.

Henri's voice was too matter of fact. His mannerisms too formal.

This felt like a trap.

"What if I change my mind?" she said, unable to keep the tremble out of her voice.

His gaze held hers. "You won't. Once it's done, there won't be anything connecting you to your sister. You wouldn't have enough information to change your mind."

Her vision blurred. Her fingers trembled as she lifted them to her cheek.

Henri's head snapped up to where Caleigh stood intently watching the exchange. "Could you get Juliette a handkerchief, please?"

"Yes, of course."

Caleigh disappeared around the corner, and Henri leaned forward. His voice was low and urgent. "When we're done here, go to the repose area and wait for me. I'll find you there."

Juliette didn't have time to acknowledge him before he sat back abruptly. Caleigh was at her side, pressing a folded square of fabric into her palm.

"Thank you." She dabbed at the corners of her eyes. She felt the weight of Henri's gaze, but she couldn't bear to look at him.

Regret sat on her tongue like a bitter pill. Asking Caleigh to bring Henri here was a mistake. She'd thought it was a clever way to get time alone with him so they could plan her escape. But she hadn't considered that Caleigh would stay, hadn't even thought about how Henri would have no choice but to give her details she'd rather not hear. She understood he was only doing what he had to, but his words knifed through her and left her bleeding.

"Any other questions?" Henri asked gently.

A stab of irritation went through her. He must know she had a thousand of them and couldn't ask a single one. She lifted her head and his eyes searched hers.

"No," she said. "I think I've heard enough." She could have sworn he flinched, but he recovered quickly.

"I better be on my way then." He stood. Juliette stared at the wall above his head.

Caleigh walked Henri to the door. He didn't look back as he left, and Juliette didn't say goodbye. Once he was gone, Caleigh joined Juliette by the fire. She laid a hand on her shoulder. "For what it's worth, I think you're doing the right thing."

Caleigh's opinion was worth nothing and she had no idea what Juliette was doing. But Henri's acting lesson wasn't lost on Juliette. She reached up and squeezed Caleigh's fingers.

"Thank you," she said, "I'm counting on it."

CHAPTER TWENTY-FOUR

H ENRI FOUND STELLA ON A PRIVATE BALCONY ON THE top floor of the east wing. Unlike the penthouse, with its stunning vistas of Belle Fontaine, this room overlooked a crystal blue lake surrounded on three sides by pine trees. The view was genuine—breathtaking without the help of any magic at all—and it was one of Stella's favorite places to come when she needed an escape.

She sat in a fancy armless chair with her back to Henri. A cup of tea and a plate of sweets rested on the low table beside her. Henri could tell by the way her posture changed that she'd heard him approach, but she didn't turn in his direction.

"I hope you came to tell me you executed the harvest I requested."

"Even better."

Finally, she looked in his direction. Arched a delicate eyebrow. "Do tell."

Henri lowered himself into the chair beside her. Despite its high back and overly fussy appearance, it was unexpectedly comfortable. Though it shouldn't have surprised him considering Stella's expensive taste.

"Juliette Berton has agreed to have all the memories of her sister removed."

"And how did you get her to do that?"

"Mostly my good looks and charm." Henri picked up one of the sugar-dusted cookies and took a bite. The shortbread melted in his mouth—rich with notes of sweet vanilla.

"Good. How did it go? Any problems?"

Henri chewed slowly before he swallowed. "I haven't done it yet. She wanted to wait until just before she leaves."

Stella's eyes narrowed. "Unacceptable."

Henri dusted the sugar from his fingertips. "Why? I don't see the harm in letting her hang on to the memories until the end of her stay."

"It means she's reluctant. And reluctant guests change their minds."

"She won't change her mind."

Stella's spine stiffened. "I hardly think you're qualified to know what Juliette Berton will or won't do."

Henri shifted in his seat, uneasy. He knew he had to tread carefully. To find a way to answer without either lying to Stella or arousing her suspicions. But he couldn't think of a single thing to say that wouldn't do either. He didn't want to answer her questions. He wanted her to answer his.

He wanted answers about Clementine. Answers about what was happening with Theo. Answers about why there was a box full of Henri's own memories in the attic.

Anger trembled inside him, and he worried it would break free. He tried to hold it down, and it trembled harder.

"Henri?" Stella's voice was soft and concerned. "What's on your mind?"

"Actually, I was wondering about my parents."

She frowned. "What about them?"

"You've never told me much of anything."

She lifted a single shoulder. "There was never much to tell." Her tone was light, but he didn't miss the hard line of her mouth, or the way she stared straight ahead, as if fixated on something in the distance.

"You must have met them at some point."

"Don't be ridiculous. If we knew who they were, you would never have been in the children's home in the first place. And you certainly wouldn't be here now."

"So, I never visited the hotel before you took me in?"

A muscle jumped in her jaw. "Of course not. Henri, where is all this coming from?"

"I don't know," he said. "I guess all the talk of Juliette and her sister got me thinking about my own family."

"Well, stop," Stella said. "There's no need to reopen old wounds. And speaking of the girl, we can't take any chances. You need to remove those memories right away."

"I've gotten to know her over the past few days and I really don't think—"

"I don't care what you think you know. This is my hotel and I make the final decision. Have I made myself clear?"

"Yes," Henri told her, "you have."

Stella's stoic expression faltered—for just a moment—and Henri wondered if she could feel it too: how the anger inside him quaked so hard it opened a fault line.

And now they stood on opposite sides of an abyss.

A buzz grew in Henri's head as he hurried through the hotel. He hadn't realized the fullness of his hope until Stella's lies had punctured it, leaving him deflated and small.

She was keeping something from him and—against all reason—he thought she might admit it if confronted directly. He wanted her to offer some explanation for the box of abandoned memories. He'd seen into his past. He knew he was at The Splendor the first time he met Clementine. Which meant Stella knew exactly who his parents were. Why would she lie?

Henri noticed a few guests staring and he gave himself a mental shake. He needed to stop walking so fast. He was drawing attention.

He slowed. Unclenched his fists.

The last thing he needed was some staff member reporting to Stella that he was running through the hotel like it was on fire.

He turned the corner and stepped into the open-air repose area. He hoped Juliette had followed his instructions. And he hoped she'd come alone. First, he checked the vine-draped pergola, but the massage table was empty. He climbed up the tree house to see if she was in the steam room. He checked the soaking pools and the waterfall. Nothing.

His pulse thundered in his ears. He needed to find her and get to the Hall of Memories. They were running out of time.

And then he caught movement through the trees. A figure paced back and forth in one of the tranquility rooms. A relieved sigh escaped his lips.

Juliette didn't notice him right away, and a warm feeling wound through Henri as he watched her. Her brow was furrowed, her shoulders tight and rolled forward. She nibbled on her thumbnail as she moved. Even anxious, she was beautiful.

She looked up as if sensing his gaze. Her expression went slack with relief.

"I was starting to worry you weren't coming," she said.

"I was starting to worry you wouldn't be here." He moved closer and took her hand in his. "I'm sorry about before. I had to make Caleigh believe—"

"I know." A shadow fell over her expression and he could see how much he'd hurt her. It made him hate himself. "It was just . . ."

"Painful?" he finished.

"Yes."

He let go of her and stuffed his hands in his pockets. "I went to see Stella. I was hoping she'd tell me the truth."

"How did it go?"

"Painful."

She frowned at the echo. "Were you able to buy us time?"

He sighed. "Not as much as I'd hoped. We need to get you out of here as soon as possible. So, what do you say? Should we go rescue Clare's memories and figure out what happened to Clementine?"

Her expression softened, "I thought you'd never ask."

Afternoon light poured through the small circular window of the attic room.

Henri and Juliette stood in front of the shelf of Clare's memories, at least a dozen boxes, each full of glass containers.

"How are we ever going to get them out of here?" Juliette slid one of the boxes to the front of the shelf as if she intended to start hauling them down the ladder on the spot.

Henri touched her wrist lightly. "Well, we're not going carry them, that's for sure."

"What other option do we have?"

Henri scrubbed a hand over his chin. "It would be easier if Clare were here. Restoring someone's own memories is relatively straightforward. It's just a matter of letting them sink into the mind, because they know precisely where to go after that. But since she's not here—" He bit the inside of his cheek, feeling suddenly sheepish. "I'd planned to implant them in your mind. Then once we leave the hotel, I can take them from you and give them to Clare."

"That would work?"

"Yes. I think so."

"You *think* so?"

"It will work," he said with more confidence. "But usually when I implant memories, I weave them into existing experiences so the guest can't tell where one ends and the other begins. In this case, we'd be trying to keep Clare's memories distinct and separate. It will likely cause you some discomfort."

Her voice shrunk a little. "It's going to hurt?"

"Not physically. Emotionally."

"I don't understand."

"These aren't some stranger's memories. You have your own experiences with Clare, and her memories of the same events might be different from yours. In some cases, they might directly contradict each other."

"So, if our memories are different, which one is right?"

"Both." He shrugged. "And neither."

Her fingers tapped nervously against the shelf. She pressed her lips together.

"It can be disorienting," Henri said. "So, you should make sure you're prepared before we proceed."

Her gaze darted around the room and landed on the boxes of Henri's memories. "Maybe we should do your thing first."

"My memories can wait. Once you're safely at home,

I'll figure out what happened with Clementine."

Juliette fidgeted with the hem of her tunic. "I'd like to know too. Unless . . . ? I don't want to intrude."

Something in her tone made his pulse flutter. He thought of how he'd felt connected to her since they first met. Seeing her in Clare's mind had made him feel as if he knew her. As if he'd known her his whole life. Now he wondered: *Was it possible his memories had done the same for her?* Was it too much to hope she might see him as something more than the fool who got duped into stealing her sister's memories?

"It's not an intrusion."

"Good." Her cheeks pinked and she looked away.

Henri pulled a box from the shelf and set it on the floor between them. He picked up a vessel made from pale pink glass and shaped like a seashell. He removed the stopper and handed the container to Juliette.

"Are you ready?" she asked.

He wasn't sure if he would ever be ready. He felt as if he were standing at the edge of a cliff, too afraid to jump. Maybe he didn't want to know what Stella was hiding from him. What if the fall destroyed him? But then he thought about the promise he'd made to Clementine—a promise he didn't recall making to a girl he couldn't remember—and he knew his only option was to jump.

"I'm ready."

Juliette tipped the memory into his cupped palms. Then she set the vessel down and put her hands on top of his.

⊙—⚹ HENRI BROKE HIS PROMISE.

For days, Clementine had been sleuthing around the

hotel, casually chatting up staff members as she tried to gather information.

Henri told her he was helping, but instead he spent the time in his room, staring at the ceiling as guilt gnawed a hole in his gut.

"I think the magic here is corrupt," she said one night after dinner. They were walking around the fountains at the front of the hotel, out of earshot from the guests who were dancing in the center of the courtyard. The weather had gone from winter to summer in a single evening.

"What do you mean it's corrupt?"

She leaned closer and lowered her voice to a whisper. "I was talking to Adrien today. He's one of the illusionists. Have you met him?" Henri shook his head. "Well, at first he wouldn't tell me anything, but all it took was a little flattery and he started singing like a songbird. He says the hotel is built on a network of underground hot springs and the magic comes from the water."

"But why would that mean it's corrupt?"

She waved a hand in front of her face. "It doesn't. But this used to be the grounds of an ancient temple. It was built here because of the magic. Adrien said there was a stream that ran alongside the temple—all the way from the tops of the mountains, through the network of hot springs and down into the valley. And once a year, when the snow in the mountains began to melt, the stream would flow into the city and magic would be everywhere. For a few weeks, everyone in all of Belle Fontaine had access to it. There was a huge festival and competitions to see who could make the most impressive illusions. Those few weeks were called the Days of Wonder. Isn't that amazing?"

Clementine was flushed and nearly breathless. Her eyes glimmered with the reflection of the light from the fountains.

Henri was at a loss for words, but it didn't matter, because she rushed on without waiting for him to reply.

"Adrien said after the Days of Wonder the magic would slowly evaporate into the air to fall as snow again in the winter. Then the cycle would start all over again. But now the magic is trapped and stagnant."

"It sounds like Adrien knows everything." Henri couldn't quite keep the bitterness out of his voice.

Clementine stopped walking and put her hands on her hips. "Are you *jealous?*"

"No," he said, affronted. And he wasn't. Not in the way she thought anyway. But he couldn't help but wish he'd been the one to get her answers. He made her a promise and he'd done nothing but avoid her like a coward. Shame licked up his neck.

"I don't believe you."

"I wish I'd done more to help, that's all."

"Don't worry," she said, "there's still plenty to do. And you're right . . . Adrien *is* kind of an insufferable know-it-all."

They both laughed. "Well, it sounds like he's a useful know-it-all," Henri said. "Did he explain why the Days of Wonder don't happen anymore?"

If they ever did.

Henri wasn't entirely convinced by this story—wouldn't he have heard it before?—but he didn't want to express any doubt when Clementine seemed so excited.

"Because someone bought the land, dammed the stream, and built the hotel right over the top so all the magic was trapped under the foundation. Whoever built the hotel is hoarding all the power that used to belong to everyone. But that's not even the worst part. Adrien said the evaporation cycle used to reinvigorate the magic—somehow it fed off the joy of so many people making illusions. But since that doesn't happen anymore, the owners had to find another way to replenish the magic so it doesn't dry up. And do you know how it gets replenished?"

He shook his head.

"It feeds on *memories*."

Henri couldn't help himself; he laughed. This Adrien person had obviously told her some ridiculous fairy tale. But then he registered her expression and his stomach dropped to the ground. Two bright red spots had appeared on each of her cheeks. Her lower lip was trembling.

"You think this is funny?"

"No, of course not. It just all sounds a little . . ." He kicked a pebble and sent it skittering across the ground. "It just seems unlikely."

"Do you have a better explanation for what keeps happening with my father?"

"No, I don't. I just—"

"Because I didn't tell Adrien about any of it, and yet everything he said would explain why my father doesn't remember discussing my birthday plans. Why he seems to change a little every time we visit. Because someone is removing his memories. And you act like you don't even care."

She spun on her heel and stalked away. Henri ran to catch up. He caught her fingers in his. "Clementine, please."

She turned, but her expression was guarded.

"I care," Henri said softly.

She put one hand on her hip, a challenge in her eyes. "Then prove it."

"I will. I'll help you find answers this time."

"Good," she said, "because if this is all true, we have to do something."

"Like what?"

"We have to find a way to destroy The Splendor. Promise me you'll help?"

"I promise."

And this time, it was a promise he intended to keep.

Henri slipped the memory back into the vessel. The room was stifling. Sweat dripped down his neck and pooled in the small of his back.

Juliette stared at him with a question in her eyes. "Was she right? Is that how the magic works?"

A pit opened in his stomach. He thought of his conversations with Stella.

"Some of it is true. I know the hotel was built on the site of an ancient temple, but the rest of it . . . I don't know."

Stella never made the magic sound corrupt. He tried to remember their last conversation on the subject.

The magic only flourished if the springs were fed.

Fed what? he'd asked.

Experiences.

What if by experiences she meant memories? Stella had made it sound like the magic simply needed the hotel to be bustling with guests for it to be replenished, but what if Clementine had been right? What if they were taking memories from guests to replenish the springs in the crypt?

What had he done?

CHAPTER TWENTY-FIVE

JULIETTE

"Henri?" It was the third time Juliette had said his name. She put a hand on his knee and he startled. He lifted his gaze to hers and he looked as if he'd seen a ghost.

"Do you need a break?" she asked.

"No, I'm fine." He answered this question the same way he'd answered all her others—with a hollow detachment that suggested his thoughts were somewhere far away.

She lifted the hair off the back of her neck and wished they could open the small window to let in a breeze. The heat had glued her clothes to her skin.

"Should we keep going then?"

Henri nodded and picked up a ruby-colored jar with sapphire blue wings for handles. This time, he removed the stopper and spilled the memory into Juliette's waiting fingers.

○—ⁿ THE NEXT TIME HENRI SAW CLEMENTINE, SHE WAS RUNNING. He was sitting on the back steps of the hotel, the marble cool against his thighs, lost in thought. He was contemplating their conversation and how to get her the information she needed. And then he looked up and saw her sprinting toward him from across the wide expanse of lawn.

He stood and hurried down the stairs to meet her. "What's wrong?"

"I just talked to Adrien again," she said. Her voice was high-pitched and agitated. "He says the owners are training you."

A fist closed around Henri's heart. He hadn't intended for her to find out like this.

"Is it true?" she asked. "Are you *helping* them?"

The truth stuck in his throat. He hated the way she was looking at him.

"Is. It. True?" she said, stabbing him with the words like they were thrust from the end of a sword.

"Yes."

"So that's why you laughed at me yesterday. Because you knew I was right and you're as guilty as they are."

"No!" he said. "I'm not guilty of anything. I laughed because I knew you were wrong."

Her eyes were filling with tears and she was slowly backing away. "I thought we were friends. But I guess I was wrong. I never want to see you again."

"Clementine, wait."

But she didn't. She hurried up the stairs and disappeared inside the hotel. Nausea pushed up his throat. He couldn't lose her. He had to get the answers she was looking for and then he would tell her the truth. About everything.

Henri started running and didn't stop until he got to the penthouse. He knocked sharply but didn't wait for an answer before he threw open the door and stormed inside.

Stella came around the corner with a dust cloth and a glass container in her hands.

"Henri? What are you doing here?"

"Is it true that you're feeding memories into the hot springs beneath the hotel?"

Stella calmly set the container and the cloth on a side table. "Where did you hear that?"

"Clementine."

"I see. And where did she hear it?"

"Adrien."

"Henri, I asked you to keep her happily occupied so her parents could have a nice vacation. Was there something about the assignment you misunderstood?"

"She's my friend," Henri said. "She thinks the hotel is changing her father. I believe her and I promised to get her answers."

Stella's mouth thinned. "You never should have promised something so reckless. You'll have to go back to her and tell her you found nothing."

"She deserves real answers."

"Oh?" Stella's voice was soft, like a snake sliding through grass—quiet, but dangerous. "And what do I deserve, Henri?"

His hands fisted at his sides. She was trying to confuse the issue, but it wouldn't work.

"Is Clementine right? Is the hotel taking memories from her father?"

"Whether she's right or wrong isn't nearly as important as whether or not you're loyal to your family."

"Loyalty has nothing to do with it. I'm not going to do something terrible just to prove myself to you."

Stella reached him in three long strides. She lifted her hand and cracked her palm across his face. Henri gasped and stumbled back.

"You will be loyal," she said, "or you will be made to be loyal."

His fingers went to his cheek. It was hot and smarting. "You can't *make* me loyal."

She laughed. "Can't I? Maybe your life has been a little too privileged, Henri. Is that why you haven't told your friend who you are? Because you're ashamed?"

Her gaze bore a hole through him and he looked away. His guilt left a bitter taste at the back of his throat. Henri hadn't intended to deceive Clementine. But when they first met, she'd assumed he was a guest. Once he knew how much she hated the hotel, it was easier to let her keep believing their families chose the same week each year for a visit rather than risk losing her friendship by confessing that he was the heir to The Splendor. He'd been a coward.

"I'm not ashamed," he said softly, though it was a lie.

"Well, you should be. Your father and I have given you every luxury imaginable, but instead of being grateful, you're thankless and insubordinate. You should have come to me the moment that girl started asking questions, but you're so concerned with how she sees you that you haven't given a single thought to how she could damage your family."

"Clementine just wants—"

"I don't care what Clementine wants!" Stella's voice thundered through the penthouse. She pressed a hand to her forehead. Took a deep breath. When she spoke again, her tone was measured. "Theo and I have poured our souls into this hotel and I won't have you ruining our life's work. Maybe you need a different history."

Something about the sudden calm in her voice made him feel trapped, like a fly in a spiderweb. Distantly it occurred to him that he shouldn't feel that way. Not with his own mother.

"What are you talking about? It's too late for a different history."

"I wonder . . ." Her gaze was faraway. "What if you were an orphan?" She said it casually, as if she were brainstorming a different paint color for the room.

"Are you . . . ?" Henri swallowed, a chill seeping into him. "Are you disowning me?"

Stella laughed. "No, darling, I'm going to *rescue* you." She brought her hands together in front of her face as if she'd just heard exciting news. "What better way to ensure loyalty than if Theo and I pluck you from obscurity—save you from abandonment—by bringing you to The Splendor to train in magic?"

A slow horror rolled through Henri. He backed away. "You can't be serious."

"It will be a fresh start, Henri. A chance to prove yourself."

"I don't want a fresh start."

"You never think you want a fresh start. But you're always happy when you get one."

Henri felt as if time slowed. As if the room held its breath.

His father had given him a knife as a young boy. A gift given only if Henri promised never to use it without supervision. Henri gave his word as he admired the gleaming steel, ran his thumb over the silky wooden handle. He kept his promise for a while, but then Stella bought apples. They sat in a bowl on the kitchen table like a bright green challenge until he convinced himself he had the skill to pare one without help. Theo had shown him lots of times before.

He held the apple firmly in his palm with his left hand and punctured the skin. He slowly pressed the fruit against the blade until the knife rested under the peel. Then he began to carefully rotate the apple.

His hand slipped. He saw what happened next in slow

motion—like a dance teacher breaking down the steps one by one. The blade sliding along the side of his finger. A pulse of anxiety as he wondered if he'd cut himself. Bringing his hand close to his face for further examination. Then a moment of uncertainty—it must have been a mistake, nothing there—followed immediately by unmistakable blooming pain and blood welling at the wound.

Stella's words in this moment felt the same. The swift cut. The slow realization. The pain.

His own mother was willing to manipulate his memories to keep him docile. And it seemed like she'd done it before.

"Father won't let you do this," Henri said. It was a grasp in the dark. One last glimmer of hope.

Stella's eyes flicked to where Theo stood framed in the doorway. "Why don't we ask him?"

"Papa?" Henri gave him a pleading look.

"Oh, Henri." Theo's expression was sad, but unyielding. "What have you done this time?"

A storm of confusion raged in Henri's chest. His gaze skipped from Stella to Theo and back again.

Theo stepped into the room and closed the door. He gave a wry smile, as if amused that the two of them were at odds again. But he could fix it. Theo always knew what to say. Theo opened his arms wide, and relief rushed into Henri, as welcome as a cold glass of water on a hot day. He ran to his father and buried his face against Theo's chest. Theo's arms closed tight around him. Henri's cheeks left wet splotches on his shirt.

"I'm sorry," Henri said, his voice muffled.

"Shhh." Theo stroked his head. "Everything is all right."

Henri closed his eyes and relished the feeling of safety. Theo's grip suddenly tightened. Henri tried to pull away, but it was too late.

Stella plunged a needle into his neck and his vision went dark.

Juliette emerged from the memory with her fist in her mouth, as if some part of her were trying to bite back a scream. The cloudy substance had disentangled from their fingers, and now it drifted toward Henri. Juliette lunged to catch it—she wasn't sure he even wanted this memory back—but she was too late. It settled on Henri's forehead and disappeared. He flinched as if reliving it all over again.

If her heart was pounding this fast, she couldn't imagine how Henri must feel. She turned to him, but he was staring straight ahead, his eyes glassy and unfocused, as if still trapped in the memory.

"Henri?"

He gave no indication he heard her. She closed her fingers around his. He took a shuddering breath and his eyes finally focused.

"Are you all right?" Juliette asked.

He shook his head, his expression bleak. "Everything was a lie."

CHAPTER TWENTY-SIX

ENRI'S EARS WERE FILLED WITH THE SOUND OF HIS LIFE shattering like a glass vessel. Everything he thought he knew lay around him in a pile of rubble—shards of jagged memories that might slice through him if he tried to handle them.

And just like a broken glass container, his life—even if he could find a way to glue it back together—would never look the same again.

Stella and Theo were his parents.

Henri thought about how often he'd wished he'd been adopted instead of conscripted to work at The Splendor, how many times he'd dreamed about sitting down to a meal with a mother or a father who loved him unconditionally. And even though he chided himself for such thoughts—he didn't want to seem ungrateful after Stella and Theo had done so much for him—he secretly held the idea of family close to his heart, like a hidden amulet on a slender cord. Tucked out of sight, but a comforting weight against his chest.

Now that dream was dead. He'd always had parents. They just cared more about their legacy than they ever cared about him. He'd given them credit for rescuing him when all they'd ever done was wound him over and over again.

"Henri?"

A hand closed around his. He blinked and Juliette's face swam in his vision.

"Are you all right?" she asked.

His gaze found hers. "Everything was a lie."

"I saw. I'm so sorry, Henri."

"I don't know what to do now." Henri hadn't meant to give voice to the helpless feeling floating inside him, but the words slipped out anyway.

Her eyes went soft. "I think we need to leave."

He knew she didn't just mean leaving this room. They needed to leave the hotel. It was clear that Stella and Theo would stop at nothing to protect The Splendor. And Henri and Juliette both knew too much to ever be safe here again.

But he couldn't leave. Not yet.

He was trying to find the words to explain, but Juliette followed his gaze to the boxes of vessels and understanding washed over her expression.

"You don't want to leave Clementine."

A shock of warmth went through him at being so quickly understood.

"I abandoned her once. I can't bear not finding out what happened to her."

Juliette darted a look toward the door. "But Caleigh will notice I'm missing soon. What about Clare?"

Henri scratched the back of his neck. "Just a little longer," he pleaded. "If we don't find answers soon, we'll go."

Juliette didn't reply right away. Her fingers twisted together.

Finally, she dropped her hands in her lap and let out a sigh. "You're right. Let's find out what happened."

Henri and Juliette opened vessel after vessel, watching just enough of each memory to decide if it had any potential for information before depositing it back in its container. Clementine was in every single one.

She was threaded throughout Henri's young life. The two of them lay on their backs in the grass and watched the night sky for falling stars. They waded barefoot through streams, pretending they were pirates crossing the high seas. They shared dishes of yellow cake with three flavors of syrup drizzled on top.

As they grew, they traded games of make-believe for debates about philosophy. They fought and laughed and sometimes cried.

And then finally, a memory that held promise for answers.

CLEMENTINE STOOD IN THE LOBBY OF THE SPLENDOR. She leaned against the wall opposite the grand staircase, her arms folded across her waist, watching guests descend.

It was clear she was waiting for someone, and anyone who knew her well would assume it was Henri.

Stella and Theo came down the stairs, arm in arm. Stella was dressed in a black velvet gown with a plunging neckline. Theo looked smart in a tailored suit.

At the bottom of the staircase, they headed straight for

Clementine. She pushed off the wall and stood up straight. Her gaze darted from side to side until she seemed to realize they were coming for her.

"You must be Clementine," Theo said warmly. "We've heard so much about you."

"I'm sorry," Clementine said, "do I know you?"

"We're Henri's parents," Stella said. "I understand you have some questions."

An expression of panic flitted over Clementine's face.

Theo chuckled. "Don't look so alarmed. Henri asked us to find you. He wants to show you something."

"Oh." Her voice was still unsure. She shifted her weight from one foot to the other. "What is it?"

Stella leaned forward and lowered her voice to a whisper. "We talked to Adrien." At this, Clementine's eyes went wide. "And that thing he told you about? We can show you. Unless you have somewhere else to be?"

Clementine's eyes sparked with interest. "Henri will be there?

Theo clapped her on the shoulder. "Like I said, who do you think sent us?"

Clementine followed them through the corridors. "So, Henri talked to you about the history of the hotel?"

"He did," Stella said over her shoulder, "and we found your theories fascinating."

"I didn't think he believed me."

"He didn't. Not at first. But after talking with us, he was convinced."

"It's nice he can talk to you," Clementine said. "Sometimes . . . I wish I could confide in my parents."

"You haven't told them about your conversations with Henri?" Theo asked.

"No. They'd just tell me I was imagining things."

Stella stopped, opened a door, held it for Clementine. "After you, my dear."

Clementine sucked in a sharp breath as she took in the stone staircase that plunged into the cavern below. "This is amazing."

"Yes," Theo said, "wait until you get to the bottom."

Clementine moved faster. Her eyes flitted from the small circle of hot springs that bubbled like a collection of witches' cauldrons to the steam curling from Lobster Lake, to the small brook that curved around the cavernous space and tumbled into a pond. They had reached the bottom step, and Clementine turned in a slow circle, trying to take it all in.

"How long have you known about this place?"

"Since we bought the hotel," Stella said.

Clementine froze. "Wait . . . I thought . . . you said you were Henri's parents?"

"He didn't tell you?" Theo pushed his fingers through his hair. "Well, this is awkward."

Clementine licked her lips nervously. "I'd like to go now."

Stella frowned. "I'm afraid that won't be possible."

Clementine tried to run, but Theo stepped in front of her and blocked her path. She took a step back. Her eyes were wide and terrified. "Please don't do this. I won't tell anyone about this place, I swear."

"I'm sorry," Theo said, "but it sounds as if you've talked of little else since you arrived."

Clementine took another step back. "Where is Henri?"

Theo shrugged. "I can't say I know for sure."

"Henri would never want this. He's my friend. Ask him, he'll tell you."

Stella took another step toward Clementine. "Did you talk to anyone else about this? Besides Henri and Adrien, I mean."

"Please." Clementine's eyes darted from Stella to Theo.

"Adrien didn't do anything. He was just answering my questions."

"Questions he shouldn't have been answering," Stella said. She moved forward as Clementine moved back.

Clementine wiped the sweat from her forehead with the back of her hand. "My parents will be wondering about me by now."

"Actually," Stella said, "they won't."

"What do you mean?" Clementine's voice trembled. Her eyes filled with tears. She looked back and forth between Stella and Theo, but when it was clear they weren't going to answer, she clasped her hands in front of her face, prayer-like. "Please. I'll never ask another question about The Splendor. No one will ever know I saw this place."

Theo turned to Stella. "Do you believe her?" His voice was suddenly conciliatory, as if he were an actor in a play and his next line was about forgiveness.

"No," Stella said, "I don't." And then she leaned forward and pressed her fingers to Clementine's temples.

Clementine gasped and her eyes went wide and startled.

Memories unspooled into Stella's fingers, twisting around her wrists like a pair of iridescent bracelets.

"That's enough," Theo said.

But Stella didn't listen. Memories poured from her hands, surrounding all three of them in a thick fog.

Theo grabbed Stella's elbow. "Let her go. You're taking too many."

She tried to shake him off, but he held fast. Slowly, the light went out of Clementine's eyes like the flicker of a candle in a stiff wind. Finally, Stella released her grip.

Clementine stumbled back. Her feet tried to find purchase, but Stella had positioned her perfectly at the edge of a boiling hot spring. Her heel slipped over the lip.

She tumbled backward.

"No!" Theo rushed forward, but he was too late.

Clementine's screams of agony only lasted a moment before abruptly falling silent.

Theo spun toward Stella. "You said you just wanted her to forget the past few days!"

"Well, I think we succeeded. She's definitely forgotten."

"Don't be flippant. You didn't have to do that."

The memories gathered and sunk into the water as if trying to find their owner. A low rumble shook the ground, and the hot spring began to burble. Theo and Stella leaped back just as a jet of water erupted from the surface of the spring. A single droplet landed on Theo's arm. He yelped as the skin began to blister.

Nausea rolled through his stomach. The girl's death must have been agonizing.

Theo scrubbed a hand over his face. "Henri will never forgive us."

"Henri will never know." Stella reached up and brushed his cheek with the backs of her fingers. "And you don't have to remember either, if it bothers you."

He shoved her hand away. "If it *bothers* me? It makes me sick. You can't keep manipulating every memory that casts you in a negative light. You're going to make Henri's memories unstable. And there's not a *chance* I'm letting you start doing it to me."

"But I hate the way you're looking at me. Like I'm a monster."

"You killed her, Stella!"

"We both know that girl was trouble. She was poisoning our son with her stories, and she wouldn't have stopped until he'd completely turned against us." She reached for Theo's hand and threaded her fingers through his. "Don't be angry, darling. This solves so many problems at once. This girl's memories will renew the magic, and Henri will be on our side again."

"He won't stay on our side. You should know by now that you can take his memories, but you can't change his heart. He's too good to ever sanction something as awful as this."

"This time will be different. Henri will owe us everything. He'll stay loyal to us, and to The Splendor."

Theo dropped Stella's hand. "Well, I'm not sure you'll be able to say the same about me."

Henri flung himself from the memory. He ran to the far side of the room and heaved, but his stomach was empty, so there was no relief. Only a wrenching revulsion, endlessly repeating. Clementine's terrified face swam in his vision. His stomach wouldn't stop moving.

Juliette made a choked noise at the back of her throat and Henri spun around. She still held the memory—it looped around her fingers like a snake—and she stared at it, frozen in horror.

"This isn't your memory." Her voice was hollow and scared.

"No." Henri went to her side and tried to help her guide it back into the vessel. But his hands were shaking so violently it took him three tries. "It's Theo's."

The container looked like betrayal: It was a deep midnight blue and the glass had raised ridges that looked like scars. Henri replaced the stopper and put the vessel back in the box.

He thought of Stella claiming Theo's memory had been slipping and his chest went tight. He thought of his own episodes. How Stella made him believe his memory magic came with a curse of forgetfulness, that the two things were opposite sides of the same coin.

No wonder Stella was always so tired.

It must be taxing work to cover up such a multitude of sins.

CHAPTER TWENTY-SEVEN

JULIETTE

EVERY MUSCLE IN JULIETTE'S BODY PULLED TAUT. SHE was a rope stretched too far and now she was fraying at the edges.

"I need to get out of here," she told Henri.

Henri's eyes roamed over her face. "I never meant for you to see something so awful. If I'd had any idea, I never would have—"

She shook her head. "I don't want to talk about it. Can you just give me Clare's memories so I can go? Please?"

"Of course." Henri pulled one of the boxes from the shelves.

A crash from below froze them both in place.

Henri's eyes went wide. He carefully lowered the box to the floor.

Juliette's heart stuttered, and then restarted at twice the speed.

Henri held up his hand. "Stay here," he whispered. "I'll go find out what happened."

She reached up and grabbed his fingers. A thrill of nervous

energy passed between them. "Be careful," she whispered.

"I will." He let go of her, ducked through the opening, and disappeared. Juliette's breath felt trapped in her throat.

Voices drifted from below. Juliette strained to make them out.

". . . glad . . . found you. Have . . . seen . . . Juliette?" Caleigh. Juliette pressed a hand against her chest. At least it wasn't Stella.

"Last I saw her, she was headed toward the repose area for a massage. Have you tried there?" Henri's voice was deliberately loud.

"I . . . did . . . wasn't . . . try . . . again . . ." Caleigh's voice was so muffled, Juliette only picked out the occasional word.

Then everything went silent.

Juliette waited. The air felt too thick to breathe.

She crept closer to the opening. The floor creaked, and she winced.

"Juliette?" Henri called. "She's gone."

A relieved sigh sagged out of her. She waited for the sound of him climbing the ladder, but the silence was like the pressure in the air before a storm.

"Henri?"

No response.

Juliette was caught in a tide of uncertainty. Questions pulled her under faster than answers could surface. Was Henri waiting for her to come down? But why would he do that when he knew they still had Clare's memories to deal with?

Had Caleigh come back? Was Henri waiting for her to leave again?

Should Juliette go down or stay put?

Panic swelled in her throat.

What if something happened to Henri?

She waited for what felt like an impossibly long time,

until she was certain Henri wasn't coming back. Finally, she realized she had no choice.

If she wanted to get out of this room, she was going to have to leave Clare's memories behind. Juliette ducked through the entrance and emerged on the landing. She let her gaze sweep over the sunlit room below, but she didn't see anything amiss. The Hall of Memories was empty.

She hurried down the ladder, and nearly tripped over a fallen broom at the bottom. This must have been the crash she and Henri heard when Caleigh came into the hall. She tried to remember if she'd seen leaning it against the shelves before they climbed into the attic. She couldn't recall.

Juliette turned in a slow circle. Where had Henri gone?

A blunt force hit the back of her head. A swift, startling shock.

And the world went dark.

Juliette dreamed.

She stood in front of the mirror in her suite, turning from side to side, examining her reflection. She wore a shimmering gown of pearlescent white with a sweetheart neckline and a sleek silhouette. Her hair was swept into a low chignon with a few soft curls framing her face. She pinched the apples of her cheeks to add a bit of color and slipped on a pair of strappy shoes embellished with diamonds. It was crucial she looked perfect tonight; she was the guest of honor.

"Are you ready?" Caleigh called from the other room. "Can I come in?"

"I'm not sure I'll ever be ready. But yes, come in."

Caleigh came around the corner and let out a gentle sigh.

"You look absolutely perfect."

Juliette blushed. "Are you sure? It's not too much?"

"You're stunning."

Juliette rested a palm on her stomach. "I guess we should go down then."

Caleigh smiled. "Yes, we should."

Juliette held her dress a few inches off the floor as they walked through the corridors. At the top of the grand staircase, she took a deep breath.

Caleigh squeezed her fingers. "Good luck."

Guests were gathered below, hundreds of them, and as Juliette started to descend, their eyes were drawn upward. A hush fell over the crowd.

And they began to applaud. Shy pride swelled in her chest. She reached the bottom of the staircase and people greeted her. They grasped her hands. They congratulated her on revealing the true nature of The Splendor. Now they knew the truth, and it was all thanks to her.

A throat cleared and the crowd parted. Henri. He came forward and took her hands in his.

"Thank you," he said. "I couldn't have done this without you."

He leaned forward and kissed her.

Juliette woke with a gasp. Someone was knocking at the door. She sat up in bed. Her thoughts were slow and sticky, like molasses oozing from a jar. The dream had felt so real. The adulation from the crowd, the dress. That kiss.

Heat crept into her cheeks.

More knocking.

"Come in," she called, the words scratching roughly from her throat, as if her voice were out of practice.

Caleigh came into the room with a tray of pastries. "Good morning. I hope you're hungry. Since it's your last morning,

I brought all your favorites."

Her last morning? Juliette tried to clear the cobwebs from her mind. And then it all came back in a rush: the attic room full of memories, Clementine's death, Henri disappearing. She scrambled backward on the bed, blankets clutched to her chest.

"How did I get here?"

Caleigh's brow furrowed. "To the hotel? I don't know. I'd assume you arrived by carriage, but I suppose it's possible you walked. Why?"

"No," Juliette said, "how did I get to this room? In this bed?"

Caleigh's eyes went wide and she laughed. "Did you visit one of the hotel taverns last night?"

"This isn't funny. I want to leave."

Caleigh's expression softened and she sat on the edge of the bed. "Of course, you can leave. You're scheduled to check out this morning." She rested a hand on Juliette's knee. "That must have been some dream you were having."

"It wasn't a dream—" Juliette said, but even as the words left her mouth, her certainty faltered. The details in her mind blurred as she tried to examine them. Coming down the staircase hadn't been real—she had no doubt about that—but what about the rest?

"I laid out your clothes for you," Caleigh said gently. "Why don't you get dressed, and then I'll make sure you get all your questions answered?"

Juliette tried to shake her residual fear, but her pulse wouldn't cooperate. She avoided Caleigh's gaze as she got out of bed and padded into the closet.

But the sight pulled her up short. It was completely empty except for a single dress: the one she'd been wearing the day she arrived. It had been washed and neatly pressed, but she recognized the thinning fabric and patched elbows. A lump rose in her throat as she ran her thumb over the frayed sleeve. It seemed like an eternity since she'd worn this.

Juliette hurriedly changed. Her dress was scratchy and uncomfortable. She'd gotten too accustomed to luxury fabrics, and now the presence of her old clothes against her skin was conspicuous.

Unease thrummed at the back of her mind, but every time she tried to pinpoint what was troubling her, the thoughts floated away. It reminded her of forgetting a word—the sensation of having it just on the tip of her tongue, but not being able to find it in time to give it voice.

"All ready?" Caleigh asked when Juliette came back into the main part of the suite.

Juliette nodded. She was ready to go home.

Home. The word rose in her mind with a face attached.

Juliette's hand flew to her mouth. She couldn't leave without Clare's memories. And where was Henri? He promised to help her. How did she get here?

"What's wrong?" Caleigh's voice was full of concern, but some instinct made Juliette suspicious. *Don't trust Caleigh.*

Juliette forced a smile. "Nothing. Everything is fine."

"Are you sure?"

"Positive. I'm just still feeling a little out of sorts."

"From the dream?"

Juliette's fingernails dug into her palms. "Yes."

"Follow me," Caleigh said. "I know just how to help."

Juliette doubted that. A bone-deep apprehension settled inside her, and every impulse screamed for her to run. But if she left now, Clare's memories were lost to her forever. So she took the same gamble she and Henri had been taking for days now.

She tried to buy just a little more time.

The decision fell on her like prison chains around her middle, tightly binding her as it pulled her forward. Caleigh led her down an unfamiliar corridor with walls made entirely of glass. The grass outside was vibrantly green. She wondered what it would feel like on her bare feet. Finally they came to a stop in front of a set of double doors.

"Wait here," Caleigh said. She went inside without knocking and Juliette could hear the low murmur of voices. A few moments later, Caleigh returned.

"You can go in now."

Juliette hesitated. Her pulse roared in her ears.

"You wanted answers, right?"

"Yes." Her dress felt suddenly too small. She tugged at the sleeves.

"Then go." Caleigh lifted her brows and dipped her head toward the door.

Juliette gathered her courage and pushed it open. Her breath caught. She'd seen Stella at least a dozen times in Henri's memories, but until now she'd never seen her in the flesh.

She was so small.

It took Juliette off guard. In Henri's memories Stella loomed. She was all powerful. Larger than life. Not this diminutive woman who stood behind a desk, offering an extended hand and a sunny smile.

"You must be Juliette. I'm Stella. It's so lovely to finally meet you."

Juliette's words abandoned her, and doubt fell over her like a shadow. If her impression of Stella was this faulty, what else had she gotten wrong? She stared at Stella's outstretched hand until the woman's smile faltered. "Have a seat," Stella said as she settled into the large chair behind the desk. "I understand you had some questions about your Signature Experience."

"My what?" But the words stirred up something familiar, and she suddenly remembered what Henri told her the first time he showed her the Hall of Memories. *Each guest gets a Signature Experience—some grand adventure that makes a dream come true . . . that is my role at the hotel.*

"No, I didn't get one of those."

"But of course you did."

Juliette's confusion must have shown on her face because Stella leaned forward, fingers splayed on the desk. "On your first night here, what did you tell Henri you wanted?"

"I didn't tell him I wanted anything."

"Are you sure?" Stella asked. "Think."

She thought of her first night at The Splendor. The awe. The luxury. Getting so lost in fantasy that everything else seemed to disappear into the background.

But then she thought of dancing with Henri. He'd asked her why she'd come to The Splendor.

Everyone comes looking for something. Adventure. Fame. Love. So what are you looking for?

"Answers." She said the word softly, almost to herself.

"Exactly," Stella said, as if this somehow settled the matter.

"I don't understand what that has to do with a Signature Experience."

"Our goal is always to give our guests precisely what they come searching for. It seemed you wanted a mystery to solve. So, we gave you one."

Doubt-laced fear ate at Juliette.

"What are you saying?"

"I'm saying everything you've experienced at The Splendor has been part of an experience tailored just to you. It's been an illusion, Juliette."

"What has been an illusion?"

"All of it."

Juliette's lungs went tight. "I don't believe you."

Stella's eyes twinkled with amusement. "Henri is getting too good at his job. It's meant to feel real. This wouldn't be The Splendor if it didn't."

No. Her mind refused to accept it. "You're lying."

"Do you know how many conversations I've had like this? Where I had to assure a guest they haven't really performed onstage as a prima ballerina, haven't gone to war and returned a hero, haven't sailed across the sea on a months-long voyage? So, now let me assure you, you didn't really"—Stella paused to check the notes in front of her, dragging her finger along the page as a smile flickered over her expression—"discover a host of secrets that will expose The Splendor and close it down for good."

Juliette's thoughts spun away from her; she chased after them. "What you did to Henri was real. I saw his expression. He was devastated."

Stella frowned sympathetically. "It seems your stay has been only half successful. Your Signature Experience felt real, but it doesn't seem like it satisfied you. I'm so sorry, Juliette. If we'd had a little more time to prepare—"

"Stop lying to me! I saw you hurt that girl. I saw—"

"You saw an illusion."

"You're saying you didn't lie to Henri about being your son? You didn't tell him he was an orphan to control him?"

"Henri isn't an orphan and he isn't my son. His parents are alive and well. They live in a fishing village just outside Belle Fontaine, and he visits them on his days off."

Juliette didn't speak, but she shook her head slowly. It couldn't be true.

"Think about it," Stella said. "That first night, he told you a story tailor-made to forge a bond between the two of you. You were both orphans. Both abandoned. But, when you still seemed unsettled, he thought you wanted the distraction of a mystery and the connection of a friend to solve it with."

Juliette reared back as if slapped. The thought that Henri might have only been pretending to care about her settled in her stomach like a clenched fist. She had thought . . . she had hoped. No. She pushed her worries away. Stella was just trying to talk her way out of what she'd done.

"Someone hit me on the back of the head." Juliette's voice was nearly hysterical. "They dragged me back to my suite so I'd think it was a dream."

Stella tilted her head to one side. "Something like that would leave evidence. Are you injured? Did you wake with a headache or a goose egg?"

Juliette's fingers went to her scalp. Stella was right. She couldn't find anything—not a bump or a knot or even a spot that felt tender.

"But Clementine . . ."

"Never existed." Stella's expression softened. "You came here because you'd gotten in an argument with your sister, isn't that correct?"

"No, I came because this place *changed* her. She didn't care about me anymore."

"And you wanted to figure out why?"

"Yes."

"It seemed you wanted a fantasy—a mystery to solve—that would give you answers about why a beloved childhood companion might unexpectedly vanish from someone's life. You were searching for some explanation for Clare's behavior, and we tried to help you as you grappled with your grief. But sometimes—despite our best efforts—a guest's mind runs away with our illusions and fills in details on their own. First, you thought Clare sold her memories of you. It would explain your sister's behavior. If she no longer remembered you, her sudden distance would make sense. But that was too painful. You couldn't accept it. So then you convinced yourself her memories were stolen."

"They *were* stolen. I saw them."

"You saw an illusion of the memories you wish she'd had. Can't you see? Clementine was a stand-in for Clare. Henri created her as a way of providing a little distance from your own loss, so you could see things more clearly. But you refused to accept Henri's illusion. Instead, your mind desperately searched for an explanation, no matter how far-fetched. Maybe it was a less painful notion that a loved one died tragically—was murdered, even—than that of two people who grew apart."

"Clare would never abandon me." Juliette's throat ached.

"She didn't abandon you," Stella said. "She grew up and moved on. It happens."

"*No.*" Juliette said the word softly to herself over and over. *No. No. No.* "Henri wouldn't lie to me like this."

"He didn't lie to you, Juliette. You came here knowing what The Splendor was. And even as Henri was creating a fantasy for you, he was trying to give you plenty of clues about reality so you could come to these conclusions on your own."

"No, he wasn't. He never gave me any reason to believe it wasn't real."

"Did he explain his work? His job as an illusionist? His ability to implant false memories that feel like they really happened?"

Juliette thought of Henri's explanations of his work using false memories in dreams.

"Yes, but—"

"Why would he tell you all that if it implicated him in

some nefarious scheme?"

"You're just trying to protect yourself."

"Protect myself from what exactly?"

"From everyone finding out about you. From losing your legacy."

"My *legacy*? Who do you think I am?"

The question sounded so sincere, so incredulous it made Juliette falter. "I . . . you and Theo own the hotel."

When she answered, Stella's voice was gentle. "A board of directors owns the hotel. I just manage it. And I don't know anyone named Theo."

Juliette's thoughts scrambled, spinning wildly from one to the next. Could any of what Stella was saying be true? And if it was . . .

"I thought The Splendor was supposed to make dreams come true," Juliette said. "This has been the worst week of my life."

Stella leaned forward and rested a palm on Juliette's forearm. "I know. But sometimes getting what we really want—what we *need*—isn't about pleasure and luxury. Sometimes the greatest fantasy is that we can accept reality for what it really is." Stella leaned back in her chair. "I understand you told Caleigh you wanted to forget Clare."

"Only because Henri convinced me to. I never would have said it on my own."

Stella arched a delicate brow. "But when she asked you about it a second time, did you verify it was what you wanted?"

Anger sparked inside Juliette.

"Did you?" Stella prompted.

"Yes, but—"

"And didn't Henri come to your suite—in the presence of Caleigh—and explain the harvesting procedure to you in painstaking detail?"

"You're twisting things! I only said I wanted to forget Clare because Henri told me it's what I needed to do."

"Perhaps, because he knew it was important for you to let go."

Juliette shot out of her seat. "No. Because you were so insistent on him figuring out what I wanted that he thought I was in danger."

"I see," Stella said in a tone that suggested she definitely did not.

"He said we had to pretend to let Caleigh into the inner circle in order to keep her out." Even as the words left her mouth, she heard how ridiculous they sounded. She felt like a rag doll coming apart at the seams, her insides spilling out like insubstantial fluff. Was she really so naive that she checked in to a hotel promising fantasy and illusion and then believed she could cling to reality? Did she actually think Henri could be falling for her when her own sister no longer cared?

Something about Juliette's expression made Stella's eyes fill with sympathy, and it was this more than anything else that finally shredded the last bit of Juliette's hope. She felt it slowly bleed away like water sinking into sand.

"I'm so sorry this didn't turn out the way you wanted," Stella said. "If you'd like to try again sometime, I'd be happy to offer you a complimentary stay."

Juliette wiped at her eyes. "Thank you, but no."

She wanted to get as far away from The Splendor as possible.

And she didn't ever want to come back.

Juliette's vision blurred as she stumbled from Stella's office.

Caleigh waited for her just outside the door. She took one look at Juliette and her eyes went wide. "Oh no. What happened?"

"Is she trustworthy?" Juliette asked, dipping her head toward the office. "Tell me honestly."

Caleigh bit her bottom lip. "Yes. I'm so sorry. This is all my fault. It was my job to take care of you and I let you down. What can I do?"

"Nothing. I just want to go home."

"Of course," Caleigh said. "I'll walk you out."

They moved through the corridors without speaking. The hotel was bustling with people. Bellhops pushed carts loaded with bags while well-dressed guests trailed behind, looking alternately blissful and reluctant to leave. Everyone was preparing to check out, but no one else was weeping.

Not that it mattered—the other guests didn't even seem to notice Juliette. Who had time to pay attention to a girl in a threadbare dress who didn't even know the difference between fantasy and reality?

Her arms felt achingly empty. She thought she'd be leaving with all of Clare's memories, but she didn't even have so much as a bag to carry. It seemed like ages ago she hurried through the streets of Belle Fontaine with nothing but a wilting reservation in her hand and anger at her back like a strong wind.

She came with nothing and she would leave with nothing.

"You know," Caleigh said, "you could always go through with it."

Juliette stopped walking and spun to face Caleigh. "Go through with what?"

"Forgetting Clare."

Juliette stared at her, mouth agape. How dare she—

"Wait," Caleigh said, "hear me out. You're in pain. But you don't have to feel that way."

"There isn't any other way to feel." Juliette's thoughts were hopelessly tangled—a jumbled mess that made no sense. But pain seemed to rise to the top, easily plucked from the heap.

"Why not?" Caleigh asked. And then, more gently: "When you go home, will anything have changed?"

Suddenly Juliette was so tired. Her memories felt heavy inside her. She hadn't realized how much she'd been leaning on Henri, how their shared glimpses of each other's history had bound them together. And now—after finding out it was all an illusion—she felt like a boat adrift at sea, lost and aimless. Maybe it wouldn't be so terrible to have a fresh start.

She sighed. "What would I have to do?"

Caleigh was about to answer when Juliette spotted a familiar face. Henri was passing through the corridor. She felt Caleigh stiffen beside her. Inhale sharply. In the span of that single breath, Juliette knew.

Stella lied.

Caleigh took her arm and tried to distract her, but Juliette pulled away.

"Henri!" She chased him down the corridor. "Henri."

He turned. Smiled. Her heart felt like a dish of butter over flame.

"What happened? Where did you go before?"

His smile faltered. He cocked his head to one side. "I'm sorry. Have we met?"

CHAPTER TWENTY-EIGHT

THE GIRL HAD HAIR LIKE A FLAME AND A FACE LIKE A windowpane. Her emotions were transparent in every expression, and Henri watched them cascade over her face as she approached him. First relief. Then anger. And finally—when it was clear he didn't know her—panic.

The panic confused him the most.

He was used to the way his episodes kept others at a distance. Memories were the glue that bound relationships together, so he was never surprised to encounter disappointment when he forgot a name or disdain when he couldn't remember some shared experience, but he'd never seen fear before. At least he didn't think so.

"We have to run," she said, grabbing his arm. "We need to get to the Hall of Memories now before Stella catches up."

Carefully, he extricated himself from her grip. A disgruntled employee then. Stella must have fired her in preparation for the next batch of new guests to arrive. "There's no need to run. Do you mind telling me what this is about?"

"I'll tell you on the way. Henri, please. I know you don't remember me, but you have to trust me. We're both in danger."

Caleigh appeared at Henri's side and shot him an apologetic glance. "Juliette, would you come with me please?"

Something prickled at the back of Henri's neck. "What's going on?"

"Just a little misunderstanding," Caleigh said. "I'll take care of it."

Juliette touched the back of his hand. "Henri, please." Something about the familiar way she said his name tweaked something inside him.

He turned to Caleigh. "Can you give us a minute?"

Caleigh's gaze darted back and forth between them. She had the distinct expression of someone caught between two equally unappealing options.

He watched the struggle play out on her face: She could either defy him when she knew he outranked her, or she could acquiesce and risk him finding out something she clearly didn't want him to know.

After a few moments of hesitation, she chose the latter.

"Yes, of course. Sorry to interrupt."

Caleigh hurried away like something hungry was nipping at her heels.

"She's going to get Stella," Juliette said. "We need to hurry."

"Wait. Tell me what's going on first."

Juliette's glare went murderous. "No. I'm done trying to convince you. Follow me or don't." She spun on her heel and stormed away. Henri had no choice but to follow.

He ran to catch up with her. His assumption she was on the staff was obviously right. She knew the path well and she seemed impervious to the illusions.

"So did Stella fire you?"

"Did she *fire* me? No, I don't work here."

"You're a guest?" Henri's voice was incredulous; it was impossible. "But then how do you know about the Hall of Memories?"

She frowned. "You told me."

He couldn't imagine what would have possessed him to do such a thing, but despite himself he believed her. Still, he couldn't just blindly follow her to a restricted area of the hotel. Not without an explanation.

"What's going on? You said you'd tell me on the way, so you better start talking."

Juliette blew out a frustrated breath. "It's a long story, so I'll give you the highlights. Stella stole my sister's memories. You promised you'd get them back for me. In that process, we discovered she'd been taking memories from *you*." She threw a look over her shoulder. "And it appears she's done it again."

A slow horror crept over Henri. Stella would never do that. His steps faltered . . . Would she? They'd reached the staircase that led to the Hall of Memories. Henri lightly touched Juliette's wrist. She stopped walking and turned to face him.

"I don't know what you're asking me to do," he said.

"I'm asking you to keep your promise."

"Juliette . . ." He trailed off as he realized her name felt familiar on his lips. A jolt went through him—forceful and startling.

"Yes?"

He'd been about to ask her the details of whatever plan they'd obviously hatched together, but an entirely different question came out instead. "Was there . . ." He tugged on the back of his neck. Cleared his throat. "Was there something between us?"

"I wish I knew."

She turned and hurried up the steps. Color rose in Henri's cheeks. What was that supposed to mean? Either there was something between them or there wasn't. His pulse sped as if his heart knew something his mind didn't.

At the top of the stairs, Juliette opened the door to the Hall of Memories and charged forward to the back wall. She pulled the rolling ladder to the center of the shelves and began to climb.

"Where are you going? There's nothing up there but storage."

"Trust me," she said, "there's a lot more than that."

He clambered up the rungs and hoisted himself onto the ledge. Juliette crawled through the small square doorway, and Henri followed a moment later.

They emerged into the attic room and climbed to their feet. A small round window bathed the room in warm sunlight. On one side of the room were shelves littered with rows of cleaning supplies—furniture polish, dust cloths, glass jars filled with detergent. Several brooms in different sizes leaned against the opposite wall. A stack of buckets sat in one corner.

Juliette let out a small gasp. Henri saw all the fiery determination drain out of her in one swift motion, like a glass knocked over by a sharp elbow.

She ran to the shelves and rummaged through their contents, tossing aside stacks of rags and small tins of beeswax. A glass jar of powdered soap fell and shattered, sending a cloud of white dust into the air.

"Whoa," Henri said, catching her by the wrist, "slow down. Let me help."

She shoved him away. "Help with what? We're too late. Stella took everything."

Juliette's eyes were wild. Her face flushed. Henri studied

her warily, and he suddenly wondered if Caleigh's apprehension was warranted: if it was less about keeping something from Henri and more about how Juliette was acting. In this moment, she didn't seem rational.

"Is it possible this room was never anything more than storage?" he asked. The Splendor had a way of braiding together reality and fantasy that made them hard to untangle. He wished he knew what her Signature Experience had been and if he'd made some misstep that caused her confusion.

"No, it's not possible." Her glare was full of daggers. "I carried Clare's memories up here myself. Boxes and boxes of them."

"But . . . we don't store memories in boxes."

"I know that," she snapped.

"So, where did you get boxes?"

"There was a stack of them in the corner." She pointed. "Right over there."

His gaze followed her finger. To the stack of buckets.

"Juliette—"

"Stop. Doing. That."

His eyes went wide. "Stop doing what?"

"Stop looking at me like you're trying to figure out if I'm lying or irrational. I'm neither. Now either figure out how to help me or leave me alone."

Inexplicably, warmth coiled through him. He didn't know why he trusted her, but he did.

"How can I help?" he asked. A tremulous smile flickered on Juliette's lips—gone as quickly as it appeared—but it was just enough for Henri to gain a flash of insight. Despite all her bravado, she was afraid he'd leave.

"Stella moved the memories because she suspected we might come back. Which means we can't stay here." Juliette's fingers twisted together, and the gesture seemed familiar to

Henri. The sensation was unnerving—like hearing a melody he knew, but not quite remembering the words. "I don't know the hotel like you do. Is there somewhere we can go she won't think to look?"

Henri thought of all the places he used to escape as a boy when he needed a secret spot away from the pressures of The Splendor.

"There's a lepidopterarium on the grounds," he said.

A smile spilled over her face like sunshine emerging from behind a cloud. "You never change, Henri. The butterfly house sounds perfect."

CHAPTER TWENTY-NINE

JULIETTE

JULIETTE COULD TELL HENRI DIDN'T BELIEVE HER. NOT
entirely. But several times during their conversation,
his eyes sparked with recognition. It seemed Stella had
removed the memories of Juliette but hadn't managed to
sever their connection. A thought percolated at the back of
her mind: Why hadn't Stella removed *Juliette's* memories? It
seemed to be her default answer for every sticky situation.
But maybe the last few weeks had spooked her. Maybe Stella
finally realized it was dangerous to remove the memories of
someone outside her control. If Juliette was asking questions
about Clare, who knew if someone might show up in a few
weeks to ask questions about Juliette? It would be far easier
to convince Juliette it had all been an illusion, send her on her
way, and remove Henri's memories instead. Juliette chewed
her thumbnail. Hopefully, whatever connection still remained
between her and Henri was enough to get them out of here.

"This staircase is creaky," Henri told her as they left the
Hall of Memories, "so watch where you step."

Juliette followed him down, careful to place her feet precisely where Henri's had been. They turned the corner at the bottom of the stairs and heard voices. Henri grabbed her hand and pulled them both into an alcove on the back side of the stairs. He put a finger to his lips.

"I'll search upstairs," Stella was saying. "The rest of you, split up and do whatever it takes to find them. Henri is not himself right now, so don't be taken in by his charm. My orders take precedence over his, no matter what he says. Is everyone clear?"

A murmur of assent followed.

"Good, then get going."

Stella's footsteps thundered overhead, and a half dozen other sets of feet took off in all different directions. Henri pulled Juliette farther into the shadows. Their backs were pressed against the wall, their palms slick with sweat.

Juliette's heart was beating so loudly, she was surprised the sound alone hadn't already given them away. She darted a glance at Henri. His mouth was tight and his body looked like a coiled spring. Juliette suspected hearing Stella discussing him as if he were a fugitive finally made Juliette's claims credible.

They waited, breathless, for what seemed like an eternity. Then finally, Henri let go of her hand.

"Let's go." His voice was low and husky.

He led her down a series of corridors, turning left when her instincts would have told her to go right. She was hopelessly turned around. If she were responsible for getting the two of them out of the hotel unseen, she'd fail miserably. But Henri knew every side corridor and secret pass-through. Unless—the thought nearly closed her throat with dread—what if Stella removed those memories too? Then again, it didn't seem like Stella was in the habit of taking any memories that would jeopardize Henri's role at The Splendor. And Henri knowing his way around the hotel was a definite benefit for Stella.

At least until today.

Finally, they entered a huge ballroom with doors on three sides.

"Almost there," Henri said. Juliette followed him through the exit and down another long dark corridor. Soon, they spilled out onto the brick pathway that led to the butterfly house.

Juliette had never been so relieved to be outside. But she knew it was only a matter of time before Stella realized they weren't in the hotel, and started searching the grounds. She and Henri hurried up the pathway and stepped into the warm enclosure. They moved into the belly of the glass structure, far out of view of anyone who might be wandering the grounds.

Finally, Henri turned to her, eyes bleak. "Why is Stella searching for me?"

"Let's sit," Juliette said, gently leading him to the same bench they'd shared just yesterday.

They sat and Juliette worried the wooden slats with her thumb. "She's searching for you because you're helping me."

"Then maybe I shouldn't be helping you." Henri's words were laced with bitterness, but Juliette forced herself to bite down on the sharp reply waiting at the tip of her tongue. She couldn't blame him for his confusion or his doubt. This place had a way of creating both.

Juliette touched a glossy green leaf with the tip of her finger. "Last time you brought me here you said you loved it because it was one of the few truly beautiful places on the grounds because it isn't enhanced by illusion." Juliette watched his face change, opening like a blooming flower. She could see that he recognized himself in his own words.

"Yes, it's one of my favorite spots."

"I know." She studied a bright blue butterfly landing on a nearby flower as she struggled to come up with the words to tell him the rest.

"You said Stella has been taking memories from me?" Henri prompted. "How could you know that?"

Juliette took a deep breath and gave Henri a quick recap of everything that had happened—from her arrival at The Splendor all the way to sneaking into the Hall of Memories on the night of the masquerade ball. Henri frowned as he listened, but he didn't interrupt her.

"When I was looking for a place to hide Clare's memories, I found several boxes of yours in the storage room. We looked at the memories together. I hoped you could see them again, but—"

"Stella moved them."

"It seems so."

A heavy silence stretched between them, thick with unanswered questions.

Finally, Henri shifted in his seat. "What kind of memories were they?"

"Childhood friends, arguments with Stella, and—" Juliette winced. It seemed unfair that she should have to be the face of such painful news. "Answers about your parents."

Henri's eyes lit up. His curiosity felt like a dagger in her heart. The truth wouldn't give him the peace he hoped for. She wondered what it must feel like to find out you'd been betrayed over and over. She thought about how scars didn't disappear simply because you forgot about the wound.

Something about Juliette's expression made Henri's face fall. "Stella wouldn't take my memories unless she had something to hide."

"No," Juliette said, "she wouldn't."

He sighed. "Then you may as well just tell me."

"I have a better idea, but you're not going to like it."

He gave her a skeptical look but indicated she should continue.

"I think you should execute a harvest on me."

A line appeared between his brows. "I don't understand. What good would that do?"

"You told me once that since I'd seen Clare's memories, they were mine now. But, Henri, I didn't just see Clare's memories. I saw yours too. Stella may have taken those boxes, but she didn't take my memory of seeing what was in them."

He shot to his feet. "Absolutely not."

"But why? It could work."

"You're asking me to take a memory of you seeing a memory? And what am I supposed to do with it? I don't have access to any memory vessels. I'd need to put it somewhere."

"Couldn't you take it out, look at it, and put it back?"

"You have no idea the amount of concentration that would take. What if I lose focus and the memory dissipates? Then it's gone forever. For both of us."

"I don't see what choice we have."

"Of course, we have a choice. Why would you risk this when it has nothing to do with your sister?"

"You think I *want* you poking around in my mind?" The thought of him seeing things she didn't intend for him to see made her want to fold her arms across her chest and disappear. Her cheeks flamed. "But you're the only person I trust, and you're never going to fully trust me in return until you see those memories. And if I have any chance of surviving this, I need you to trust me."

Henri sat heavily and dropped his head into his hands. Juliette wasn't sure if he was more reluctant about executing a harvest on her or actually seeing memories he'd rather leave alone. Perhaps ignorance was bliss. But when he finally lifted his gaze to hers, his expression was gentle.

"Fine," he said, "I'll do it."

CHAPTER THIRTY

HENRI

ENRI HAD NEVER HARVESTED A MEMORY AT SUCH CLOSE range before. Juliette leaned back with her head resting against the top of the bench. Henri tried to summon his magic, but it sputtered out before it reached her. He moved farther away—maybe the proximity was a problem—but that was even worse. He couldn't focus.

Juliette lifted her head. "What's wrong?"

Henri scratched the back of his neck. "I don't know. It might help if I'm in contact with you."

She shot him a quick, self-conscious look. "I assumed that's how it worked. Go ahead." She leaned back and closed her eyes.

His hand trembled as he touched her temples. Her skin was warmer than his, and softer too. She smelled like citrus.

His magic finally settled, the threads sinking into Juliette's mind. Memories swirled beneath his fingers, most of them fresh and tinged with pain.

He started with her most recent memories: the surge of

relief she felt when she saw him and realized Stella lied; the waterfalling disappointment when he didn't remember her; the sharp stab of fear that followed.

He watched with growing discomfort as Stella tried to convince Juliette her time at The Splendor had been only illusion. He felt her disbelief melt into an aching dismay, felt her heart shrivel at the thought that Henri had been pretending. A pang hit him square in the chest, and he had to resist the urge to stop what he was doing and defend himself. No matter how skilled he was at illusion, he wouldn't have done what Stella was implying.

Henri worked his way back until he saw his own memories in Juliette's mind.

They were vivid and fresh; they slipped into his fingers as easily as an egg from a cracked shell.

Clementine.

The name settled inside him with a familiar echo. Then horror crushed his lungs as he watched her die. His own emotions fused with Juliette's. Now he understood the panic in her eyes.

Memories poured into his fingers, almost more quickly than he could take them in. He watched his relationship with Clementine in reverse—friendship, and connection, and shared secrets.

He couldn't stop.

All of Juliette's memories since she arrived at The Splendor rushed at him. Her sorrow over Clare, her unease at the way the hotel seemed to be designed to make her want to forget. Meeting Henri.

It was strange to see himself from someone else's perspective. To watch Juliette go from doubting him to opening up to him to something more. Something she seemed to be hiding from herself, even in her own mind.

Henri's energy flagged, but now that he knew what Stella was capable of, a new sense of urgency overtook him. He needed to give these memories back to Juliette and get her out of here.

He needed to get himself out of here too.

He worked as quickly as he could, his exhaustion growing by the second. He was nearly back to where he started—with only Juliette's most recent memories remaining—when he heard a noise that snapped him back to the present.

The door to the butterfly house had just creaked open.

The blood froze in his veins.

He only had moments to spare. He glanced back and forth between the memories swirling in his palms and Juliette. If he kept going with the implantation, they'd be caught. If he let the memories go, they'd dissipate.

"Hello?" Stella called, her voice full of false cheer.

Henri let go of the memories and swatted them away. They rushed to the ground and sunk into the dirt. He grabbed Juliette's shoulder and shook her. She'd fallen asleep, and she woke confused and disoriented. She wouldn't remember coming here.

"No matter what happens, follow my lead, understand?"

She sat up straight. "What's going on?"

Henri gave her a sharp, silencing look. "There's no time. Tell me you understand."

She bit her lip, but she nodded.

"We're over here," Henri called, forcing what he hoped was a casual tone.

Stella's footsteps filled Henri with dread, but when she reached where they sat on the bench, he turned and gave her an amused smile.

"Juliette here has quite the story."

"I'm sure she does." Stella turned to Juliette, who still

wore an expression of dazed confusion. "But I'm here with an offer she won't be able to refuse."

Juliette's gaze sharpened. "What kind of offer?"

"It seems your sister's memories were removed after all. Would you like them back?"

Juliette inhaled sharply. "Yes. Yes, of course I would."

Henri's pulse spiked. Juliette didn't know what she was up against. He hadn't been able to replace her last conversation with Stella or her memories of seeing what happened to Clementine. And if Juliette heard the *after all* in Stella's statement, she hadn't shown it. In her mind, the fact that Clare's memories had been removed was not in dispute.

He needed to warn her, but if he gave any indication he was on her side, any hint he'd seen what Stella did to Clementine, he knew Stella wouldn't let Juliette leave alive.

"I'm so glad to hear it," Stella said, "and I'm terribly sorry for the misunderstanding. If you'll follow me, we'll take good care of you."

Henri wanted to scream. He'd seen this all play out before with Clementine. Stella offered her what she wanted most, and Clementine gullibly followed like a lamb to the slaughter.

Now Juliette was about to do the same. Her eyes sparked with hope and it seemed she'd forgotten all about him. At this point, the best way to protect her was to stay by her side and pretend he didn't know anything more than Stella thought he did.

At least until he could find a way out of this mess.

Juliette followed Stella and Henri trailed behind. When Stella stopped to hold the door open for Juliette, she gave him a curious look.

"We don't need you for this, Henri. I can take care of Juliette myself."

Yes, he thought, *I'm sure you can.*

Instead, he said, "I think I'll come along anyway if you don't mind."

Her expression turned hard. "Actually, I do mind. We have new guests coming today and you have work to do."

"Oh." Juliette stopped midway through the door. "I'd feel better with Henri there."

Stella's grip on the handle tightened. Her knuckles paled. Henri could see her weighing her options. If she insisted on Henri staying behind, she risked losing Juliette's trust. But clearly, she didn't want Henri present for whatever she was about to do. He tried to keep his expression neutral, like he was curious and nothing more.

Juliette watched her expectantly. Finally, Stella seemed to accept she had no choice.

"Of course," she said sweetly, "if that's what makes you most comfortable."

Henri gave a noncommittal shrug, as if he weren't concerned one way or the other, but inwardly he laughed at the irony: How could Stella deny a guest such a simple request when she was in the business of making dreams come true?

Stella led them into the hotel, and Henri's mind scrambled for some way to keep her from taking them to the crypt. Once Juliette was down there, he wouldn't be able to protect her. Too much could go wrong. His lungs ached from holding his breath.

But Stella didn't go down. She went up.

Juliette shot Henri a look of pure joy as they climbed the staircase to the Hall of Memories. He wished he could pull her aside and explain that Stella's promises were lies, but the most he could hope for was that somewhere inside her was an echo of the truth.

If he could find a way to force Stella to leave him alone with Juliette—if only for a moment—he might be able to convince her they needed to run. He knew it would be almost impossible to persuade her of anything that would require her to walk away from the possibility of getting Clare's memories back, but he would have to find a way. Her life depended on it.

The moment he stepped into the room, Henri's blossoming hope died on the vine. Theo was here.

And he was holding a syringe.

CHAPTER THIRTY-ONE

JULIETTE

SOMETHING WAS MISSING.

Juliette felt it the way she used to feel the absence of a recently lost molar—the constant probing with her tongue, a searching that bordered on obsession until finally the void became normal. Her thoughts kept circling, probing, but she couldn't figure out what was gone.

She'd been reluctant to follow Stella, but the promise of getting Clare's memories back had hurried her footsteps despite her misgivings. And Henri had insisted she follow his lead; he wouldn't have put her in danger, would he? But the sensation that *something* was missing nagged at her. What was it?

It must be a memory. The last thing she remembered was sitting with Henri in the butterfly house. *There's something I need to show you.* She had been about to bring him here. To prove to him that Stella and Theo had been lying to him about who his parents were. Had she actually shown him the memory? Did he know his parents were guests at the hotel and Stella recruited him for his magic? Or did he still think they found him in an orphanage?

Maybe she did show him and that was the gap in her memory. But then why would she have woken up in the same place, on the same bench in the butterfly house? If Stella was trying to cover her tracks, she hadn't done it very well—Juliette was wearing completely different clothes than before. She ran her fingers along one sleeve. This was the dress she was wearing when she arrived at The Splendor.

Something was wrong.

She darted a glance at Henri, but he was gaping at a man who stood in the center of the room.

The man startled. "Henri . . ." Juliette caught a glint of something metal in his hand before it disappeared behind his back. "I wasn't expecting you."

"No," Henri said, "it seems not."

"What's going on?" Juliette was slick with dread. A lock clicked behind her, and she spun around. Stella stood between her and the door. She'd just walked into a trap. "Where are my sister's memories?"

"They don't belong to her anymore. Now, if you'll cooperate, we'll have you on your way home in no time."

"Cooperate with what?"

Theo took a step toward her, and this time she saw the needle nestled in his palm. Sudden understanding pinned her in place. She'd spent a week mourning the loss of her relationship with Clare, but now she was about to lose her sister for good.

"Wait!" Henri stepped between her and Theo. "Don't do this."

"*Son*—" Theo started, but the word made Henri go rigid. "Don't. Just give me the needle."

"You know I can't do that."

"What else do you know?" Henri's voice was low

and dangerous. "Do you know that Stella regularly takes memories from you too? Or did you only know about how she does it to me?"

Theo's expression faltered. His gaze flicked to Stella.

"That's ridiculous." Stella's face was impassive, her tone unconcerned. "Henri, you're not in your right mind at the moment."

He spun to face her. "Because you've been manipulating my mind for years!"

"Henri—"

Henri turned to Theo and held out his hand. "Give me the needle."

But Theo was looking at Stella. "Is he telling the truth?"

"Of course not. He's grasping at straws because he got too close to a guest and he can't bear the thought of being without her. He'd say anything right now."

Juliette's cheeks flooded with heat. Was that true? She didn't remember.

And then she realized this was the game Stella constantly played. It must be so easy to win when you can see the cards in every other player's hand, but they can't even see the cards in their own. Stella was the only person who ever knew the full truth, so she controlled the narrative.

Juliette had always thought the power was in creating fantasies, but the real power was being able to see reality when no one else could.

And Stella had far too much power. They'd never find a way around her.

But Henri hadn't given up.

"Think about it," he said, still facing Theo. "Do you remember a single disagreement? Some argument where the two of you compromised? Or does she just alter your memory whenever you cross her?"

"That's enough!" Stella said. "Theo, immobilize the girl. Let's get this done."

"Do you?" Henri pressed, ignoring Stella. "One single disagreement in all these years?"

Theo dimmed but didn't speak. Henri kept pushing.

"Is it possible your marriage is so ideal because it's not really a marriage at all, but a fantasy? Could it be you're just a husband made of clay, sculpted to fulfill Stella's wishes? And when you fail, she pounds you down and molds you into something better."

Theo's face was like seeing the moon at midday, leached of light and color; Henri's expression was full of regret, as if he knew he'd wounded Theo, but he also knew he had no choice.

Juliette was so fixated on the two of them, she didn't see Stella move toward her until it was too late.

CHAPTER THIRTY-TWO

A STRANGLED GASP DREW HENRI'S ATTENTION, AND WHEN he looked up, his heart leaped into his throat.

Stella clutched Juliette to her chest. Juliette's eyes were wide and frightened.

"I don't need the needle to take her memories," Stella said, "but she'll be more comfortable with it than without. You decide."

"I don't understand why you're doing this," he said softly. "Juliette hasn't done anything to you."

"I don't understand why *you* can't be loyal to me." Her gaze flicked to Theo and back again. "Either one of you."

Henri thought of the memory Juliette had seen. *You will be loyal, or you will be made to be loyal.* For years, he'd been feverishly working to earn Stella's approval. Hoping if he gave her enough evidence he was worthy, she'd treat him like the son he longed to be. The irony was a bitter pill to swallow: He'd always been her son, but it wasn't a son she wanted. She wanted an unquestionably loyal servant, and he could never give her that.

His fantasy choked out one last breath before it died, and it allowed him to see the truth for what it was: Earning Stella's love was impossible. Her heart was a hollow space with a hole in the bottom. No matter how much he poured in, it would never be full.

"This isn't about loyalty," Henri said softly. "It's about doing what's right. Taking Juliette's memories accomplishes nothing."

Stella tightened her grip on Juliette. "She knows too much."

Henri frowned. "We *all* know too much." But he could see from the hungry gleam in her eyes, she intended to fix that.

Henri wished he knew which shelf held Theo's memories. He thought about seeing himself in Juliette's mind, brow furrowed in concentration. How hard he had to focus not to let his own memories sink into his mind before she could see them too.

If he could get Theo's memories close enough, they'd likely find him without Henri's help. He needed an ally. And a way to distract Stella.

"Theo," Stella said, "bring me the needle, please."

A pregnant beat of silence. And then Theo gave a quick nod of assent and started toward her. Henri was out of time. He swept his arm across the nearest shelf, knocking the vessels to the floor.

Breaking glass shattered the silence and sent sprays of colored shards in every direction.

"No!" Stella screamed. "What are you doing?" But in her moment of panic, she let go of Juliette, who rushed forward and started helping Henri toss vessels from the shelves. A few of the containers didn't break right away, so Henri picked them up and slammed them to the ground until they burst apart like ripe watermelons. Memories floated in the air like a fog rolling in from the sea. Henri gathered them by the palmful and shoved them in Theo's direction.

"Stop!" Stella rushed forward and yanked on Henri's arm. "You don't know what you're doing!" But he was too strong for her, and he shoved her away while he continued to on his path of destruction, sending dozens of vessels crashing to the floor with each sweep of his arm. Henri thought Stella had given up until he heard Juliette let out a yelp of pain. He turned.

Stella had Juliette by the hair and was dragging her away from the shelves. Juliette flailed and kicked, but since Stella was behind her, she couldn't land a direct enough blow to do any real damage. With a grunt, Stella yanked Juliette's hair so hard she fell to the floor. Then Stella knelt on her chest to hold her down. She placed her fingers on Juliette's temples and closed her eyes. Henri rushed forward and knocked Stella to the ground. Juliette scrambled to her feet and backed away. Henri kept his eyes on Stella, but he heard glass breaking in the background.

And then, from the corner of his gaze he spotted Theo, who was transfixed by the cyclone of memories swirling around him. Several threads had perched on his head and were sinking into his temples. Henri's breath caught.

It worked.

Now he just needed Theo to come through for him. To remember past wrongs and finally make the choice to right them.

Sudden movement pulled Henri's attention to Juliette. She was scaling one of the bookcases, sweeping vessels from each of the shelves as she went. But she'd made the case top heavy, and as she climbed, it started to tip.

"Juliette, careful!"

But Henri was too late. He felt as if he were watching it in slow motion: the bookcase tilting, Juliette losing her balance and falling backward through the air, the sickening sight of the shelves following her path to the floor. Brightly colored glass fragments rained from the ceiling. Memories gathered like storm clouds.

Juliette screamed. Her leg was trapped.

Henri ran to her and hefted the shelf up with such force that he sent it careening into the one behind it.

He knelt down beside Juliette. "Are you hurt?"

Juliette started to answer, but before he could take in what she was saying, a swirl of memories assaulted him. Henri as a toddler chasing a puppy through an open field; Henri as a child perched on a stool in the kitchen while the cook let him lick various emotions from spoons in the form of cherry cobbler and chocolate pudding; Henri the first time he met Juliette—holding her in his arms while he made her believe she was dancing.

He tried to fasten himself to the present—to help Juliette—but he was disoriented. His childhood streamed into his mind like a swelling river, and Henri was caught in the current.

He watched Stella teach him how to cast illusions. Her wide-eyed delight when he made a tiger fly a kite, her murmurs of appreciation when a rosebush came to life, the blossoms changing colors as they twirled through the garden. *You don't know how lucky you are*, she said, pressing a kiss against his forehead. *I grew up a scared little girl with no power at all, but* your *life will be different. You'll have so much power no one will ever be able to hurt you.*

New memories of Clementine poured into his mind, blending with the ones he took from Juliette. He watched himself meet Clementine, grow to love her, and then mourn her when she suddenly disappeared.

Dark memories crowded out happy ones. He was six years old and had spent the day near the creek, forming turtles out of mud and then animating them to rival one another in swimming competitions. He ran into the lobby of the hotel, excited to tell his mother how he'd been able to sustain the illusion for the entire race, all the way until his favorite turtle stood, victorious, on a podium made from river rocks.

But Stella took one look at the mud he'd tracked onto the gleaming marble floors and flew into a rage. She screamed at him until tears trickled down his cheeks, and then she shamed him for crying. Later that night, she tucked him into bed. *I lost my temper*, she said, *and I wish I hadn't. What do you say we make it all better?*

Henri nodded. He thought she'd hug him then, or maybe tell him she was sorry. But she put her fingers to his temples instead. It was the first time, but it wasn't the last. Stella harvested his memories every time he questioned her too harshly, every time they argued. Whenever she didn't get her way.

Henri watched himself uncover the seedy underbelly of the hotel over and over again. And each time, he woke with gaps in his memory and a new appreciation for The Splendor.

It was too many memories at once, and a crushing pressure built in Henri's chest. Pain in every flavor—guilt, sadness, grief, loss.

And something sharp at his neck.

Slowly the room came into focus. Juliette on the floor, holding her leg. Theo off to one side, needle still in hand. But Stella knelt behind Henri—he could feel her breath on his neck.

She was holding a jagged piece of glass against his windpipe.

CHAPTER THIRTY-THREE

J ULIETTE FORGOT THE PAIN IN HER LEG WHEN A FEW OF
Henri's memories brushed through her mind on the way
to his. She recognized their shape, even as she knew
they didn't belong to her. It was as if her mind had already
created a space for them—a few empty chairs at a table set
with silverware and laden with food.

She must have seen these memories before.

Bright sparks of panic flicked down her spine as the events
of the last few days slid back into place for a moment. She
watched Stella move Clementine toward the hot springs as
she took her memories. Saw her murder an innocent girl. The
memories moved through Juliette and found Henri, but they
left an impression behind like an indentation in a recently
vacated seat, still warm to the touch. Juliette's mind was
filled with the image of a face hovering above Clementine,
shimmering with rage.

Stella wore the same expression now as she stood behind
Henri with a vivid orange shard of glass pressed against

his throat.

"Please," Juliette said, "don't do this." A pit had opened in her stomach. Would Stella really kill her own child to save The Splendor?

The hair at Stella's temples was damp with sweat. Her eyes were wild as they darted around the room. The air was hazy with memories.

"You don't know what you've done," she said. "You need to put these all back."

Juliette looked helplessly at the churning mist, not sure how she'd even begin to comply. She didn't know *why* Henri had begun breaking vessels, but she trusted him enough to follow his lead. And she definitely didn't have the first clue how to reverse what she'd done.

"Stella—" Theo's voice was labored, as if he could barely force himself to speak. If Stella heard him, it didn't show.

"Just do it!" she screeched in Juliette's direction.

"We can't." Henri's voice was strained. "Not until you let me go."

"Be quiet!" Stella's hand trembled and a thin trickle of blood inched toward Henri's collarbone. "You can't be trusted right now. Not until you learn to be loyal."

Stella's gaze found Juliette's and held it. "I can't let you remember any of this."

"I know," Juliette said. "Just don't hurt him."

Stella tilted her head to one side as if considering her options. Her hand steadied on Henri's neck. "Come closer."

Juliette swallowed and climbed to her feet. Her leg screamed in pain.

Henri made a choked noise at the back of his throat. Juliette met his gaze. His eyes flicked toward the door and then back to her. *Run*, he mouthed. But she gave a small, sharp shake of her head—she wasn't about to leave him.

She limped to Stella's side, ignoring Henri's frantic expression.

"Sit," Stella told her, and she obeyed.

Henri's breath came in short, shallow gasps, and Juliette wondered what had happened to weaken him so much. It must have been the memories. She'd only had a few brush through her mind, and she felt weaker than normal. She couldn't imagine if hundreds of new experiences suddenly appeared in her mind, all jostling for attention.

"Stella?" Theo had said her name several times, but something about his voice now—maybe the tenderness of it, or the way it held just a hint of a question that made him seem vulnerable—finally got her to look at him. Theo was still holding the needle. He held it up and pinched it between his thumb and forefinger. "Allow me?"

Juliette's stomach turned to stone. Henri cried out in protest. But Stella's expression melted into relief—Henri wouldn't offer the loyalty she demanded, but Theo would. She smiled serenely at him, as if he'd just offered her a bouquet of roses.

Henri struggled to get out of Stella's grip, but she dug the glass deeper into his neck. He was already weak and now bleeding.

Juliette's fingernails pressed crescent-shaped marks into her palms. Her mind jumped between how to make sure Stella didn't slice through Henri's jugular to defending herself against Theo. Distantly, she wondered if Clare would ever find out what happened to her, if she'd ever think to wonder. Juliette's pulse was loud in her ears. The urge to survive crested inside her like a wave. If she went down, she'd go down fighting.

She shifted her weight and prepared to kick Theo in the

chest with her uninjured leg. He lunged. Juliette's foot shot out, but Theo was faster, and she caught only air.

The needle glinted in the sunlight as it sailed past her.

And plunged into Stella's neck.

CHAPTER THIRTY-FOUR

STELLA'S MAKESHIFT WEAPON CLATTERED TO THE ground, spattering the front of Henri's shirt with blood as it fell.

Stella slumped to one side.

"It took you long enough," Henri said, taking Theo's offered hand.

"I'm sorry." Theo gave him an apologetic frown and pulled Henri to his feet. "Those memories—" He shook his head like a dog trying to dislodge water from its ears. "Took me a bit to get my bearings."

Henri too.

Fresh shock pulsed through him, as if Clementine had been gone moments instead of years. But he couldn't think about that right now. And maybe it was for the best. The adrenaline was a gift that kept the grief at bay.

The memories in the room had grown restless. They were pressing against the windows and slithering under the doors.

"We have to get out of here." Henri turned to Juliette and

helped her to her feet. Her eyes were tight with fear. She was trembling.

"I thought . . ." Her gaze skipped to where Stella lay on the floor, motionless, but still breathing. "I was sure . . ."

"I know." Henri pushed a lock of hair off her forehead. "But I wouldn't have let her hurt you." The moment he said it, he knew it was a lie. He had let Stella hurt her, and so many others.

He would never make that mistake again.

He had so much he wanted to say, but they were running out of time.

"Can you walk?" he asked.

"I think so." Juliette winced as she put pressure on her leg, but she stayed upright.

The memories grew more demanding. They flung themselves against the stained glass. Henri remembered letting go of Juliette's memories in the butterfly house—how, when he'd swatted them away, they'd sunk into the earth as if they were searching for the water. He thought of the eruption when Clementine's memories followed her into the hot spring.

Those were a few memories. This room held thousands.

He didn't know what would happen if the swirling mist made it to the crypt before the three of them made it out of the hotel.

Theo scooped Stella into his arms, and Henri gave him a searching look.

"I can't just leave her here," Theo said. "No matter what she's done, I'm not that heartless."

Henri sighed. The four of them then.

"What's going on?" Juliette asked. Her voice was strained. Worried.

"If these memories make it to the hot springs, they might cause an eruption. We need to warn the guests and the staff and get everyone as far from here as possible."

Henri opened the door and they hurried down the stairs as quickly as they could, considering Juliette's injured leg and the fact that Theo was carrying Stella.

It wasn't fast enough.

They were overtaken almost immediately by a thick fog of memories that clogged the stairwell and obscured their view.

Theo stumbled into Henri and nearly sent him sprawling. Henri clutched the banister with one hand and Juliette's arm with the other. But then the air cleared. The memories had formed into a single, focused stream—a gauzy rope of recollections headed straight for the crypt. Henri grabbed Juliette's hand and started to run. He didn't look behind him to see if Theo was keeping up.

They passed by a group of illusionists who were preparing for the next batch of guests to arrive. They were creating tiny, colorful birds that perched along railings and light fixtures, chirping out compliments to anyone who passed by.

"What a stunning dress, Juliette!" a tiny wren called out. "You're a vision!"

Henri swatted the bird out of the air, and it vanished. All five of the illusionists froze and gaped at him.

"Get everyone out of the hotel," he said. No one moved. "Do it now!"

They all sprang into action.

"Everyone out!" Henri shouted as he continued to run through the corridors. Some of the guests had already left, but others milled about, chatting with one another as if reluctant to relinquish the fantasy.

Henri's warnings weren't going to be enough.

"You have to destroy the illusions," Juliette said. She was out of breath and grimacing against the pain in her leg. "They'll all leave if you expose the hotel for what it really is."

"They won't," Henri said. "They already know it's an illusion."

Juliette shook her head. "They've been told, but they don't *know*. Trust me. Just do it."

Henri concentrated. Could he really bring down the illusions of the entire hotel? He focused on the filmy bits of magic that clung to the walls, ceilings, and furnishings. And with his mind, he started to tug.

Juliette sucked in a sharp breath. "Keep going."

He did.

And the guests began to scream.

CHAPTER THIRTY-FIVE

JULIETTE

AFTER THE HOURS JULIETTE HAD SPENT TRAINING herself to see through illusions, she thought she'd achieved some level of competence.

She was wrong.

As Henri peeled away the magic, it was like watching an heiress strip off a pair of fancy satin gloves only to reveal a network of festering sores underneath.

The Splendor wasn't just plain. It was decrepit.

Cobwebs gathered in corners. The floorboards were full of holes. Vases of flowers turned to broken pots filled with handfuls of ugly weeds. All around them, guests and staff cried out. Frightened. Confused. Repulsed.

But she'd been right. They all began to move toward the doors.

Henri and Juliette took off at a run. The ground rumbled ominously beneath them. Henri kept shouting at people to hurry, but it was unnecessary. The transformation of the hotel was expelling them far faster than Henri's warnings ever could.

Guests and staff alike poured through the grand double doors in a steady stream.

Juliette and Henri emerged outside. The marble steps had transformed into crumbling stone ruins. The fountains were cracked and dry, filled with dirt instead of water.

The scent of rot hung thickly in the air.

They ran past the dirt path that once looked like a cobbled circular drive and made it all the way to the edge of the property. Right before the path dipped toward Bella Fontaine, Henri tugged her hand. They stopped.

"I just—" He pulled his fingers through his hair. "I need to take a minute."

She understood. He needed to say goodbye.

They turned around, and even though she was prepared, the sight still snatched the breath from her lungs.

The Splendor was in ruins.

The stone was cracked and dirty. The grounds were overgrown. Discolored curtains billowed from windows without glass. Only the top level of the hotel looked untouched by the ravages of time or the power of illusion.

A pang of sadness hit Juliette in the chest.

Since she was a little girl, she'd dreamed of coming here someday. It was a wish that had gotten all tangled up with her longing for family and her relationship with Clare. For her entire childhood, she'd believed somewhere out there—beyond the walls of the children's home—was a fantasy so spectacular it would make up for her less-than-perfect reality. She thought she'd find it within the walls of The Splendor, but from almost the moment she arrived, all she wanted was to make it back to Clare.

Still, seeing her glittering dream desecrated, like rotten fruit at the base of an apple tree, felt like a bigger loss than she would have imagined.

If it felt this bad to her, it must have felt so much worse to Henri. This was the only home he'd ever known. She stole a glance at him. His expression was bleak.

She squeezed his hand. "I'm so sorry."

He shrugged. "It always looked this way to me."

And then she understood. He wasn't mourning the loss of a fantasy; he always knew the true nature of The Splendor. He was grieving because the things that were supposed to be real weren't.

"Henri, I—" But the words died in her throat as another giant rumble shook the ground. A cacophony of screams split the air. Anyone who was walking started to run; those who were already running sped up.

"We should get out of here," Henri said.

In the distance, Juliette spotted Theo headed straight for them. He still carried Stella in his arms and her head bounced up and down with every movement. His face was scarlet, and his brow glistened with sweat. Juliette could tell the moment Henri saw him because his whole body went tense. Still, he waited until Theo reached them.

"I need your help." Theo sank to his knees and pulled in deep gulps of air. "Henri . . . please."

"What do you expect me to do?" Henri asked.

A vibration built beneath the earth. All three of them turned toward the hotel, which seemed to tremble slightly like a child shivering in a sudden breeze. A gushing noise rushed into the air. And then the impossible happened.

The Splendor exploded.

CHAPTER THIRTY-SIX

THE FORCE OF THE ERUPTION KNOCKED HENRI OFF HIS feet. A column of water shot up from the ground, sending pieces of the hotel flying in every direction—wood, furniture, and bits of fabric all soared through the air. Steam curled toward the sky.

Henri lay on his back, watching the geyser in fascinated horror while specks of dust fell around him like rain. It was years too late, but finally he'd kept his promise to Clementine. He'd destroyed The Splendor.

It took him a moment to come to his senses, and then panic set in.

Juliette. Her name bubbled from his throat—he sensed the frantic rise of it, felt his lips shape the word, but the sound never reached his ears. It was as if a blanket of silence had fallen over the whole world. The lack of sound was absolute.

Where was Juliette?

Henri pulled himself into a sitting position and surveyed his surroundings. His pulse sped. Juliette was lying motionless a few feet away. Blood trickled from her forehead.

For the space of one breathless moment, he thought she was dead, and a fist closed around his heart, clamping down with such force he felt the blood in his veins go slow and sluggish. But then her eyes fluttered open. Widened as she took in the destruction.

Her lips moved. *What happened?*

Henri's pulse stuttered and his blood roared back to life. He had a thousand things he wanted to tell her, but not one of them answered her question. She touched her forehead and her fingers came away bloody.

Henri's ears began to ring. He pressed the hem of his shirt to Juliette's head to stem the bleeding. She winced. He lifted the fabric and examined the wound. Relief exhaled out of him when he saw it wasn't serious—a minor cut probably from a bit of flying wreckage.

"Are you all right?" His voice was muffled to his own ears, but she seemed to hear him. She nodded.

Sound came alive slowly—a sleepy beast lumbering awake. And with it, renewed horror. The injured moans of those who had been struck by debris. The shouts of people calling out for loved ones who had gone missing. The continued gushing of water from the gaping hole where The Splendor used to be.

After a few minutes of pressure, Juliette's bleeding stopped. Henri lowered his shirt and sat beside her in the grass.

"Thank you," she said softly. His ears were still buzzing faintly, but he heard her. "Are you . . . ?" Her hand found his knee. "Are you all right?" He knew she wasn't asking if he was injured, and he grappled with how to answer. His heart was a small stone in his chest. He should feel something at the loss of the hotel—sadness or regret or elation—but he only felt numb.

"I'm not sure." It was as honest of a reply as he could manage.

"Henri!" The voice made him swivel. Stella was lying on the ground, and Theo was kneeling beside her. In the chaos, Henri had forgotten all about them. "Come help me," Theo called. "Please."

Henri scrambled to his feet and Juliette followed. Stella was motionless. He bit his lip and looked away.

"We have to do something," Theo said, "before it's too late."

Henri felt as if each of his feet were planted on opposite sides of a widening chasm. He was slowly being torn apart and he had to choose to leap to one side or the other. Did he want Stella to survive? Could he live with the guilt of letting her die? Was it a bigger risk to let her keep her power and her ambition or live with the responsibility for taking it away?

Bitterness crept into his heart.

"Do what?" Henri's gaze flicked to the geyser. "Give her the same send-off she gave to Clementine? Because that's what she deserves."

"You don't mean that," Theo said. "Son—" Theo's voice broke. Henri wanted to walk away, but he couldn't force his feet to move. He thought of Stella training him, ruffling his hair as she passed through the room, smiling affectionately when he did something that made her proud.

His heart wasn't made of stone, he realized, but of ice.

Ice could melt. But it could also shatter. He couldn't bear to help save Stella.

He couldn't bear not to.

He raked his fingers through his hair and knelt down beside her. "What do you want me to do? I'm not trained as a healer." He pressed two fingers to Stella's neck, but he couldn't feel the flutter of a pulse beneath them.

Theo tugged Henri's hand away. "It's too late for that. She's already dead."

Oh. Cold shock hit Henri square in the chest. He didn't know if it was grief or gratitude.

"How?"

"I don't know if it was the explosion or if there was something stronger than usual in the syringe." Theo's eyes went tight. "But please help. I want to know *why*."

Understanding flowed through Henri. Theo wasn't asking him to save Stella. He was asking him to harvest her memories. Theo's anguish must be laced with confusion. But Henri didn't think he could tolerate seeing inside Stella's mind. Her betrayals were painful enough from a distance.

"I'm sorry. I can't."

"Please," Theo said, "I need to know what she took from me. I need to know who I am."

Juliette laid a palm on Henri's arm. "Maybe Theo's right. Maybe understanding her motivations would help. You both deserve closure."

Henri felt as if he'd swallowed a hot coal. It burned his throat, then sat like fire in his belly. He didn't want to understand Stella. He wanted to hate her. And yet, no matter how hard he tried, he couldn't force himself to walk away. Even in death, Stella had some cruel hold on him.

"There's no shame in being relieved," Theo said, as if he could see the shape of Henri's thoughts. "But maybe if we understand . . . maybe someday we can forgive her."

He glanced up at Theo. "Is there anything you could see that would justify her betrayal? Do you actually think you could ever forgive her?"

Theo was quiet for a long moment. Henri could practically see the battle raging within him.

Finally, he sighed. "No."

A silent understanding passed between them. Stella had betrayed her family too brutally and too often. Forgiveness was out of reach, at least for now. But still Theo was desperate to understand; determined to keep the door of redemption open. Maybe he could give his father this one last thing. Even if he couldn't give it to himself. Henri moved closer to Stella and took a deep breath.

Magic leaped into his fingertips the moment he placed them on her temples, as if the power had been kept on a leash before and now it was ready to run free.

Maybe this would be easier than he thought.

But the moment he sunk into Stella's mind he realized the futility of what Theo had asked him to do. Stella's life was like a hopelessly tangled ball of thread—her memories of The Splendor were all wrapped up with Henri and Theo, with her ability to perform magic, and even her perception of herself. How could he possibly unravel any of it in a way that made sense?

One summer when Henri was small, he'd spent the afternoon climbing trees and had gotten a hunk of tree sap stuck in his hair. Stella had tried every trick to remove it— butter, olive oil, ice—but nothing made it budge. Finally, she'd sighed.

"We can't coax it out, so we'll need to cut it out." Henri's eyes had gone wide, and Stella laughed. "Don't worry. It will grow back eventually."

Maybe Henri would need to take the same approach now. He wasn't skilled enough to sort through her memories and find only the parts that would make sense of her actions. He'd need to remove whole years and let Theo draw his own conclusions. He needed to hope understanding would grow eventually.

He sorted through Stella's mind, diving through layers of memories until he found the initial spark of the idea for The Splendor. Stella had been young—only about Henri's age—

when her parents told her about the Days of Wonder: how magic sometimes flowed into the valley when the blossoms were just coming on the trees, and how people ran through the streets conjuring illusions with breathless delight. *Imagine the power if someone could harness that magic.* It had been a stray thought, but it wouldn't leave her alone until it had grown into an obsession. She ached to find the source of the magic. To own it. To control it. Henri started with that memory, and gently he began to pull the threads that would unravel everything that came after.

It was painful work. He wished he could remove the memories and give them to Theo without bearing witness to her vulnerabilities. He didn't want to see the kernel of humanity in her quest for perfection. He didn't want to know Stella secretly worried she wasn't good at relationships, and so when she realized she could start over anytime she wanted— erase any trace of her mistakes in the minds of the people she loved—she couldn't resist.

But her constant revision of history meant she never got better at apologizing or changing or trying again. She only got better at cutting out anything that might threaten her reputation.

It was easier to hate Stella when he thought her motivations came from malice and not from a persistent nagging fear that no one would love her without coercion.

Henri always thought Stella was immune to the illusions of The Splendor, but it turned out she was living in a fantasy as much as any of the guests: a world where no one ever remembered her mistakes.

Henri tugged at the memories and watched them unravel into his fingers. Stella was always in pursuit of a second chance.

But this time, she wasn't going to get one.

CHAPTER THIRTY-SEVEN

JULIETTE

JULIETTE WATCHED HENRI WORK, FASCINATED BY THE way the memories gathered in his fingers as if he were pulling stuffing from a child's toy.

She wondered what he saw in Stella's mind that turned down the corners of his mouth and made his shoulders sag.

Her heart clenched. She missed seeing memories with him, her fingers brushing up against his, the effortless connection of a shared experience.

When Henri finally opened his eyes again, he looked around as if he were expecting to find a memory vessel. But they had all been destroyed, along with everything else inside The Splendor.

"Hold out your hands," he said, and Theo obeyed.

Henri and Juliette both watched as Theo experienced the memories, his expression full of shock and pain and sorrow. When he finally finished, he rose to his feet, wordless, and walked all the way to the edge of the crater. The fountaining water had slowed. The geyser had diminished in height, though it still burst from the ground below. Juliette and Henri watched as he released the memories—reverently—as if he were scattering ashes.

Juliette knew the moment the memories sank into the hot springs below because the geyser suddenly gained force, doubling in height for a few moments before shrinking again.

Theo returned to where Juliette waited with Henri and Stella's lifeless form.

"We'll need to find a burial spot," Theo said.

"You'll need to find one on your own," Henri said. "There is no 'we' anymore."

Theo's expression registered surprise and then pain. Oh. He'd been prepared to say goodbye to Stella, but he hadn't expected to lose Henri too.

Juliette's heart went out to him, but she'd seen enough memories—both Henri's and Theo's—to understand. Theo hadn't known everything Stella did, but he'd known enough. And when he had a chance to protect Henri, he didn't.

"Where will you go?" Theo asked, his voice catching a little on the words.

Henri's gaze slid to Juliette, and then back again. "I'm not sure."

Butterflies swarmed her stomach at the thought she might factor into his plans. Then again, maybe he just meant he intended to help her reconcile with Clare before he moved on.

"Will I see you again?" Theo asked.

"I'm not sure about that either."

Theo shifted his weight from one foot to the other. "I should have done more."

"Yes, you should have."

"I'm sorry."

"I know." Henri's voice was gentle. It held no bitterness, but it made no promises either.

Theo scooped Stella into his arms and gave Henri one last lingering glance before he walked away. He looked like a broken man.

Of the two of them, maybe Stella had the easier path. She died before she had a chance to realize that she'd lost everything. Theo would lose just as much, but he'd be alive to feel the full weight of all that could have been.

Juliette hoped he could start over and find some measure of peace. And maybe someday he and Henri could find their way back to each other.

After everything she'd been through, Juliette should have expected Belle Fontaine to look different, but somehow, the change still surprised her. As she and Henri walked through the streets, they passed the same cafés with striped awnings and wrought iron tables, the same bakeries with fancy desserts displayed in the windows like bite-sized works of art, the same flower shops overflowing with blooms. But the city seemed transformed, and Juliette couldn't quite put her finger on why.

Perhaps beauty didn't have the power over her it had before. Or maybe she knew behind the pretty glass displays that something far uglier might be lurking.

Henri was quiet beside her, and a heavy silence stretched between them like an ice-covered branch about to snap. They were safe but not settled, and the sensation prickled at her skin like an itch.

Several times Henri took a quick inhale, as if he were about to speak, and then seemed to change his mind.

"You don't have to come with me," Juliette said, finally, "not if you don't want to."

Henri stopped walking and a spasm of pain flitted across his expression that made her realize she'd misinterpreted his silence, and she wished she could snatch her words out of the air and make them disappear.

"Would you prefer to go alone?"

"No, that's not what I meant. I—"

"I would understand," he said. "She's your sister, and after everything I've done, I have no right—"

Juliette touched his elbow. "Henri, what's going on?"

"I never apologized for taking Clare's memories." She cocked her head to one side. Hadn't he? She'd spent so much time living inside *his* memories, she felt as if she could read him like a favorite book splayed open on her lap. His regret had been written all over his face for days, and it never occurred to her that he hadn't given it voice. "I'm so sorry, Juliette."

"You didn't know what Stella was really doing when you helped her."

"No, I didn't"—Henri stuffed his fists in his pockets— "but I should have. I've been so angry at Theo for not seeing through Stella's lies. For believing her excuses even when he did see through them. For not protecting me. But I did the same thing. I trusted her and I let her use me as a tool to hurt people. If I can't forgive Theo, how am I supposed to expect you to forgive me?"

"Maybe you don't expect it. Maybe you just apologize and hope for the best. At least that's my plan with Clare."

Henri frowned. "What are you talking about. What do you have to apologize for?"

Juliette sighed. "I spent my whole life wanting to escape reality. When Clare and I were little, I thought other children—the ones with homes and parents—lived a perfect fairy-tale existence. I was convinced if I could just find the secret key to their life, I'd never be sad again.

It's why The Splendor was so appealing."

"You thought it was the secret key?"

"It sounds silly, doesn't it?"

"Of course not. But what does this have to do with Clare?"

Juliette spotted a stray bit of grass poking up between two cobbles and nudged it with her toe. "I was so anxious to have a fantasy that I turned Clare into one."

Henri's brows pulled together. A silent question.

"I treated her like she only existed in relationship to me. As if her entire purpose was to make sure I was happy. I never would have admitted it to myself, but I had her on such a high pedestal, she was bound to fall sooner or later. And when she did, instead of working through it, I ran away."

His expression gentled. "She didn't remember you. That's hardly the same."

"Still, what would have happened if I'd stayed? What if I'd loved her enough to let her be flawed?" Juliette thought of Clare's words the last day she saw her. *You've been entirely too needy lately.* The words had stung, but they'd been true. "I wish I'd just let her climb down from her pedestal and learn to love me again as an equal instead of someone she always needed to take care of."

"But what if she never did?" Henri asked. "What if losing those memories changed her forever?"

Juliette smiled. "How many times did Stella harvest your memories to keep you in line after you'd discovered what was really going on at The Splendor?"

"At least a dozen."

"See? She could make you forget, but she couldn't really change you. In your heart, you want to do what's right, so no matter what Stella did, you managed to find your way to the truth again and again. And I hope Clare will too. I want a real sister, not some romanticized fantasy version. Fantasies might be perfect, but they can't love you back."

"So, does this mean you forgive me?"

Juliette threaded her fingers through Henri's and squeezed his hand. "Yes." She nudged his shoulder with her own. "Besides, I'm not really interested in having a relationship with someone flawless. It's too much pressure."

Henri froze. "So . . . you are? Interested in having a relationship?"

Juliette's cheeks flamed. She hadn't meant to be so direct. "Oh . . . I . . . I just meant . . ." She shook her head. She was too flustered to find the right words.

Henri laughed. A low, rich sound like the lowest notes of a melody. "We could talk more about my flaws if it would help."

"I think it might."

"I have another idea." Henri let go of her hand and moved to face her. He slid his palm beneath her hair and cradled her neck, his thumb idly tracing her jawline. Juliette's pulse went erratic. She felt her skin heat beneath his fingers.

His eyes searched her face. A question. She moved closer.

Henri lifted her chin and kissed her.

His lips were feather soft against hers—a barely there sensation that made her whole body feel awake.

And then the kiss deepened.

Juliette's fingers tangled in Henri's hair. She no longer felt entirely in her own body, and she wondered how something so clearly real could feel so much like an illusion. Henri kissed her until she was mindless, and then intensely present. Lost and then found again. Warmth flowed into her and she no longer understood why anyone searched for any fantasy at all when a real moment could feel this spectacular.

It was late by the time Henri and Juliette finally turned onto the street that led to her old neighborhood.

Their kiss had turned them slow and syrupy, and they'd moved through the city at a more leisurely pace afterward, as if they both wanted to hold on to the moment as long as possible. Juliette felt like she was floating, her feet barely skimming along cobbles that were bathed in the soft glow of the oil streetlamps.

But when the flat came into view, all the air went out of her and she abruptly fell back to earth.

A single window was illuminated. Clare sat at the kitchen table, absently sipping a cup of tea. Juliette's throat closed at the sight.

She wished she were returning with memories—a whole history housed in colorful glass that would put everything back the way it should be. But she was empty-handed; all she had to offer was herself. She didn't know if it would be enough.

Henri squeezed her hand. "Are you ready?"

"No, but if I wait until I'm ready, I'll never go in."

"I'm right behind you."

Juliette took a deep breath, climbed the steps, and knocked.

At first there was nothing—no scrape of a chair pushing back from the table, no footsteps padding to the doorway, no click of the tumbler in the lock. Maybe Clare had taken one look out the window and decided not to answer. Juliette's rib cage felt too tight to house both her heart and lungs—they seemed to demand more space than she had available.

The moments inched forward. Juliette seemed to hear

them rushing through her ears like a pulse. Just as she was about to turn around, the door swung open. One long, silent beat passed as the girls stared at each other. Clare's eyes were wide with surprise, and Juliette knew hers must be tight with anxiety.

And then Clare threw her arms around Juliette.

It was so unexpected that for a moment Juliette just stood there, pinned in place, certain she was dreaming. But even if it was a dream, it was a good one, and she didn't want to waste the moment. She hugged Clare back.

"You left without saying goodbye." Clare's voice was soft, her breath warm against Juliette's cheek.

"You wanted me to move out." Juliette pulled away and searched her sister's face. Did she remember?

"I should never have said that. I wasn't myself." Clare pulled at a loose thread on her sleeve, twisted it around her finger. "To tell you the truth, I'm still not."

Confusion washed over Juliette. "But you're happy to see me?"

"Of course, I'm happy to see you." Clare's expression turned stern. "Where have you been?"

"The Splendor."

The color drained from Clare's face. "Oh no. I think"— she bit her bottom lip—"I think something bad might have happened to me there."

Juliette couldn't help how disappointment seeped into her and spread like spilled ink. "You still don't remember much about me." Somehow when Clare had embraced her she'd thought . . . she'd hoped . . .

Clare's eyes filled with tears. "No. But I think I remember remembering. Does that make sense?"

Juliette thought of the sensation after Henri had removed her memories: the unexplained absence made her mind turn in circles, searching without ever finding anything.

"Yes," she said softly, "it does."

"I haven't slept well since you left." Clare swiped at her eyes. "I know I told you I thought you should find your own place, but when you didn't come back . . . I couldn't focus. I couldn't eat. I was heartbroken without really understanding why. That's when I started to suspect something had happened at The Splendor to make me forget. My heart knew I loved you even if my head didn't."

Juliette's vision went hazy. Her eyes spilled over. She was right that people returned to who they were over and over again. But her failure still sat in her stomach like a stone. "They took your memories. I tried to get them back, but . . ."

"So, that's it then? I'll never remember?"

"Well, I might have a solution." Juliette turned and motioned for Henri. "Clare, there's someone I'd like you to meet."

CHAPTER THIRTY-EIGHT

ENRI KNEW WHAT JULIETTE WAS ABOUT TO ASK HIM, just like he knew the shape of her jaw, and the slope of her shoulders, and the way her fingers couldn't be still when she was nervous.

And he knew she was going to be heartbroken when he had to tell her no.

They gathered around the table in the small kitchen. Juliette sat across from Clare, her arms resting on the smooth wood. The hope on her face as she clutched Clare's fingers was an aching thing.

"Everything will be fine." Juliette's voice was high and excited. Her cheeks were flushed. "Luckily, I saw all your memories before they were lost, so Henri can help me share them with you. Tell her, Henri."

The words felt like a blow to the gut. "I'm sorry," he said. "It won't work."

"Why not? It worked when we did it before."

"Yes, because we were at The Splendor. The magic comes

from the water. I won't be able to access it here."

She stood. "Then we'll go back."

He touched her arm gently. "It won't work. Stella wanted to build the hotel on the hot springs to trap the magic." He swallowed. "Because when it's not trapped, it evaporates. Remember?"

Even as he said it, he realized she didn't.

She'd seen Clementine's explanation of the Days of Wonder, but it was one of the memories Henri removed. And even though Juliette said Henri's memories had skimmed through her mind on the way back to his, it was clear she didn't remember the details.

So, he explained. He told her about how magic used to flow into the valley for a few days in the spring, available to everyone for a short time before evaporating and starting the cycle anew. Stella had used the hotel as a dam, trapping the magic in one place, but now The Splendor was gone. And so was the magic.

Color leached from her cheeks as he spoke.

Her face crumpled. "So, there's nothing we can do? Your abilities are just . . . gone?"

"I'm sorry. Maybe the magic will return next spring when the snow melts. Or maybe it won't return for years."

"Or," Clare said, her voice cutting through the despondent mood that had taken hold of the room, "maybe we don't need magic at all."

Juliette turned. "What do you mean?"

Clare smiled gently "There's more than one way to share memories." She patted the chair next to her. "Sit, Jules. And tell me our story."

Juliette did.

They talked for hours, all through the deepening night until the faint light of a blush-pink dawn touched the horizon.

Juliette told Clare everything she remembered about their childhood—whispered secrets, embarrassing moments, shared dreams. She threaded her tales with love and nostalgia, affection and humor.

Juliette held her sister's hand and wove a magic every bit as powerful as anything Henri had ever created.

He had the strange sensation of feeling both part of their story and completely outside it. He'd seen every single memory Clare had of Juliette. He was so familiar with them, he could have relayed each one by heart. But the bond the sisters shared was utterly foreign. He couldn't imagine loving someone so deeply that the feeling refused to leave even when it had no memories to cling to. Watching them reminded him of trying one of Amella's emotion-laced desserts and getting lost in someone else's nostalgia. He was forever tasting but never enjoying an entire meal.

A wave of sadness threatened to pull him under.

But Juliette's voice kept him afloat. She was telling Clare about the masquerade ball.

"And then I traded costumes with a woman named Emilie, whom I'd met at the clothier's. I wore her fairy costume and she dressed as the peacock. After we traded, Caleigh started watching her instead of me, and I was able to sneak away to the Hall of Memories." Juliette's gaze flicked to him. "It was even enough to trick Henri. And he nearly scared Emilie to death when he told her she was in danger."

Juliette turned to Henri, her eyes bright. "Remember?"

Something warm and tender stretched between them— the gossamer cords of a history that was just beginning. He could feel how over time it would strengthen and grow and bind them together. His past hadn't been rich with the kind of connection he longed for, but his future could be. His fingers closed around hers.

"Yes," he said, "I remember."

Time passed. One season dissolved into another. Occasionally, Henri and Juliette passed the ruins of The Splendor on their way to get croissants at the bakery, or window-shop in the market district, or stroll through the park. Each time, Henri looked up with a knot in his stomach, but the cratered hill remained dormant. Eventually, he started to breathe easier.

Maybe the magic really was gone forever.

Then—a few years later—a particularly warm spring followed what had been a particularly snowy winter. The snow in the mountains melted faster than normal. The spring thaw made the rivers rise.

And magic flowed into the valley.

All of Belle Fontaine was breathless with wonder.

Booths sprung up overnight—vendors selling candied apples and spiced nuts and hair wreaths made of flowers and silk ribbon.

Children ran through the streets, conjuring dragons who battled one another and unicorns who sipped from puddles of liquid gold. Men and women rushed home from work to create firework displays and intricately carved ice sculptures that danced through the city. Trees in unlikely colors sprouted through the cobbles and grew to impossible heights.

Henri, Juliette, and Clare wound through the streets with the same awe as everyone else.

But Henri's wonder was tempered by worry.

He watched as a man swept his hand through the air, and the sky split in half—night on one side and day on the other. Henri longed to reach for the magic—to feel it sliding through his fingers, full of power and potential—but he was afraid of what would happen if he did. Would it be like greeting an old friend? Or would it remind him too much of a life full of pain?

And there was something else. Another fear he didn't want to acknowledge that kept darting around at the edge of his mind, demanding to be noticed even as he tried to push it away.

"What's wrong?" Juliette asked, seeming to sense his hesitation.

"After everything that's happened, this doesn't make you nervous?"

Her gaze flitted to Clare, who was admiring the small owl perched on her palm. Her eyes were wide with delight at the marvel she'd conjured, and she leaned down and spoke softly to the creature, who seemed to answer with a low hooting sound. Juliette smiled and turned back to Henri.

"Why would I be nervous? Isn't this what the magic was always meant to be—something rare and special and shared by everyone?"

He was quiet for a stretch, and although he could tell Juliette hoped for a response, she didn't press for one. He loved that about her—how she allowed him plenty of time to gather his thoughts without feeling rushed.

He pulled a bit of magic from the air, created a red rose, and tucked it behind her ear. It felt good to use his magic again. Like coming home. "You're right. I don't know what I was afraid of."

But then he caught a glimpse of someone in the crowd. Someone with Theo's sandy hair shot through at the temples with just a hint of silver. For a moment Henri wondered if it was an illusion. If he'd used another thread of magic without realizing it and conjured his father from memory.

He blinked and looked closer, but Theo didn't vanish on closer inspection. He was really here. An ache built in Henri's chest. He wondered if Theo missed him like Clare missed Juliette. If there was an empty space inside where his son used to be. He resisted the urge to run to Theo to find the answer; despite the passage of time, the thought of a reunion was still too painful.

Theo's gaze swept past him without pausing—maybe you didn't see what you weren't looking for—and then it landed on a woman in the crowd who was staring at the crater at the top of Splendor Hill with a familiar hungry expression.

A chill inched down Henri's spine. This was the fear that had been simmering at the back of his mind since the day The Splendor exploded.

He remembered what Juliette said about people always returning to who they were. He knew she'd been right—it was precisely why Stella's death came with both sadness and relief. If she'd survived, she would have eventually found another way to harness the magic. But a thirst for power wasn't unique to Stella, and sooner or later someone new would rise up and take her place. As he watched the woman, he could practically see the wheels turning in her mind. She had the same expression he'd seen on Stella's face so many times before, and he was certain she was contemplating where the magic came from and how she could be the one to trap and control it.

And he could see the way Theo was attracted to her ambition like a moth to flame. How he was drawn to it even though he must have known it had the power to burn him.

He hoped Theo walked away. He hoped the woman never figured out how to use magic. And he wished he had the power to stop them both.

But a life without risk or fear was a fantasy.

Later, he and Juliette sat on a blanket under the shade of a giant oak tree, with a picnic basket resting between them. He told her about spotting Theo at the festival.

Juliette didn't ask if Theo had seen him too, or if he'd been fixated on the magic, or why Henri hadn't approached him.

Instead her expression softened. "Do you miss him?"

"No. Yes." He shook his head. "I guess I miss the father he should have been."

"I miss what my childhood should have been too."

It was a strange feeling—total contentment with the present, laced with lingering disappointments from the past. He wondered if it would always be this way. If no future happiness could completely heal old wounds.

Henri reached for the picnic basket and laid out an array of food—small loaves of bread, a variety of cheese, sliced fruit.

"What do you want?" he asked.

Juliette's lips curved, as if the question triggered some memory. "Do you remember when I first came to The Splendor and you were frantically trying to figure out what I wanted? Besides getting Clare back, I mean?"

Henri laughed. "I remember. You know, I never did figure it out."

"How could you? Even I didn't know what I wanted back then."

"And now?"

"I want to love with reckless abandon. Travel the world. Lie on my back in the grass and watch for falling stars. I want to have real experiences and a big, full, messy life."

He let out a contented sigh. "That sounds like perfection."

Juliette smiled. Her expression was full of uncomplicated joy. "There's no such thing."

Henri could think of only one way to prove her wrong—he leaned down and kissed her.

It was fantasy. It was reality.

It was perfection.

ACKNOWLEDGMENTS

I'M SO GRATEFUL TO ALL MY READERS, BOTH THE NEW ONES and those who have been with me since the beginning. I appreciate you all!

To my tireless agent, Kathleen Rushall: thank you for years of wise career advice, comforting words, and enthusiastic celebrations. You're the best!

To Lauren Knowles, who adopted *The Splendor* and loved it as her own: thanks for both your sharp editorial eye and your kindness. I've loved working with you! And thanks also to Ashley Hearn, who made me a better writer.

The entire team at Page Street is amazing and I'm so grateful to each of them for their role in helping bring *The Splendor* to life: my publisher, Will Kiester; associate editors Tamara Grasty and Jenna Fagan and editorial director Marissa Giambelluca; publicity wizards Lizzy Mason and Lauren Cepero; and designers Laura Benton and Meg Baskis—thanks for making the cover stunning!

Also, special thanks to copyeditor extraordinaire, Juliann

Barbato, who was an absolute joy to work with.

I'm blessed with an embarrassment of riches when it comes to fellow writers who are unfailingly supportive and wonderful: Addie Thorley, Becky Wallace, Kate Watson, and Katie Nelson. I'm lucky to call you friends!

To my mom, my in-laws, and my aunts, uncles, cousins, neighbors, siblings, and friends: I appreciate all your support over the years. Hugs to you all.

And finally—most importantly—thank you to my husband, Justin, and our three children, Ben, Jacob, and Isabella. You guys make my life magical.

ABOUT THE AUTHOR

BREEANA SHIELDS IS AN AWARD-WINNING AUTHOR OF fantasy novels for teens, including The Bone Charmer duology (Page Street), the Poison's Kiss duology (Random House BFYR), and *The Splendor* (Page Street).

When she's not writing, Breeana loves reading, traveling, and playing board games with her extremely competitive family. She lives near Washington, D.C., with her husband, her three children, and two adorable but spoiled dogs. You can find her online at breeanashields.com.